John Bulloch

George Jamesone, the Scottish Vandyck

John Bulloch

George Jamesone, the Scottish Vandyck

ISBN/EAN: 9783337240370

Printed in Europe, USA, Canada, Australia, Japan

Cover: Foto ©Raphael Reischuk / pixelio.de

More available books at **www.hansebooks.com**

GEORGE JAMESONE

HIS LIFE AND WORKS

"Le Genie, est la premiere chose que l'on doit supposer dans un peintre. C'est une partie qui ne peut s'acquerir ni par l'etude, ni par le travail ; il faut qu'il soit grand pour repondre à l'etendue d'un Art qui renferme autant de connoissances que la peinture, & qui exige beaucoup de tems & d' applications pour les acquerir."

De Piles (1715).

"I paint the living and they make me live."—*Kneller.*

"To saunter through the portrait gallery [at Clarencieux] and hear dealers appraise the Lelys and the Lawrences, the Vandykes and the Jamesones . this was Trevenna's paradise."—*Ouida*, in "Chandos."

GEORGE JAMESONE

THE SCOTTISH VANDYCK

BY

JOHN BULLOCH

WITH TWO ILLUSTRATIONS BY GEORGE REID, R.S.A.

EDINBURGH: DAVID DOUGLAS

1885

TO

CHARLES ELPHINSTONE DALRYMPLE, Esquire,

F.S.A., SCOT.,

TO WHOM CHIEFLY BELONGS THE HONOUR OF BRINGING TOGETHER

THAT INSPIRING COLLECTION OF HISTORICAL PORTRAITS

EXHIBITED AT THE MEETING OF THE BRITISH ASSOCIATION

AT ABERDEEN IN 1859,

AND CONSPICUOUS AMONG WHICH WAS

THE FIRST CONSIDERABLE GROUP OF GEORGE JAMESONE'S WORKS

EVER SHOWN TO THE PUBLIC,

I inscribe this Book ;

WITH THE SURE CONVICTION

THAT OF ALL MY MANY KIND HELPERS

NOT ONE

WILL GRUDGE HIM THIS REPRESENTATIVE PLACE.

CONTENTS.

ERRATA.

Page 54, 12th line from foot, after Urquhart *insert* Tutor.

Page 106, 15th and 19th lines from foot, *for* Helen *read* Mary.

Page 106, 14th, and page 170, 11th line from foot, *for* Kincorth *read* Tillycorthie.

PREFACE.

AT this, the last stage of my work, it is less necessary to
state the motives which led to my undertaking the responsibility of adding one book more to our already groaning shelves,
than to explain why I have taxed so severely the patience of my
subscribers by its long delay.

When about to proceed to press, two years ago, the fortunate
discovery of some serious mistakes as to the genuineness of a
few of the pictures I had tabulated, led at once to the resolve,
that, with growing knowledge of them, I ought to pass under
my personal review the whole series—both those I had seen
before and those I had never seen at all, but had taken on
trust. In a matter like this, authenticity was of the first
importance, although to gain it involved vexatious delay.

A secondary but not unimportant advantage has, I trust, been
gained by my efforts to acquire a more perfect knowledge of
Jamesone's works. His own somewhat conjectural life becomes
thereby more rounded and better understood. His personality
and power, which refused to develop themselves to uninformed
eulogisms, stand confessed in the light of his numerous works.
I hope these advantages may be held to compensate for the
delay.

In the course of the work there have not been wanting
voices warning me off the field as a barren one, not likely to
yield any reasonable fruitage. But these have been quite out-

numbered, not only by words of encouragement, but by deeds of helpfulness. Seldom has author been so helped, and it becomes at once a duty and a pleasure to express my deep obligations to all who have aided me so willingly.

Specially am I bound to return my grateful thanks to the noblemen, ladies and gentlemen, who possess Jamesone's pictures, for the extreme readiness with which they granted me permission to inspect those works ; and but for whose courteous co-operation the execution of the Catalogue in its present form could not have been accomplished. If it is not so complete as I could desire, the blame is largely mine.

To my late friend, Andrew Gibb, Esq., F.S.A., Scot., I am indebted for kind encouragement and direction. Of his large resources of information I was ever made a welcome sharer. To Charles Elphinstone Dalrymple, Esq., John F. White, Esq., and William Alexander, Esq., I am under much indebtedness for counsel, information, and wholesome criticism ; as also to George Reid, Esq., R.S.A., whose practical aid is conspicuous in the two illustrations which so greatly enhance the value of the volume.

It does not take much authorship to learn that a book is not a finality, and conscious of many defects in this humble contribution to the history of early Scottish art, as exemplified in " Jamesone, who burst forth at once with meridian splendour," I now commit it to public judgment.

JOHN BULLOCH.

ABERDEEN, *16th April*, 1885.

GEORGE JAMESONE,

THE SCOTTISH VANDYCK.

CHAPTER I

𝕴ntroductory.

A VERY brief sketch of the graphic arts in Scotland, before the dawn of the 17th century, may fittingly introduce a biography of GEORGE JAMESONE, her first native artist, worthy of the name.

Early traces of painting in Scotland are very rare. This is not to be wondered at, when we remember that the struggle for bare subsistence was so engrossing. It was a hard life, and men had little inclination and less encouragement, being so far removed from the stimulating influence of the more civilised centres of population, to think much of the cultivation of the fine arts.

John Barbour relates an incident in The Bruce which gives to Queen Margaret, wife of Malcolm Canmore, the credit of some knowledge of the art of delineation. It was at the time that Scotland was being invaded by the English, and its strongholds taken, that she prophesied, by means of a cartoon, the particular method by which Edinburgh Castle was to be overthrown, about 1080 :—

> And off this taking that I mene
> Sanct Margaret, the gud haly queyne
> Wyst in hyr, throw reweling [revealing]
> Off him that knaws, and wate all thing.
> Therefore in sted of prophecy,
> Scho left a takyning rycht joly

That is yeit in till hyr chapele.
Scho gert weile portray a castell,
A leddre wp to the wall standand
And a man wp thar apon climband.
And a wrat oucht him, as auld men sais,
In Frankis, *Gardys wouys de Fransais.*

Here we have the portrayal very clearly specified, but the methods by which the royal limner executed her "takyning" (token, or intimation by sign) are not indicated. The result was probably a very primitive outline in monochrome. It may be noticed here that the scarcity of words relating to the art of painting is itself a proof of how little it was practised in Scotland in early times. At a later period the word depaynt came in, derived from the French *depeindre*, to paint.

Amongst the few remains of ancient art left, it is now impossible to tell whether they are the work of native Scottish artists or of foreigners —although probably of the latter. Perhaps the very earliest specimen of portraiture extant occurs in an Anglo-Saxon MS., bearing the early date of 1159. The initial letter of this MS. is the letter M., drawn in the ecclesiastical form of two rounded compartments divided by an upright line ℚ. In one of these divisions there is a portrait of David I., the venerable founder of Kelso Abbey, and in the other of Malcolm IV., the reigning King, a lad of 17 years of age. "The portraits are supposed to have been done, in 1159, by one who had the appearance of the two [originals] fresh in his memory."*

In the Trinity Hall of Aberdeen there is a painting of King William the Lion. The picture, as now beheld, was entirely repainted, in 1715, by one White, at a sum "as cheap as possible, not exceeding 50s, sterling." The picture extends to the knees, and the King is represented with a very curious helmet and a long white beard reaching to his waist. In his right hand he holds a book, and in his left a long rod. Below the painting runs the following inscription :—"St. William King of Scots, surnamed the Lyon, the first Founder of the Trinitie Friers at Aberdeen wher he had his Chapell the cheif place of retirement for his

---

* Cosmo Innes's Sketches of Early Scottish History.

devotions. He reigned 49 yeers begining 1165, dyed at Striviling 1214 & was buried at Aberbrothick."

Of course no real value attaches to this picture as determining the early condition of art. It can be held only as proving that at an early date portraiture was attempted. The renovator of the painting has been the destroyer of its artistic and archæological value.

There exists some very ancient painted panelling at Cullen House. It forms part of the ceiling of a room to which it has evidently been adapted, as the scenes represented appear to have been cut to allow the panels to fit their new position. On the back of one of the panels the date 1325 was discovered by a workman who was making some alterations a number of years ago. The painting bespeaks an early date. The drawing is very bad, but the colours are still wonderfully fresh but crude. The painting is in tempera, and the subjects are classical.

A most interesting specimen of a more recent date is to be found in the ancient Church of Houston, in Renfrewshire. On the south wall of the aisle there is a large frame of timber on which there are two pictures seemingly done in oil, but much decayed. On the right side is a man in complete armour resembling that of a Knight Templar, with an inscription in Saxon characters over his head, some words of which are effaced :—" Hic jacet Dominus Joannes Houstoun de eodem, miles, qui obiit anno dom. M'cccc." On the left hand is a picture of his lady, also much effaced, and over her is inscribed :—" Hic jacet Maria Colquohoun sponsa quondam dicti Domini Joannes, quæ obiit septimo die mensis Octobris, an. Dom. M'cccc quinto." Pinkerton argues from this the prevalence of painting in Scotland at the period.

In 1861, an interesting discovery of a fresco wall was made during the removal of part of the old Church at Turriff. A mason, in pulling down a built-up window, was astonished to find that he had unveiled a fresco painting of a mitred abbot on the window bay, with an inscription above—" S. Ninianus."* A similar fresco was found on the opposite splay, but was destroyed by the falling of the wall. It represented an Episcopal figure, fully habited, his

---

* The fresco is carefully described in the preface to The Book of Deir, where it is reproduced in chromo-lithography.

pastoral staff in his left hand, his right hand being elevated in the act of benediction. It is believed that these pictures were part of a series that surrounded the church.

In the history of the Abbots of Kinloss, Ferrerius asserts that certain pictures there, apparently in oil, were executed about the year 1540. The historian adds that the artist also painted the chamber and oratory of the Abbot, Robert Reid.*

It is related of Prior James Halderstone, who died in 1413, that he adorned the church of his monastery with engraved stalls and painted images—" tam in sculpturis stallorum quam picturis imaginum."

Still another instance of the not infrequent use made of painting for church, monumental, or memorial purposes, is to be found in that of Blackfriars Church at Stirling, where the Duke of Albany and his two sons, who were buried there on the south side of the great altar, had paintings done of their *persons* and coats of arms.†

Elgin Cathedral, too, had been in pre-Reformation times decorated with paintings. Spalding mentions a picture of the Crucifixion on the west side of the choir, and one of the Day of Judgment on the east side.

In 1493, Alexander Reid, Provost of Aberdeen, had his portrait painted, but still by an unknown hand. As a mark of the esteem in which he was held, the portrait was placed in the Kirk Session-house, where it hung till 1640, when the officers of a regiment then quartered in the town had it removed, as "smelling somewhat of Popery."‡ The proposal to put the Provost's picture in the Session-house may have arisen from some benefaction made by him to the church.

It is said that James I., besides being a poet and musician, was also an illuminator of books and painter of miniatures. His cultivation of the polite arts was probably due to his long captivity in England. In the "King's Quhair" he addresses Lady Jane Beaufort in these words, referring probably to her efforts at gardening and floriculture :—

> Or are ye' very Nature the goddess
> That have *depaynted* with your heavenly hand
> This garden full of flowers as they stand.

* The New Statistical Account of Scotland.   † The Iconographia Scotica.
‡ Kennedy's Annals, Vol. I., p. 178.

After his restoration, and following the example of Robert the Bruce, James invited and encouraged artists of all kinds to settle in the kingdom. It is doubtless to some of the Flemish artists, thus induced to come to Scotland, that we are indebted for such works of art as have been enumerated. These have been chiefly ecclesiastical, yet we can see in the following story how in those early days art was made to subserve more utilitarian ends.

Bowar, the continuator of Fordun, relates how, "about 1430, a Highland robber having taken two cows from a poor woman, she swore that she would wear no shoes till she had complained to the King. The savage, in ridicule of her oath, nailed horses' shoes to her feet. When her wounds were healed, she proceeded to the royal presence, told her story and showed her scars. The just monarch [James I.] instantly despatched orders to secure the thief, who being brought to Perth and condemned, the King commanded that he should be clothed in a canvas frock, on which was painted the figure of a man fastening horse shoes to a woman's feet. In this dress he was exhibited through the streets for two days, then dragged at the tail of a horse to the gallows and hanged."

The short and troubled reign of James II. is blank in artistic record or achievement, although the former stimulus might have been expected to have been sustained, owing to the King's marriage with Mary of Guelders.

James III. was distinguished by his love of the fine arts, especially of architecture. The noble picture of him and his Queen at Kensington shows the presence of a master hand. On the rich head-dress worn by the Queen are the letters P. ANAG, which have ever been a crux. If they are the artist's name, they nevertheless do not reveal the man. Pinkerton, writing of this picture, says:—" Hardly can any kingdom in Europe boast of a more noble family picture of this early epoch, and it is in itself a convincing specimen of the attention of James III. to the arts. Its probable date is 1484."

There exist tangible proofs of the fact that James IV. encouraged painting, in the following extracts from the "thesaurer's" accounts, showing sums due to his "craftismen fyne" :—

"Item to David Prat ye Payntour, in compleit payment of ye Altar Paynting as resting awind to him ij lbs iy s."

"Item being Kinges command to ye Inglise Payntour quhilk brocht ye fuguris of ye King Queen and Prince of England, and of our Quene xx fr. or xiiij lbs."

"July 23, 1515 Item deliverit to Alexander Chalmer Paynteour for ane hundethe and xl Payntit Armys to the Obsequys of our souerane lord King James the Fred, price of ilk pece tuelf pennys, summa viij lb."

There is a portrait of James at Abbotsford, dated 1507, in Holbein's style; but it may have been painted in France during the King's travels. One John Prat, a "payntor," lived about this same time, and a priest, Sir Thomas Galbraith, was chiefly employed in the illumination of manuscripts.

James V. inherited all his father's fine taste, as his palace at Stirling proves, long reckoned one of the wonders of Scotland for its decorative carvings. These were done by native artists. He also bought foreign pictures, and employed native painters, as the following notes of disbursements show, viz. :—" 1535 October 24. Certaine fyne Picturis of Flanderis coft fra John Browne to the King's grace, price thereof xvij libs." And in 1541 " Item to Andro Watsoun paintour for ye painting of v dufan armes, v. li."

February 14th " To the Quenes Payntour to by colouris to paint with in Falkland xj. li."

July 10 "To the Quene's Payntour for his wageis to August first, next to come." This artist's salary was paid monthly.

A picture of James and his Queen, Mary of Guise, is in the possession of the Duke of Devonshire. The artist is unknown.

Brought up in France where painting was in a forward state, Mary had artistic tastes, which she turned to good account. Before she was married to James, she had secured his portrait. "This fair ladie . . . . past to her coffer and teuk out his picture quhilk shoe had gottin out of Scotland be ane secreit moyane."

During the unhappy reign of Mary, Queen of Scots (1543-1567), the fine arts in Scotland may be said to have been extinct for any specific trace of them that comes down to us. Genuine portraits of herself seem all to have been painted during her early youth spent in France. There is a great dearth of portraits of the remarkable men of that remarkable period, and it seems a mere fortuity that we possess . those of the Regent Murray and of John Knox. The reformers of that day preached a vigorous crusade against all images in stone or on canvas, lest they should be a temptation to the people's return to idolatry.* They went further, and destroyed every carving and painting used in religious worship.†

Though but few works of art have come down to us executed in that period, pictorial representation was not quite neglected. Buchanan relates that after Darnley's death " libels were published and pictures made " and hawked about, bringing home the guilt of the deed to the Queen and her confederates. Put in this graphic way, they winced under the charge, and instituted a rigorous search for those who made it. Among other efforts to discover the guilty, all painters and writing masters were naturally suspected and unsuccessfully examined. Again, when the Protestant Lords took the field against Mary, they adopted the same method of at once wounding her sensibilities, and of sustaining the popular prejudices against her. They flaunted in the Queen's face a great standard on which the catastrophe of the Kirk of Field was emblazoned, and underneath the figure of the dead Darnley were the words—" Judge and revenge my cause, O Lord." Art applied to such base uses, only shows what primitive ideas people then had of its real scope and ends.

The reign of James VI. forms an epoch in the history of painting in Scotland. Portraits and historical subjects became more common, and a

---

* England at this period was advancing in taste. Elizabeth's *amour propre* was so wounded at the unattractive manner in which artists executed her portraits, that she issued a proclamation forbidding any to be painted but by " special cunning painters."

† The same *animus* existed among the Puritans of England, who, however, went further still. They considered one-half the fine paintings idolatrous and the other half indecent. Parliament decreed that all pictures in the royal collections representing Our Saviour or His Mother should be burnt. Sculptured Nymphs and Graces, the work of Ionian chisels, were handed over to Puritan stone masons to be made decent.

token of the dawn of civilisation may be seen in the fact that in a few instances the wealthy began to collect works of art for the decoration of their houses. The unfortunate Ruthven, Earl of Gowrie, is said to have built a " fair gallery," and decorated it with pictures. Notwithstanding the numerous portraits of James, he was personally averse to them being painted.

During the Regency of Morton, one Arthur van Bronchorst, who explored the gold mines in Scotland, became one of His Majesty's sworn servants to paint small and great pictures to the King ; and, in 1594, Hadrian van Son is styled painter to the King in a privilege granted by James to a ship belonging to this artist, " whom for many reasons we greatly favour and wish him well." It is quite evident that these gentlemen were something more or something less than artists. There must have been, in the one case, a division of affection between art and a love of gold, and, in the other, between art and merchandise. James, however, appreciated their efforts in painting, and gave them such encouragement as his extreme poverty and the parsimony of his Parliament allowed him. Prince Henry seems to have possessed something more than a passing feeling for art, and had he not been cut down in the flower of his youth would, in all probability, have given much stimulus to the cultivation of art. " He loved," says Cornwallis, " and did mightily strive to do somewhat . . . . . in sculpture, limning, and carving, and in all sorts of rare and beautiful pictures, which he had brought with him from all countries."

Other references might be given to art and artists in North Britain, but the " paintit broddis " displaying portraits or " conceptis " were either the imported work of foreign artists—first those of France and then those of the Low Countries—or the work of native painters, whose highest skill appears to have been equal only to the emblazoning of a coat of arms.

The removal of the Court to London, in 1603, gave a decided check to the progress and encouragement of art, which, after that event, had no exponent, so far as native talent went, until from the far north the star of Jamesone's genius rose, and his works began to attract notice by their excellence.

To Jamesone must be conceded the precedence of all native British artists. For, while England was made familiar with art, in a way that Scotland knew little of, it was still the result of foreign art or foreign artists. On Macaulay's authority, as far on as the close of the reign of Charles II., there is not a single painter or statuary whose name is now remembered. It is strange that in England a plenitude of art should have resulted in such sterility of native talent, whereas, obversely, out of the comparative barrenness of Scottish art should have sprung so early, an artist so well endowed as George Jamesone. It is with a sincere feeling of gratitude that we think of the splendid legacy to posterity in his numerous portraits. There may be two opinions as to the art value of Jamesone's pictures. There can be but one as to their historical importance. " I have to tell you, as a fact of personal experience," says Carlyle in a letter to David Laing regarding the project of a National Exhibition of Historical Portraits, " that in all my poor historical investigations, it has been and always is, one of the most primary wants to procure a bodily likeness of the personage inquired after ; a good portrait if such exists, failing that, an indifferent if sincere one. In short, any representation made by a faithful human creature of that face and figure, which *he* saw with his eyes, and which I can never see with mine is now valuable to me. . . . . All men, just in proportion as they are ' historians ' (which every mortal is who has a *memory* and attachments and possessions in the Past), will feel something of the same—every human creature something."

There is a natural instinct to perpetuate the memory of the illustrious dead. With our own rude forefathers in pre-historic times the feeling found expression in raising a cairn, and it became the inherited duty of posterity to keep adding a stone to it. The same feeling prompted the ancient Egyptians to embalm their dead, and to render their effigies in their own peculiar manner. In the higher civilisations of Greece and Rome it led to the execution of that marvellous sculpture which has given to all time such a *vraisemblance* to their life and literature. The modern developments of portraiture in sculpture, painting, engraving, and photography, attest the survival of the same instinct in increasing strength.

CHAPTER II

State of Society at Jamesone's Birth.

A T the time of George Jamesone's advent into the world, there are several reasons for the belief that there were certain conditions favourable and others unfavourable to the creation and development of his artistic genius. In the preceding summary sketch of the state of art prior to his day there is not much to be seen of a kind to suggest to or foster in his mind the artistic idea. What little of the work of native artists he had seen was more likely to deter rather than promote any efforts of his own in the same direction.

Among the general conditions of life not favourable to the introduction and pursuit of art may be reckoned the great ignorance that prevailed, especially touching matters of æstheticism. Men's minds were pre-occupied with graver questions. Not only had the peace and faith of the country been recently threatened, but the national existence had been imperilled. A feeling of unrest following the averted danger had scarcely subsided, and that was not a congenial soil for the growth of art. The sword was happily sheathed, but it was still deemed mightier than the pencil, and martial prowess was more valued than skill in painting. The individual struggle for existence, too, was very severe, and admitted but small attention to the refinements and embellishments of life. In short, for such art as George Jamesone introduced there seemed to be little demand ; for the artist, no niche in the social economy of the times. One unfavourable factor to the progress of the fine arts has already been mentioned. The Union in 1603, by withdrawing the King and Court, and many of the nobility, from Scotland, weakened and impoverished the country, and dealt an undoubted blow to that phase of the nation's advancement.

On the other hand, it has to be admitted that during the entire period of Jamesone's life, although polemics prevailed in Church and State, it

was a war of words, and did not reach its more acute stage of open
violence until he had succeeded in educating his countrymen to a
better appreciation of art. It was a lull between crucial times, and in
that lull Jamesone popularised painting in Scotland so effectively that
the impetus has never been lost. A growing connection and intimacy
with the Continent was also helping to widen the interest of Scotsmen
in the study of art. Merchants and scholars were frequently passing
over to France and the Netherlands, where art was to be seen in high
perfection, and it became not an uncommon thing for them to bring
home their effigy in oil by a foreign master.

In Aberdeen, Jamesone found the conditions for entering on the
career of his choice to be about as favourable as could be found any-
where in his native land. It was an old historic town, round which
clung many interesting traditions, whose picturesqueness could not fail
to stimulate the imagination and quicken the sensibilities. It was
pleasantly situated, and the diversified beauties of its surroundings of
ocean and forest, river and rich meadow lands, were attractive and
educative. Within its bounds were the venerable University buildings,
and still more venerable Cathedral of Saint Machar and Church of
Saint Nicholas. The entire population did not perhaps exceed 5000 or
6000, but certain circumstances may be recalled to justify the opinion, if
need be, that the citizens were for the age in an advanced state of
culture.

For centuries before, as a cathedral town, the presence of a bishop
and his court, consisting of a numerous retinue of resident clergy, could
not fail to leave a certain impress, and impart a certain humanising tone
to society. The gorgeous ritual of Saint Machar's and Saint Nicholas'
had so familiarised the people with a sense of the beautiful in worship
that we know it was with some reluctance that they adopted the balder
forms of the Reformed services. In the possession, too, of King's
College and, at a later date, of Marischal College, Aberdeen was an educational luminary and a centre of diffusive light for the whole northern
portion of the kingdom. Scholarship was in the ascendant, and
the leaven of learning, caught from intercourse with resident professors,
and the groups of ardent students who were attracted to their classes,

also added opportunities at least for culture. Whatever superiority of refinement was possessed by the nobility and gentry of the north, was shared by the inhabitants, inasmuch as no family of distinction was without its town mansion. This, with the not infrequent visits of Royalty itself, accustomed the people with modes of life and the ministries of art, of which it was scarcely in mimetic human nature to resist the civilising effects.

Yet another element conducive to social and material progress consisted in contact with the outer world, already hinted at. Aberdeen was essentially a seafaring town. From immemorial times an extensive foreign trade was carried on with the seaport towns on the north-west coasts of the Continent. Home and foreign vessels plied constantly, and conducted an important exchange of commodities. The outward bound carried the far-famed salmon of the Dee and the Don, pickled pork, raw hides, as well as coarse textiles in woollen and linen goods, the product of primitive looms; and worsted stockings, the noted product of the lissome fingers of the " shank-wives " of Bon-Accord. The homeward bound brought not only the natural products of more genial climes, but the manufactures of peoples who had made very great progress in the mechanical and in the fine arts. Rich fabrics, consisting of plain and brocaded silks, the result of French skill, and fine-figured linens, from the weavers of Ypres, as well as velvet from Utrecht, were imported and bought for personal wear. Clocks, watches, jewellery, silver plate, articles of *vertu*, arms, arras, books, medicines, stoneware, and much else that Europe excelled in, were freely imported. The " skeely skippers," who navigated the Aberdeen ships or foreign bottoms across the chopping North Sea, conducted much of the merchandising, and became personally enriched thereby. But, for many obvious reasons, the merchants visited the Continent in person, preferring the *vis-a-vis* transaction, albeit conducted in broken Dutch or French, in the city of Amsterdam or Paris, to the less satisfactory results of a long-winded correspondence. Commerce did not exhaust the passenger traffic of the time. There was likewise a steady intercourse with the Continent by the professional classes. Students, having completed their University career at home, went abroad with the design of finishing their studies,

Young men of rank also went abroad, either to visit at foreign Courts or to enrol themselves in foreign military service. They usually returned in the course of a few years, bringing with them many notions, habits, and customs, which spoke of an advanced state of society. In most instances personal intimacies were formed, and afterwards sustained by an occasional interchange of visits.

These appear to have been among the influences at work at the close of the 16th century in the gradual preparation of the soil for the nurture of the native artist. And at this juncture George Jamesone appeared. He betook himself to painting the portraits of the men and women who made the history of his times, and has thereby helped us the better to understand that history.

CHAPTER III.

His Family Connections.

FROM time immemorial it has been customary to trace pedigrees and family descent. However desirable it might be to make out a genealogical deduction, the lapse of well nigh three hundred years makes such a task in George Jamesone's case a very hopeless one. For all we know he was the first distinguished member of his family.

In searching the records of the period prior to the artist's birth, his patronymic is not found to be a common one in Aberdeen, but, as if to compensate for its infrequent appearance, it is spelt, when it does occur, with a most ingenious diversity of orthography. There seems to have been no fixed standards of spelling at that time—hence we have Jamesonn, Jamesoun, Jamesoune, Jameson, Jamesone, Jamison, Jamieson, Jamesonne, Jamissoune.

In 1554, reference is made to "Williame Jamesone, dekyne of the masonis," who conducted business on his own account. A contract, dated 18th June of that year, between him and the Dean of the Guild, is for somewhat extensive repairs to the Tolbooth, namely, "the bigging beyting and mending of the battelling . . . and reforming and mending twa vindowis therof . . . and makand the said tolbuith vattirthicht sa far as concernis the mason craft, for the quhilkis the said den of gild sell gif him xl poundis." Other references to the "dekyne" show him to have been a prominent man in his day, engaged in various works of a public kind, such as the superintendence of the work of the Bridge of Dee. What is to be understood by this is, that this noble structure, conceived and begun by the munificent Bishop Elphinstone, and completed by his worthy successor, Bishop Dunbar, from working plans furnished by that most cultivated ecclesiastic, Alexander Galloway, parson of Kinkell, was gratefully accepted as a gift by the community of Aberdeen, who, in the person of Deacon Jamesone, found a practical and responsible man to keep the structure in thorough repair. Its age was about a quarter of a century.

There is no certain proof of it, but it is not an unlikely supposition that the worthy "dekyne," who had this important trust committed to him, was none other than Jamesone's paternal grandfather. The simple fact that he was of the same craft as the artist's father gives some degree of probability to the suggestion.

It is satisfactory to be able to quit the region of doubt and conjecture for the sure ground. That the artist was the son of Andrew Jamesone, master mason in Aberdeen, is at least one fact in his life that has never been questioned. In the public records of the times Andrew Jamesone's name is frequently referred to, as carrying out various important building operations about the town, much as if he had naturally succeeded his reputed father in similar employments, sometimes planning, erecting, and repairing. His position seems analogous to what we now designate City Architect, and adviser of the Council in matters connected with the structural crafts. Whether he succeeded to it or created a business for himself, by his own industry, skill, or business capacity, his position was highly respectable. Not disdaining, perhaps, to work with his own hands, he was an employer of labour, and had the direction of certain public works under his control.

He appears at times to have conducted his business under a co-partnery. In the year 1607, in concert with William Massie, he entered into a contract to execute such extensive repairs as almost amounted to a rebuilding of the Bridge of Don, venerable even then. It is described as having become "very ruynous and liklie to fall." The work was done at three periods, after intervals of two years. The first contract price was £3333 6s. 8d. Scots, with a trifle for extras. The contracting parties were the "maissonnis foirsadis," and Bishop Blackburn, Principal Raitt, and Provost Cullen. The third specification of the work, provided for the repair of the "waist part" of the bridge, "beginnand at the new wark alreddie biggit," and for the building of the "haill butreissis on ilk syd of the said brig." The work was done at the sight of David Cargill, Andrew Watson, and David Anderson, Master of Kirk and Bridge Works—the last-named being Andrew Jamesone's brother-in-law.

In 1610, he is again referred to in the burgh records. Under date 15th August of that year he signs a contract with the town for rebuilding the Bow Brig over the Denburn. It was to be of "twa bowis," or arches, and as the bridge lay in the way of the most important access to the town, it behoved to be a structure of some little pretension. The contractor is designated "Androw Jamesoun, masoun." The contract price of 250 merks was paid in three instalments, presumably according to the amount of the work done, and in discharging the bill Jamesone gratefully adds to his signature—"I hald me weill content and payit." A very pleasant ending, and one that doubtless betokened the fact that his employers were as "weill content" with the workmanlike way in which he had fulfilled the contract as the mason was with his merks. Jamesone's bridge was but one of several structures which successively spanned the Denburn at that spot. In one generation it was a bridge of "ane bow," and in another of "twa bowis," till in our own day the "stane and lyme" has been replaced by lattice iron girders over the Denburn Valley Railway, which has metamorphosed the whole scene. From such references it is not difficult to conceive Andrew Jamesone's social position and status in the town. He must have been a well-to-do, enterprising, reliable man. He was a Burgess of Guild, and took an active and leading part in questions affecting the interests of his own craft. In the common indenture entered into between the town and the various crafts, in the year 1587, Andrew Jamesone is found to represent and sign for the masons.

He was married, in 1585, to the artist's mother, Marjory Anderson, a young woman of equal rank with himself, and of a respectable family. The marriage entry runs—

"Thair is promess of marriage betwix Ando Jamesone, Marjore Anderson." It is under date 17th August.

Her father was Gilbert Anderson, an eminent merchant in Aberdeen, a Burgess of Guild, and one of the magistrates of the town. His name occurs frequently in the transactions of the day. The surname Anderson was a most common one, and there can be little doubt that the family was of the "old blood of the town." Gilbert Anderson is recorded to have married Janet Moir on the 29th May, 1576, and as his daughter's marriage with Andrew Jamesone occurred nine years later, she, with her brother David, must have been the fruit of an earlier union. She is spoken of as the eldest of her father's family. The other members of the family were Alexander, Janet, and Christian, probably the half-brother and half-sisters of Marjory and David. Nothing is known of the two daughters, Janet and Christian, but the two sons, Alexander and David, rose to be men of some distinction. Both had a decided talent for mathematics, of which the former was a professor. At his death his mathematical instruments, and books were bequeathed to Marischal College as a proper depository. David turned his attention to applied mechanics, and, as the "command servand of the toun," was able during a long course of years to render it many valuable services. Parson Gordon's opinion was that he was "the most skilful mechanic that lived in Scotland." He was, indeed, a remarkable man, and there is, perhaps, no name more prominent than his in the civic activities of his day. His precise official position was what is now designated town's surveyor or civil engineer. He is described as a plumber, but the truth is he was a master of many crafts, a sort of Board of Works—so versatile that he earned at last the *soubriquet* of "Davy-do-a'-thing," by which he is still known. In his capacity of Dean of Guild and one of the magistrates of the burgh, his scientific knowledge and his practical ingenuity, which knew not the purgatory of defeat, found ample scope. From the "macking ane orloge in the common clerkis chalmer" to the designing of a steeple for the Church of St. Nicholas, and fixing up the weather cock with his own hands, or the carrying out an important harbour improvement, he was a useful and successful public servant.

Any reference to David Anderson is sure to suggest the oft-told story of how he applied his inventive genius to the removal of a huge stone known as Knock Maitland or Craig Metellan, which had dangerously obstructed the fairway to the harbour mouth. It was a source of continual anxiety and damage to the shipping interest until Anderson, as harbour engineer, took the difficulty seriously in hand and succeeded in overcoming it. His plan was a very simple one, and the wonder is that it had not been adopted long before. It consisted in

securing, at low water, a number of empty barrels to the stone. Their
buoyancy on the inflowing of the tide lifted the whole mass out of its
bed. It is said that Anderson seated himself on one of the barrels and,
with a sense of mingled triumph and humour, sailed up the harbour with
flying colours, and dropt the suspended block where it could do no more
harm. This exploit was met with grateful acclaim by the citizens, and
the 300 merks it cost was deemed a safe investment.

By such incidents is David Anderson best remembered, but they do
not cover the entire area of his services to his native town. He gave in
other directions proofs of his power. Into these we cannot enter, but
as a permanent official, it is clear that he played an important part in
the management of the town's affairs, and enjoyed a well-earned respect.

By his marriage with Jean Guild, Anderson became connected with
an important local family. Her father was Matthew Guild, described as
a wealthy armourer. He was a sturdy supporter of some of the use-and-
wont convivialities of his early days, and, in consequence, got himself
involved in a prosecution by the more rigid disciplinarians of later times.
A portrait of this worthy hangs in Trinity Hall among other distinguished craftsmen. It is asserted to be a copy of an earlier picture
by Jamesone. It would be nearer the truth to say that it is a copy by
Jamesone of an original which he could not have painted, since Guild
died when Jamesone was still a boy at the Grammar School. Jean
Guild's brother was the well-known Dr. William Guild, whose attitude
during the stormy period of the Troubles has been keenly contested
by men of all shades of opinion. His name need only be mentioned
in this connection as being thus distantly related to George Jamesone.
Dr. Guild was a year older than Jamesone, and is very likely to have
companioned him both at school and college.

The foregoing detail of the family connections of George Jamesone
point out definitely that socially they were highly respectable, and in
possession of fair means. , To be environed by a circle of such friends
was an unspeakable advantage, especially for one who had need of
all the sympathy and encouragement so necessary on entering a field
entirely new, the fruitage of which was entirely problematical. This
goodly inner circle of substantial relatives, with their respective groups

of friends and town's folks, with whom they were in close association, made an outer circle more or less interested in the novel work and future success of the young artist when he opened the first studio in Aberdeen, and began to paint the portraits of the burghers of Bon-Accord.

In the course of time it had come to be forgotten in what part of the town the Jamesone family had a fixed residence. Within the present century a growing interest in the painter has led to various speculations as to where he was probably born. One tradition points to the Mutton Brae, the western declivity of St. John's Hill. No houses, however, existed there at that early period. The Shiprow, old even in Provost Davidson's day (for there he kept his *taberna* in the year of the Brim Harlaw), has been surmised to be the locality of the Jamesones' residence. There is no better ground for thinking so than the existence of a passage there called Jamieson's Court. But here there is nothing in a name. Another and more definite tradition has pointed to "an old Flemish building which projects into a narrow street," without naming it, as the home of Andrew Jamesone, and the birthplace of his illustrious son.

The building that best answers this description is obviously the ancient turreted mansion on the north side of the Schoolhill, and in close proximity to the church and churchyard of St. Nicholas. A somewhat troublesome search, some ten or twelve years ago, for the title-deeds of this old property was rewarded by the discovery of Andrew Jamesone's proprietary interest in it. In these deeds, the property is described as "that temple tenement of land lying within the burgh of Aberdeen upon the north side of the Schoolhill thereof, betwixt the land sometime of the altar of Saint Lawrence and Ninian of old founded by the barons of Drum," and is further described in one part "as sometime of the heirs of Andrew Jamesone," and in another, "of the deceased Andrew Jamesone." Complete confirmation of this has recently been got in the Burgh Sasine Books by Mr. Alexander M. Munro, to whose courtesy extracts therefrom are given in the Appendix (p. 187). Andrew Jamesone's first sasine is dated 27th May, 1586, just two months before the birth of his first child. The land is carefully described, but no mention is made of a house, which naturally leads to the supposition that the house in question was erected by Andrew Jame-

sone as a family house, in keeping with his means and social position.
The contiguous property was owned by Andrew Jamesone's relatives,
Jean Guild, and her husband, David Anderson, his brother-in-law, and
was ultimately bequeathed to the town for educational purposes.
Whether any tenement existed on the Andersons' property is not
known, but Jamesone's own house, in its substantial massiveness, has
survived all its contemporaries in the quarter, the passive witness of many
changes and of stirring historic scenes enacted in its neighbourhood.

This picturesque reminder of bygone centuries and generations of
men is, unfortunately, doomed by the exigencies of modern commercial
enterprise to vanish from the scene, and that, probably, ere this year is
out. Fortunately, the building was sufficiently attractive to Mr. Billings
to induce him, from an architectural point of view, to give it a place in
his " Baronial Antiquities of Scotland." That engraving is suggestive of
restoration, inasmuch as in all its lines, and in the details of its fine
mouldings, the masonry seems fresh from the chisel of its builders.
Still more fortunately, the picture presented *en face*, etched from a
beautiful drawing by Mr. George Reid, R.S.A., will survive as a more
realistic delineation of Jamesone's birthplace.   A front view of the
house shows between the two turrets a blank square within a stone
moulding.   This had probably contained a coat of arms, a usual
appendage on buildings of this description. See Appendix, page 190.

Various idle traditions attach to the house.   Among others, Queen
Mary is said to have lodged in it, and also that Samuel Rutherford, the
banished minister, lived in it during the two years that he was a prisoner
on parole in Aberdeen.   It has been long known as the manse of St.
Nicholas, and it is not improbable that at some time or other it may
have been occupied by some of the incumbents of the church.   The
motto " Domus optima cœlo " is said to have been at one time inscribed
over the doorway. Of this no trace now exists.   There is an outer and
an inner deeply-moulded doorway.   The former, facing the street, had
been protected by an iron gate, and gave access through the house to
the wooded garden behind which stretched to the margin of the loch.

The artist, as ultimate heir of his father and brother, fell into possession of the whole " foreland " and tenements, and there continued to

Jamesone's House . Schoolhill . Aberdeen   R.

Chromlith. et Imp A Dumont Paris

live, work, and rear up his family. It is said that he built his studio as an addition to the house, behind it, with the advantage of a steady north light. It has long since disappeared, and on its site an ordinary dwelling-house stands. On its east and west sides are inserted corresponding carved stones, thus—

1729
I · A
I · I

These initials might be those of John Alexander and Isabella Jamesone, respectively the son-in-law and daughter of the artist, but the date forbids. During some alterations on the property, about 1850, a coin of Hieras II., King of Syracuse, was found among the rubbish. An added interest in this circumstance is derived from the fact that Jamesone, who was well known to be a collector of coins and antiquities, may have once possessed this coin. His antiquarian taste was probably acquired whilst under the personal influence of Rubens, who had a *penchant* for the antique.

The artist's parents, as we have already seen, were married in 1585 —exactly three hundred years ago—and their first child, a daughter, was born in the following July. On the last day but one of that month, she was baptised according to the following register :—

  " The penult day July 1586 andro Jameson marjore anderson [had a] doithar in mareage callit elspaitt.—James Robertson, edward donaldson, elspatt cultis, elspatt mydiller, witnesses."

How the social and religious life of the people of the 17th century was hedged about by municipal and ecclesiastical enactments may be seen in the following statute affecting the baptism of children :—

  9th September 1573 " Ordainit that the fader off the barn that is to be baptised, and, in his absens, the neirest freind off the barne, or the gosseppis, cum the day befoir the barn is to be baptised, and shew the Redar, to the effect he may aduerteis the Minister quhidder the barn be gottin in matrymony or no."

In this Andrew Jamesone had no difficulty in satisfying the " Redar."

Hitherto it has been generally believed that George was the next

born and eldest son of his parents. This mistake has doubtless arisen
from the circumstance that early searchers had found him so styled in
documents of a certain date, subsequent to the death of an older brother
named Andrew. The true reading of such a phrase would therefore be
"eldest [surviving] son of the quondam Andrew Jamesone." Referring
to the sasine of 3rd December, 1607, it clearly states that the property
in question was "in gratiam et favore delecti filii *seniores* legitim Andre
Jamesoun." Without any record of the birth or baptism of Andrew,
junior, it remains to suppose that he may have been born during the
autumn of 1587. In September of that year Andrew Jamesone appears
as witness to the baptism of probably a brother's child, but his wife,
Marjore Anderson, is conspicuous by her absence from among the gossips
on the occasion. From this it may be inferred that only urgent family
reasons hindered her from countenancing the baptism of her niece :—

    "The x September 1587 alex‘ Jameson and Isbell cruickshank [had a]
        doithar in mareage callit elspaitt ; andro Jameson andro Knowes,
        elspat gordon, margaret gray, witnesses."

Passing now to the birth of the artist, in the absence of any bap-
tismal register, the same perplexity is met in fixing the exact date.
His position in order is clearly defined in the fourth sasine quoted in the
Appendix. He is there styled "delecti filii sui *secundo* geniti Georgii
Jamesoun." Allowing a similar period to elapse between Andrew's
birth and his own, as has been supposed to elapse between Elspet's and
Andrew's, it is left to conjecture George to have been born before the
close of 1588—a very notable year in the country's history.

At its dawn, if there was not an actual reign of terror, very grave
anxieties clouded the minds of men. All eyes were directed to Spain
who, drawing on her then splendid resources, was equipping that mighty
Armada intended to lay renegade Britain low. Before the year was
out, and ere yet young Jamesone saw the light, his parents may have
seen the gale-driven remnants of the ill-fated fleet drifting help-
lessly past the town, up the North Sea, to certain destruction on
the rock-bound coasts beyond. The conflict was one of religious
opinions, and in Aberdeen, proof of the strained relations between
the rival faiths may be seen in the fact that at that time, by a *lex*

talionis, the Town Council decreed that all adherents of the old faith were to quit house and home by a certain day, leaving their heritable property confiscate to the burgh. The animus thus generated in society survived long after the crisis which occasioned it had passed away. After the first excitement had subsided, the currents of life flowed back into their wonted channels, ruffled only by those events which lent them a piquancy, sometimes pleasant and sometimes otherwise.

In Aberdeen, during the first decade of young Jamesone's existence, there were a few occurrences, mostly of a spectacular kind, which would make an undoubted impression on his mind. Amongst these were no fewer than three royal visits of King James. That of 1589 would pass unheeded, but those of 1592 and 1594 might reasonably be expected to interest him. On the last named occasion " his Majestie remanit v or vj weekis," and only left "for skearsitie of wiueris." To a boy of seven the spectacle of the King, his courtiers and soldiers, would be far more than the object of the visit—the chasing of Catholic Lords—would be to his father. Another important event connected with royalty was the equipment of a vessel of the port, to form the town's contingent to the fleet which accompanied James to the Continent on the occasion of his marriage. This vessel was named the Nicholas, and no pains was spared to render her worthy of the occasion. She sailed on 16th April, 1589.

Aberdeen, always loyal, had a more than ordinary interest in this wedding, on account of the important part which one of the citizens had in bringing it about. This was George, fifth Earl Marischal, who, in this year, had the honour of being appointed Ambassador Extraordinary to the Court of Denmark, where he stood proxy for King James in his espousals with the Princess Anne. The Earl conducted the embassage on a magnificent scale, and out of his own pocket gallantly defrayed all the charges.

Before passing from these references to King James, it may be mentioned that Jamesone has been credited with having painted his portrait. There exists no evidence in support of this. Jamesone probably had no other opportunity of seeing or delineating the royal features than the occasions mentioned. The portraits of the King ascribed to Jamesone possess nothing of his characteristic mode of treatment. The tradition results from the same ignorance which attributes to Jamesone so many old portraits, the artists of which are now unknown.

In this same decade the Earl Marischal gave further proof of his great wealth and liberality in a way that laid Aberdeen under lasting obligations to him. This was his establishment, in 1593, of a new College and University. In that year, exactly one hundred years after King's College had been established, the Earl founded Marischal College, and endowed it at first with funds sufficient for the maintenance of a principal, three professors, and six scholarships for students of merit, and afterwards increased his benefactions for its extended usefulness.

Its great hall is adorned with many portraits, several of which are by Jamesone's hand, including those of the noble founder himself and Robert Gordon of Straloch, who was the first graduate of the College. Indeed, but for Jamesone we should now be without any representations whatever of these two remarkable men.

There were two events, in 1594, which would appeal to the boy's imagination and love of the picturesque. One of these was the riding of the town's outer marches with more than usual pomp and circumstance. Both his father and uncle would take a prominent part therein, considering their intimate connection with the civic business. This would bring the great event very much home to the boy. He would see Provost Collieson, the Magistrates, Council, Officials, the Trades, and other burghers of Bon-Accord, all bravely mounted, muster at the Tolbooth and troop down the Shiprow, through the Green, and furth the town by the Bow Brig, with banners flying and music playing. He would also eagerly watch their return in the evening, after having satisfied themselves that the ancient landmarks had not been removed.

The other event was the observance of a "Wappinshawn" on the Woolmanhill, a little westward of his father's house. It is more than likely that its revival at this period resulted from the recent raids of rievers from the wilds of Birse, who, by approaching in their lawlessness the very gates of the town, taught the "indwellers" the necessity of not neglecting the arts of defence and of standing to arms.

The numerous witch-burnings of the period may be adverted to as affording some insight to at least one phase of the social and religious condition of the people. It is difficult to realise the credulity of those men who, with a remorseless zeal, could sacrifice, within a year or two, the lives of dozens of poor, and certainly harmless creatures on the altar of Superstition. With a view to the entertainment or admonition of the people, the witches were burned in batches. It is to be hoped that young Jamesone did nothing more than hear that such cruel and degrading things were done.

In 1597, the most noted historic event that occurred in the town was the reconciliation of Lords Huntly and Forbes with each other, and both with the Church and the State. An imposing ceremony in Saint Nicholas Church and subsequent civic festivities were matters of universal interest to the citizens, and the meaning of it all, not beyond the reach of a boy of ten who had probably been a witness of what took place.

CHAPTER IV.

His Education.

OF the principal occurrences noted in the preceding chapter, Jamesone had been simply an intelligent eye witness. At the age of ten he reaches a new era in his life, in passing from gaping spectatorship to take his personal share of the activities of the boy-world —the school. Only a few paces from his father's door, the Grammar School had been familiar to him from his earliest days. And although there were no primary schools leading up to it, there had been some degree of preparation for it, if but the horn book for a primer, learnt at his mother's knee, and the Bible, as a text-book of higher education, under his father's teaching.*

Before formally entering the Grammar School, pupils were probably initiated in the art of writing, and also in arithmetic. It was attended by the sons of the better-to-do citizens, as well as by boys from a wide country area, many of them the sons of the country gentry, who had received some previous training, either at the hands of the parish schoolmaster or of the family tutor, usually some poor probationer of the Church. The Grammar School of the burgh was a very ancient institution. Proof of its existence, and superintendence by an ecclesiastic of the day, is obtained before the close of the thirteenth century. It was flourishing two centuries before the establishment of King's College and three centuries before that of Marischal College. In 1597, when Jamesone's father introduced him to it, Thomas Cargill was the Rector. The

---

* One David Mackenzie had thought fit to open an elementary school in the town, but, in 1593, the magistrates, thoroughly imbued with a monopolising spirit, ordered him to desist. This action was taken at the instigation of the Rector of the Grammar School, whose influence in educational matters can be seen in an act of Council four years after, by which no other school but the Sang School was to be permitted, except under his licence and control.

post was no sinecure. The scholars partook of the turbulent character of the times, and conflicts, not always confined to a war of words, sometimes took place between the masters and the pupils. The latter had very pronounced opinions as to their rights and privileges, and very jealous of any abridgment of them. On one occasion we find them appealing in Latin to the Town Council on a question of holidays, of which the Rector of the day (1569) had, with more zeal than discretion, deprived them.

Unfortunately such classic modes of obtaining redress were not always adhered to. They sometimes revolted altogether, taking the law into their own hands. and the school into their own management. On these occasions the little rebels had usually to be bought off by concessions to their demands. In order to guard against these ebullitions of youthful spirit, the Council enacted "that in all tyme comying all gentilmannis soneis to landward as burgessis soneis within this burgh, the scholar and barne sall, be the maister to quhome he is enterit, be presentit to the prouest and baillies or euer he be receivit within ony schuill of this burgh and sall set caution of burgessis, induellaris of Abirden that the scholar presentit sall obey the magistrat and maister and sall nawayis vsurpe aganis the ordinance of the consell wnder the paine of ten poundis more of penaltie to be paid be the cautioner for the barne transgressing."

There are many such references to the school, which characterise the "maneris" of the little community into which Jamesone was introduced, and but few which indicate the nature of the studies pursued.

In its infancy the school was entirely supported by the municipality. When, however, Mr. William Carmichael was appointed to the Rectorship, in 1573, his salary was set down at the humble figure of 50 merks, along with the sum of two shillings "ilk raith" or quarter from each scholar, which was probably the origin of the system of school fees. His successor was appointed on similar terms, his defined duties being to impart "knowledge and maneris," and in the subsequent election of a teacher, in 1603; the course of instruction for the youth embraced "the airt of grammer, gude letteris, and maneris." To acquire these, the school was attended not only by boys belonging to the town, but largely

by boys from the country, more especially such as intended to follow it
up with a view to some of the learned professions.   This naturally
suggests the idea—Which of these did the parents of Jamesone have
in view as the destination of their son ?   There was the Church, the
Bar, and Medicine.   It may have been that nothing definite was in
view, but simply that, having the means to provide the best education
that could be had in a town of educational facilities, young Jamesone
was to be privileged as his father had never been, and fitted for what
course his talents best suited him.   That it should have been that
which he ultimately pursued, it is safe to predict, was not in all their
thoughts.

The Grammar School was regarded as an educational luminary in
the North of Scotland, and here the young portrait painter would make
acquaintance with a crowd of contemporaries destined, like himself, to
play a not inconspicuous part in the history of the period.   The school
stood in that western suburb to which it gave its name—the Schoolhill.
It adjoined the Convent of the Blackfriars, and in the same vicinity
was the Sang School, standing in the Waster Kirk Gate, next the
church, exactly opposite the modern No. 35 in that street now called
the Back Wynd.

Latin formed a very important element in the school course of
instruction, and before finishing the four years of its curriculum, scholars
were usually able to converse in it freely.   Indeed, at College they were
prohibited from using any other.

On leaving school, in 1601, Jamesone had a choice of two Colleges.
There was King's College, in Old Aberdeen, and Marischal College, in
the new town.   His name does not occur in the lists of students or
alumni of the former ; and, as regards Marischal College, it is unfortunate that the first volume of the College records has been lost,
where it would have appeared, if at all.   It is most probable it would
have been found there.   There would seem to be something like a
fatality about the actual records of Jamesone, which throws a conjectural element into his life.   More of this will be seen as we proceed.

University life in the beginning of the seventeenth century partook
somewhat of the conventual character.   Students from a distance took

up their residence in it, very much as is still the usual custom at the great English Universities. This residential arrangement began at the period when these seminaries were entirely in the hands of Church-men, and more exclusively than now the nurseries of men designed for the Church. Their practical seclusion from the outer world was deemed favourable for the successful prosecution of studies adapted to their sacred calling. The practice had the undoubted advantage of securing to young men far from home an abode under a rather stricter surveil-lance and protection than could have been secured without it. Students, like Jamesone, living in the town had less need and were not obliged to reside in College.

The students carried the independent, not to say turbulent, spirit of their school-days to the more advanced academies of learning, to check which, nothing is so apparent as the disciplinary character of the College rules. Quarrels among the students themselves, collisions between the students of rival Colleges, conflicts between town and gown, had all to be guarded against. Consequently arms and offensive weapons were forbidden to be worn, and breaches of the rigid rules of the College were visited with corporal punishment, pecuniary fines, or expulsion. The masters wisely endeavoured to give useful direction to the youthful expressions of the rude health and strength of the students by seeking to develop their physical education in the en-couragement of such exercises as running, leaping, wrestling, fencing, archery, golfing, football, swimming, and other healthful and manly sports.

But, however agreeable in themselves, these pastimes were not the serious occupation of the students' curriculum. The range of studies was narrower than now, but there was more time and scope for its thorough mastery, because greater concentration on the subjects studied. The curriculum was, as it is still, a four years' one before graduation.

The first year's work consisted in acquiring a knowledge of the elements of Greek, besides reading critically some of the easier authors in that as well as in the Latin tongue, to compose and declaim in those languages. Besides this, the session finished with a short compend of

Logic.   It was the custom of the Regents to dictate to the students
their observations on such parts of the writings of Aristotle, Porphyry,
and others, as were read in their class.   Indeed, one of the College rules
was that in public conversation students were to speak only Latin or
Greek.   The second year's work consisted in following up the study of
Logic, begun in the first, along with that of Metaphysics.   The work of
the third year was a study of the elements of Arithmetic and Geometry,
the works of Aristotle, and Cicero's De Officiis.   Students successfully
passing this three years' course took the B.A. degree.   In the fourth
year the Principal engaged the students himself.   Besides having
the supervision of the whole University, one of his duties was to
conduct a religious knowledge class by giving Bible expositions
for an hour every Monday.   He also illustrated the physiology of
Aristotle, beginning where the third Regent left off, gave a short expli-
cation of Anatomy, taught the principles of Geography, Chronology,
and Astronomy, and introduced the students to the Hebrew Grammar.

At the close, the degree of Master of Arts was conferred on such
students as the Principal found deserving of that distinction.   For
Jamesone to have come creditably through the mental discipline of such
a curriculum, was to be endowed with a liberal education.   Even for an
artist such a scholarly training was valuable.   A mind thus informed
and accustomed to the nice distinctions, analogies, and characteristics of
the subjects of study, could not fail to give intelligent direction to eye
and hand when grappling with the practical details of his art.   Whatever may have been the measure of his bias towards art, it lost nothing
that was worth preserving in being subject to the chastening restraints
and the classical influences of a thorough University education.

So much for the course of study, which, although gradually widening
in range, did not differ much from that of pre-Reformation times.   That
it should have partaken so much of a purely classical character is probably due to the fact that an intimate knowledge of Latin and Greek
was essential at an age that knew scarcely any other culture than
what these languages embodied.   The College session was a long one of
nine or ten months.   It began at Michaelmas, and did not end till July,
with but a brief break of a few days at the new year.   The working

day was also prolonged. It began at the early hour of six or seven, a practice attaching to the residential system of College life. The classical text-books were all imported from the Continent, and the sale of them, at high prices, was conducted by the Professors ; thus the first booksellers to whom from time to time " kists of buiks " were consigned.

We glean from the history of the Family of Rose what a student member of that house paid for his books at a somewhat later date. A Horace cost thirty-two shillings ; Virgil, thirty-six shillings ; Juvenal and Perseus, twenty-four shillings ; Buchanan's Psalms, thirteen shillings and fourpence ; and the Confession of Faith, twenty shillings.

The ordinary students were distinguished, as they are still, by a picturesque red gown, but the bursars or exhibitioners wore a black one, with a girdle round the waist. The gowns of the University secured their wearers against the jurisdiction of the town, of which the University was independent.

At Michaelmas, 1603, then, arrayed in one or other of these, Jamesone would enter Marischal College. Its situation was scarcely farther from his father's door than was the Grammar School, but in the opposite direction. To reach it, he would simply have to traverse the Upper Kirk Gate, passing through the Port, which stood about half way up that thoroughfare, then turning the corner of the Guestrow, would at once be confronted with the College gateway in the Broad Gate. The College buildings were the confiscated Convent of Grey Friars, the only portion of which now remaining is the chapel, and that in a modified form.

Apart from the benefits of study, Jamesone would naturally largely extend his acquaintanceship. A certain proportion of his school-mates would enter College with him, but there he would also meet many students whom he did not know before, and in whose society his mind would receive stimulus. There he formed some of the friendships of his life, such, for example, as that with Arthur Johnston, the precocious little Latinist from the village school of Kintore. They were precisely of the same age, and in the warm, joyous, poetic temperament of the cadet of Caskieben, eager for the friendships of life, Jamesone found a congenial companion. Time brought its separation, but that

they continued good friends is more than to be surmised from the
mutual services afterwards rendered by the painter to the poet, and by
the poet to the painter.

School and education over, Jamesone, a youth of 17 or 18, is face to
face with the question which, to parents and guardians, is often the first
really serious one in the upbringing of youth—What to turn to as the
serious business of life. Such have as yet been the conditions of society,
that with the great mass the answer is usually determined by reasons
altogether apart from the wish of parents or the special aptitude of
youth. Necessity compels a too-early answer, too early for the development of any bias that may exist, or too early to distinguish between a
mere transient taste and the more permanent bent. Jamesone, however,
much as an excellent education may have widened his horizon, and
fitted him for pursuing any of the usual lines of professional or commercial life, followed none of them. His inclination towards art stript
these of their interest, and over-leapt the obstacles that lay in the way
of his desires. These obstacles were, perhaps, more of a negative than
a positive character. They did not absolutely prohibit his pursuit of
art, but they threw him on his own resources. Happily his circumstances did not compel him to cast his lot in an uncongenial sphere,
but granted him the necessary leisure, slowly and painfully, to acquire
that dexterity which he ultimately attained. He could have had no
teacher, properly speaking, and, as we have already seen, but few examples, and most of these very primitive, to spur him on to excel.

Kennedy, in his " Annals of Aberdeen," speaks of Jamesone as
" endowed by nature with an uncommon genius for portrait painting,
which he discovered at an early period of his life." This may be so, but
there is one most important element in Jamesone's case that favoured
and helped to develop this natural bias. In his father's house, drawing
was familiar to him from his infancy, and the use of the pen and pencil
a circumstance of daily occurrence. How early in his career Jamesone
became habituated to the use of drawing utensils we shall never know,
but in his circumstances it is not unreasonable to suppose that they
formed a source of pleasure from his boyish years. A little later
his skill might find a useful outlet in assistance rendered to his father.

No doubt a wide gulf lay between the preparing of building plans and portrait painting, but still they are allied, and it is not difficult to imagine how, with an innate artistic feeling and taste for pictorial delineation, a perspective or front elevation of an architectural design would assume the character of a picture by the introduction of a few effects. If these suppositions are correct, we might expect to find Jamesone's earlier efforts to consist of pictures of this character. Just one such exists. It is a view of King's College, which hangs in the Senatus room there. It is generally attributed to Jamesone, and represents the front view of the College as it had existed in his day. From the badness of the drawing and its false perspective, we should be glad to know that it is not his work. Yet, if we suppose it to be little more than a front elevation done by him as an architect's apprentice, it is not, on the whole, a discreditable picture. The figures in the foreground are tolerably good, and the colouring is pure, forecasting future attainments as a colourist.

Architecture itself is one of the fine arts, and capable of giving expression to some of the noblest qualities in art. Jamesone practised it under such strict limitations, that in becoming an artist proper he is a noted type of that class who pass the border line of one trade or profession and merge it in an allied and higher one. Hogarth, the silver engraver, becomes the picture engraver and painter. David Roberts, the house painter, becomes the etcher and artist. The handicraft grows too narrow, and the artisan developes into the artist.

Allan Cunningham's remark that "Of George Jamesone much less is known than we could wish," is specially applicable to the decade of his life, from 1608 till 1618. But what is to us a period devoid of biographical incident must have been to him one of great industry and progress. It was the period of his early manhood—full of experiment, enterprise, and energy. As yet his sitters must have been limited to members of his own family and people, of purely local connection and celebrity. Each canvas finished, whether that of a portrait or other composition, would be a forward movement, a gain in knowledge of what or how to delineate. Who first encouraged the young artist with the responsibility of perpetuating their features on canvas or panel we do not know, but a test of his quality as a faithful painter would quickly justify their trust in him, and induce that current of popularity which never forsook him, but went on ever broadening till his death.   As practice gave increased facility of execution, the period in question must have been one bringing satisfaction both to painter and patrons—to him in the exercise of the art of his choice, and to them in the society of one to whose success they were contributing something.

Jamesone's merit, in a great measure, consists in this, that without examples worthy of mention, without a master of any kind, and, probably, with but very poor materials—with nothing, in short, but his own sense of the beautiful, and a strong determination to arrest it by his brush—he reached such a degree of excellence.   His progress must necessarily have been both a series of inventions and a train of discoveries.   And, alongside these, there must have been many experiments, and not a few failures.   The difficulties with which he was environed would have caused many a less resolute man to pause, and finally to abandon the pursuit.   But no, here is something that ought to be done and that can be done, and by me, with such means as I possess. In this spirit he set to work, and in it he conquered, not only his own disabilities, but much of the prevailing ignorance on the subject of art, till he reached one inevitable mark of success, in an ever-increasing popularity and demand for his work.

Ten years, then, of assiduous work brought their legitimate rewards of improvement and appreciation.   His long apprenticeship, however, only revealed to him the necessity for a *wanderjahr*, where he could see and learn from the masters of the art very much that would advance and perfect his own practice of it.

Something like a fatality seems to exist in obliterating almost every historical proof of Jamesone's early career and movements.   It follows us when we seek to verify the tradition that he went to Antwerp and entered the study of the famous Rubens, where he met, among others, the brilliant Vandyck, the prince of portrait painters.   But whilst there is no positive evidence, there is at the same time no moral doubt.

The only doubt on the subject of his having studied abroad is as to the date. What tradition has said all along is, that Jamesone went to Antwerp and lived with, and studied under Rubens, and that he had Vandyck for a fellow-pupil. And, as a tradition, it is not to be set aside simply because there is no authentic proof to support it. There is the inferential proof of manner. As has been well said by John Hill Burton, " His [Jamesone's] pictures are Flemish as broad as they can stare."

There is much obscurity regarding the time when Jamesone went abroad, as to how long he remained there, and the date of his return. Cunningham asserts that, after remaining several years with Rubens, he returned in 1628. Kennedy, again, maintains simply that he returned to Aberdeen in 1620. It is less difficult to show Cunningham to be in the wrong than to prove Kennedy to be in the right. For one thing, Jamesone's pictures, dated from 1621 onwards, prove him to be busily engaged pursuing his art at home during those very years that the former would have us believe him to be with Rubens. Besides, he was married in 1624, and it is not likely that he would absent himself for a series of years in the circumstances, and it ought to be remembered that Vandyck left Rubens in 1620, and was only intermittently in Antwerp thereafter, so that Jamesone's association with him must have been slighter.than the circumstantial evidence of his portraits warrants us to believe.

Among the varying opinions as to the date when he went abroad, we incline to the view that it was probably in 1618. If so, then it was as a man of thirty years of age that he went to increase his attainments in painting. His experiences of difficulties to be overcome would at that age be well realised.

He was ripe for instruction, and " I am not sure," says Dr John Brown, " that it is not an advantage to be not young before seeing and feeling some things." Jamesone was no raw youth who knew not to set a palette when he thought of visiting Antwerp and the Continental masters ; not one who had not travelled the road before and to whom everything was equally new and strange ; but one who had been over the ground and had still many specific inquiries before his round of knowledge had any claim to completeness.

The Reformation was the precursor and cause of the political revolution which gave liberty to Holland, and both together had no unequivocal effect on art within the domain of their operation. The revolt against Romanism meant a displacement of Church art; the revolt against Spain meant a replacing of it by wholly new styles and schools. It was an enfranchisement of art as well as of religious and political creeds, a *Renaissance* much needed to give art a larger scope and a wider life. Nowhere had the adoption of the new ideas been more whole-hearted than in Holland, and among no people had they achieved such emancipations as amongst the Dutch, though they might well have exclaimed, " With a great price obtained we this liberty." Limiting our consideration to the subject of painting, it made a new departure. In leaving the field of religious teaching and of Church legends, and entering the more realistic one of actual life, it exerted a new influence on the masses. The gain was not merely in the greater humanness, so to speak, of the subjects painted, but in the greater fidelity to nature with which they were treated. The former subjects of angels, and principalities, and powers, came to be judged too good for human nature's daily food ; and painters, with a love of truth that cannot be over-rated, set to work on such materials as they had, to find in many cases that under a commonplace exterior they had been entertaining angels unawares.

From what has already been said of the intimate connection between Aberdeen and the Continent, it is easy to be seen that, as the home of art, Jamesone's attention was drawn to it. Many of his fellow-citizens had been there, his college friends had been across, and from them he would learn what was passing. Of Antwerp especially he would hear much. Its many artists, chief among whom was Rubens, who had established himself there, converting his abode into a school of art, would be familiar to him by name at least. Specimens of their works would be brought home and admiringly studied, and perhaps copied, till at length the idea would grow that the nearest road to success was to visit Antwerp.

CHAPTER V.

Study at Antwerp.

ANTWERP was one of the Continental towns with which Aberdeen had from very early times maintained a close commercial intimacy. Only in point of population was it surpassed by any other European city. Its commercial enterprise was unrivalled. Its fleets traded with every part of the known world, laying them under contribution for all that could add to its enrichment and delectation. Its free institutions were the envy of most and the admiration of all. During the first three-quarters of the 16th century, it is certain that no other city in Europe wielded a more potent influence in the world than Antwerp, or proved a source of greater attraction and stimulus to those adventurous spirits who courted her society.

Evil days fell on Antwerp, and she was trampled upon by the Spanish Fury, which decimated her ranks and reduced her supremacy, so far as commercial importance was concerned. It was besieged, plundered, and sacked. Writing, in 1616, Sir Dudley Carleton, the intimate friend of Rubens, says :—" I could never set my eyes in the whole length of a streete uppon forty persons at once. . . . . In many places grasse growes in the streetes." Art alone continued to maintain its supremacy. Eight years before this, Rubens had set up his studio in Antwerp, and contributed not a little to re-animate the town with some of its former glory, whilst he earned for himself undying fame. There were other artists of merit in Antwerp at that period, but he was pre-eminent and by far the most popular.

His position was unique. He was a man of wide and varied culture, all which became tributary to his art. Of great strength and nerve, with unlimited confidence in his own powers, and possessing an immense capacity for work, he produced, in response to demands for it from all quarters, a constant succession of pictures. They were of all kinds—

from the dainty little things he loved to paint on panels, to colossal compositions on canvas—and they comprised every variety of subject. Too great to be jealous, in the remotest degree, of his contemporaries, he not only spoke generously of their efforts, but made his princely home a sort of *rendezvous* for all who chose.   For his brother artists he kept alike an open table and an open studio.   Thither flocked many of the " masters " of the Painters' Guild of St. Luke, of which Rubens was at one time the dean.   Among others were Snyders, Jan (" Velvet ") Breughel, Van Uden, engraver as well as painter ; John Wilden ; not to speak of his numerous pupils, chief favourite among whom was Anthony Vandyck, who is said to have lived in Rubens' family.   His studio was an academy in itself, and Rubens entered into many a friendly partnership in work with these men—he, contributing the design and figures ; they, the landscapes, animals, and accessories. That these artists were his collaborateurs was avowed by him and well known, although sometimes resented.   " I have engaged," he writes to Sir Dudley Carleton, " as is my custom, a very skilful man in his pursuit, to finish the landscapes."   Now he undertakes a commission to paint a picture entirely of his own hand; and, again, a picture is spoken of as " a peece scarse touched by him."

Courted by wealthy clients, " his demands ar like yͤ Lawes of Mides and Persians, wᶜʰ may not be altered," says one negotiator who elsewhere speaks of him as " yͤ cruell, courteous Paynter."

Such was the *entourage* and characteristics of the great Rubens when Jamesone ventured himself into his presence, a humble pupil from the little, northern Scottish town of Aberdeen.   To him it was a new world, a very Paradise of painters.   There was much to see in the shape of finished work, much of work in the making, much to observe of the differing characteristics of the various masters and their peculiar methods of working, and so many men to associate with, artists like himself, and with whom he might for the first time exchange ideas on the subject which had been the passion of his life.   Tradition has gone absurdly out of its way to account for Jamesone's becoming a pupil of Rubens by connecting his domestic history with that of his illustrious instructor.   The picture known as the *Chapeau de Paille* is a portrait of

Rubens' second wife, whom he married when he was 54 and she 16. Some of the French lives of Rubens call her Helena Fremont, but the more accurate Germans give her name as Forman. This was not an uncommon north-country name, and the tradition is that she was an Aberdeenshire girl, and a relative of Jamesone's. Helena Forman is represented as rising from the humble position of a house maiden in the great artist's family, and then bringing her kinsman to participate in her fortunes. The story is not true in any particular. The lady was the daughter of Daniel Fourment (merchant), and Rubens' niece by marriage, being the child of his first wife's sister, Clara Brandt.* Besides, Helena's marriage with Rubens did not occur till at least 1630 —ten years, probably, after Jamesone had returned to Aberdeen. There is no need to invent reasons for Jamesone's visit to the Continent. The attractions were obvious enough, and verified, doubtless, by many a wit- ness. So clear is Allan Cunningham on the point, that after Vandyck he holds Jamesone to be Rubens' ablest scholar. This is, perhaps, a too partial estimate arising from a too limited knowledge of Jamesone's works. But if there is something of Rubens in paintings by Jamesone, such as his peculiar-looking varnishy shades, there is much more of the characteristics of his fellow-student ; and hence it is that of the two cognomens, the Scottish Vandyck and the Scottish Rubens, applied to Jamesone, the former is the happier and more generally recognised. That the work of Vandyck and Jamesone has frequently been mistaken for each other, is a fault that may readily be forgiven. Confining the comparison to the common ground of simple portraiture, there is a dignity, an expressiveness, and a finished life-likeness in the works of Vandyck which Jamesone seldom reached. At the same time there were occasions on which Vandyck forgot himself (he had many weak moments), and there were occasions on which Jamesone excelled him- self, and in this approximation of treatment and qualities lies the chief element of perplexity in deciding, in the absence of any specific ken- marks, to whom the credit of certain works belongs. That Jamesone should have been more largely influenced in his style by Vandyck than by Rubens, more the pupil of a fellow-pupil than of their common

* Edinburgh Review, January, 1863, p. 142.

master, is not to be wondered at, especially with such marked individuality as Vandyck possessed. The fire of emulation is frequently caught from, say, a fellow-pupil, whose attainments are not so much beyond one's capacities or comprehension as the master's are. We are not, therefore, surprised to miss in Jamesone the peculiar glory of Rubens, his richness of colouring, and the full sweep of his "tempestuous" brush, nor to find instead the thinner and more spiritual painting, and the more elaborate detail of Vandyck. In the careful attention to the hands of his sitters—a characteristic of Vandyck —Jamesone *sometimes* reminds us of his fellow-pupil.

However long or short the period that Jamesone spent on the Continent, we are driven to adopt Mr Kennedy's statement as the correct one, that he returned in 1620. He was at that time a man of thirty-three years of age.

As to the advantage to himself of his training abroad, there can be no question. He could not be a witness of the methods of such masters as he met in Antwerp ; he could not view the *chefs d'œuvres* which were displayed in church and hall ; he could not copy such pictures as attracted him, nor suffer the friendly criticism to which his work would be subjected, without learning much and without unlearning more. To every point—drawing, colouring, technical details, pigments, and so forth—this double process had applied. His return would, therefore, be with added knowledge, increased skill, higher aims, and with greater confidence to prosecute his work.

CHAPTER VI

Establishes his Reputation, 1620-1630.

JAMESONE'S return home from the Continent was the signal for a renewed interest in his life and work. To the novelty of having devoted himself to the study and practice of painting as a profession was now added the further element of interest, that in order to perfect himself in it he had gone abroad and studied under the greatest masters. This proof of the earnestness with which he sought to pursue the business of his life naturally increased the feeling of curiosity in his unique position. Sir Paul Menzies, the Provost of Aberdeen, soon became an influential patron. It is said that he even introduced him to King James, whose portrait Jamesone painted, as well as other notables of his Court. This statement, it is to be feared, is true only in part. That Sir Paul, who was Jamesone's personal friend, should have taken a lively concern in the artist's progress may be accepted without hesitation ; that he was even so proud of his attainments as to introduce him to the King is possible ; but if we are asked to believe the tradition that he painted the King, on the strength of the portraits of James attributed to Jamesone, it may be safely rejected.

It is not to be doubted that Jamesone was now a public man, a notable figure in his native town, and his familiar personal appearance, his comings and goings, his traces of travel, would be all freely commented on. On all these matters he would unconsciously gratify his friends and fellow-citizens ; but he would do more. He would show his studies done abroad as evidences that the real object of his travel had not been in vain. The display would consist, among others, of his ten Sybils and the four Evangelists, copies, doubtless, of pictures seen at Antwerp. The merit of these would be appreciated, and their improvement on former efforts gratefully recognised by all, whilst to a large number they would be a first lesson and revelation of what Art

7

sought to accomplish. But, satisfactory as were these specimens of work, Jamesone was soon able to give further practical proofs of his growing powers. Thus the interest in the artist became widespread. That of itself was encouraging. It was a great point gained. His enterprise, whatever may have been early opinions regarding it, was no longer a doubtful one. And a still greater stimulus to his best efforts was the degree of confidence with which sitters flocked to his studio. These were no longer confined to narrow local limits, but embraced a wide range. They were men of the town and men of the gown, men of the sword and men of the pen, noblemen and noblewomen, gentlemen and gentlewomen, poets, statesmen, no matter what their creed, nor whether they changed it or abode loyally by it. There was the little child of a few summers, the blooming bridegroom in his later teens, and the old man within a measurable distance of the natural term of life.

One of Jamesone's very earliest commissions on his return home was that of Sir John Stewart, afterwards the Earl of Traquair. It is not quite easy to understand what led this visitor from the Borders to sit for his portrait thus early in Jamesone's career. It is dated 1621, and in that year he had just returned from the Continent, where he had been pursuing his studies, and where, possibly, he may have met Jamesone. Or, having married into the Southesk family, he may have become familiar with the name of the rising artist when on his visits to Kinnaird Castle. There can be little doubt that the bulk of Jamesone's sitters came to his studio to be painted. This was a simpler matter than for him to transport himself with all his materials, including his easel, canvases, and "mullers," to distant country seats. Besides, many of his sitters in his native county at least had residences in the city.

When the Earl of Montrose had his portrait painted by Jamesone, he was a mere youth of seventeen, a St Andrews student, but even then a bridegroom. His home was at his uncle's, Sir Robert Graham, the Covenanting laird of Morphie, near Montrose, who, himself, also sat to Jamesone. The boy bridegroom rode all the way from Morphie to Aberdeen, a distance of forty miles, to give the artist sittings. With such persons Jamesone was not merely an artist, but a cultivated gentle-

man.   Education had increased his correspondences.   Between the
travelled Traquair, as well as the St. Andrews undergraduate, and
Jamesone there was much in common.   Conversation would not flag
for want of topic.   The portraits spoke for themselves as to the skill of
the artist, and the sitters could testify to the personal qualities of the man.

How much more than a merely passing interest Jamesone's under-
takings excited, is evinced by at least one circumstance.   He had
engaged to paint the portrait of Lady Ann Campbell, the youthful
and beautiful wife of George, Lord Aboyne, afterwards Marquis of
Huntly, and with a feeling akin to jealousy for the reputation of the
artist, in executing so delicate and trying a task, his friend, Dr. Arthur
Johnston, addressed to him an encouraging poem in that language, in
the graceful manipulation of which his own fame rests.   His well-known
version of the Psalms is the rival of George Buchanan's.

The following is the poem referred to :—

*Ad Jamisonum Pictorem, de Anna Cambella, heroina.**

> Illustres, ars quotquot habet tua, prome colores,
>   Pingere Cambellam si, Jamisone, paras.
> Frons ebori, pectusque nivi, sint colla ligustris
>   Æmula, Pæstanis tinge labella rosis.
> Ille genis color eniteat, quo mixta corallis
>   Marmora, vel quali candida poma rubent.
> Cæsaries auro rutilet : debetur ocellis
>   Qualis inest gemmis, sideribusque, nitor.
> Forma supercilii sit, qualem Cypridis arcus,
>   Vel Triviæ, leviter cum sinuatur, habet.
> Sed pictor suspende manum ; subtilius omni
>   Stamine, quod tentas hic simulare, vides.
> Cedit Apollineo vulsus de vertice crinis,
>   Cedit Apellæa linea ducta manu.
> Pinge supercilium sine fastu, pinge pudicos
>   Huic oculos, totam da sine labe Deam.
> Ut careat nævo, formæ nil deme vel adde,
>   Fac similem tantum, qua potes arte, sui.

The portrait of the lady whom Jamesone was honoured, and thus

* Arthur Johnston's Poems, p. 607, Amsterdam, 1637.

encouraged to paint, gives evidence that the artist rose to the occasion.
It hangs by the side of that of her husband at Gordon Castle.   It has
been painted with great care, and in a more solid manner than was
his wont—the result of a good many sittings, either at the artist's own
studio, or, as the town house of the Huntlys was in Old Aberdeen,
Jamesone, to convenience so fair a sitter, may have gone thither to
work.

A vague tradition has been handed down to us that Jamesone was a
poet himself.   If so, Time has not dealt so kindly by his literary off-
spring as with the products of his artistic genius.   We are not even
informed whether his muse affected the classic forms of expression as
did Dr. Arthur Johnston's, or whether those of more familiar tones.
The bare existence of such a tradition proves that strong interest in
Jamesone, as a public character, which desires to chronicle the out-
standing events of his life, or, in the absence of trustworthy data, a wish
to fill a hiatus even with a fiction.

In this decade Jamesone did a large amount of excellent work.
During its earlier years the sitters were chiefly local and north-country
people, but towards its close there are obvious signs that his influence
was extending, and that the south-country nobility and gentry were
beginning to avail themselves of the facile brush of their countryman.
Among the former were two portraits of his friend, Arthur Johnston,
and his scarcely less talented brother, Dr. William Johnston; Professor
James Sandilands, of King's College; Urquhart of Cromarty and his
wife, and Alexander Fraser, Laird of Philorth.   Among the latter were
the Earl and Countess of Tweeddale, Sir Robert Carnegy of Dunnichen,
the Earl of Buchan, and Lady Mary Erskine, Countess of Marischal and
Panmure.   This last picture was done the same year that Lady Ann
Campbell was painted, and is one of the very finest portraits that the
artist ever executed.   The lady appears to have been a very attractive
subject, and certainly the artist's whole-hearted endeavour had been
directed to the production of a very excellent portrait.   Nowhere does
Jamesone so nearly approach Vandyck as in his treatment of the
pictures of the ladies he painted.   They possess the same pale-faced
characteristics and blending of delicate flesh tints that have given to

the work of both artists a wonderful vitality and freshness. Vandyck pursued this practice advisedly. "I paint for Time," he was known to say, "and Time will darken them, and posterity will thank me for it." And so it has, for, after the lapse of two centuries and a half, we mark with how little paintiness they shine forth from their frames.

The Erskines were very good friends to Jamesone, and patronised him largely. More than a dozen members of the connection sat to him, but in none of the portraits has he been rewarded with such an assured success as in Lady Mary's.

By this time his career as a successful painter is established. Each fresh commission leads to others, and we find him the busiest of men. At home his studio is well occupied by a succession of patrons ; abroad, he is busy in the castles and residences of the nobility and gentry of Scotland, where we find numerous traces of him. Wherever he goes he is a welcome guest, quietly and quickly executing his work, leaving us little other evidence of his personality than that "sunshine of pictures" he has hung on the walls for Time to look at and to cherish. As a rule, few lives give more trouble to the biographer than the busy artist. We may follow his footsteps, as we range his pictures, in chronological or any other order, but we too often long in vain for a glimpse of the man himself. It is by Jamesone's works we know him best, as a diligent, painstaking, honest, genial man, extenuating nothing, setting naught down in malice, but conscientiously performing his work up to the full measure of his knowledge and capabilities.

It is not strange, amidst all this portrait painting, that, at last, a beautiful young lady should have contrived to impress her image so indelibly on the painter's heart that he must needs marry her. This event makes a very pretty picture in the artist's career. At the ripe age of thirty-seven he had long survived the uncertainties of his profession as a means of livelihood, and had, indeed, achieved a reputation and attained a position of comfort, if not of wealth, which, from a prudential point of view, fully warranted this step. For all we know, Jamesone's parents were now dead, and he, left with the cares of a household in addition to the cares of his painting room.

Prior to the marriage, the rather formal ceremony of Hand-fasting was the use and wont. This was a purely private affair among the friends and high contracting parties, where the marriage contracts, if any, were signed, and the arrangements for nuptials made. It was "ordainit be the Assemblee [that is the kirk-session] that nether the Minister nor Redar be present at contractis off mariage making, as thai call thair hand-fastings, nor mak na sik band . . . but that the names off the promenaris be gevin in to the Redar, to proclame the bannis thairby, and that na money be tane thairfoir."

Nothing whatever is known as to the family of Jamesone's bride, but it may be inferred that they were town's people, as the name occasionally occurs about the period. All preliminaries over, the marriage took place according to the following formal entry :—

"12 of Novr. 1624　George Jamesonne Issobel toche."

His wife was a lady, as might be expected, possessed of considerable personal charms. The best proof of this comes from the artist's own hand in a lovingly-painted family group, executed a few years after their marriage. Considerable perplexity has been caused as to the existence of the original painting. It was originally engraved by a descendant of the artist's, who assigns to the picture the date 1623. The group consists of Mrs. Jamesone, who occupies the foreground, with Jamesone himself and a child of eight years of age in the rear. The date is thus obviously wrong, and should probably be 1633. Horace Walpole, in his "Anecdotes of Painting," presents an engraving of this fine picture, copied from the original described, as in the possession of Sir George Chalmers, the artist, also a descendant of Jamesone's. It is extremely doubtful if this picture now exists, or, if so, in its original condition.

In the meantime we are thrown back to some extent on the engravings of this happy domestic group. Mrs. Jamesone's head is enveloped in a snooded tartan plaid, with a close cap underneath, having a vandycked border. She possesses very regular features, and a stately, matronly air. Her breast and neck are covered with a fine linen collar, trimmed with lace, and she holds in her beautifully painted hands a bunch of roses. This is the only portrait of the artist's wife, and it is a very pleasant one. Two inferences may naturally be drawn from the picture. The artist makes much of his wife. It is *her* picture, and in this he is revealed as an affectionate husband. His own modesty is also betrayed in the subordinate position he occupies in the rear. There are in all three portraits of himself—the one in the group just referred to, that in the possession of Major Ross, his descendant, and that in the deeply interesting picture attached to this work, and now engraved for the first time from Mr. Reid's beautiful drawing of it. Jamesone has done little more for himself in the way of characterisation than he did for so many of his contemporaries. But by these three witnesses he stands consistently revealed, a gentleman possessed of affection, *bon-homie*, and goodness of disposition, bespeaking the indulgent husband and father, and the faithful friend. In all three is the same smile on the lip, the same mild eyes, always shaded by the broad hat, in which he constantly represents himself. He is said to have had weak eyes that loved the shade. This circumstance, aggravated by intense application, was the real reason for his wearing his hat as he did, rather than that in doing so he merely wished to copy his master, Rubens, or that King Charles, having sanctioned it in the Royal presence, he ever after wore it at work and in company.

Jamesone had at least six children, the fruit of his marriage with Issobel Tosche, first three daughters and then three sons. The former, of whom there exist no baptismal registers, were probably all born before 1629, and their names were Mary, Isabella, and Marjory. They all survived their father. The sons, named William and Paul, with one unknown, all died in early life.

The birth of Jamesone's first son and heir was an auspicious event in the artist's household. The baptismal entry reads :—

" 1629 George Jamesone and [Issobel] toche ane son baptized be Mr.
robert baron the 27 day of July callet william, Mr. Patrick dore,
robert alexander, androw meldrum, william gordon, god-fathers."

The best known of this little group was the officiating minister, Dr. Robert Baron. He was the younger son of a Fifeshire family, and graduated at St. Andrews, where he attracted the attention of King James as a distinguished student. Baron held the Chair of Philosophy for a short time at St. Andrews, but, on the advancement of Bishop Patrick Forbes to the See of Aberdeen, he succeeded the Bishop in

the care of the parish of Keith.   In 1624, he was appointed one of the
clergy of Aberdeen ; and next year, when the Chair of Theology was
established in Marischal College, Baron was appointed the first
incumbent.   He was a voluminous author, and ranks as one of the
famous group of Aberdeen doctors.   Having maintained a consistent
opposition to the principles of the Covenant, he escaped formal expulsion along with the rest of his party, if not danger to his life, only by
flight to Berwick, where he died in 1639.   Before his death he was
appointed to the See of Orkney, but never entered on its duties.   Notwithstanding Baron's uncompromising attitude to the opposite party, he
passed through the conflict without incurring any personal odium.
Baillie, who may be taken as an exponent of the views of that party,
mourns Baron's sad death with unaffected sincerity, for he speaks of
" the good Dr. Baron " as a " meek and learned person."

The first-named godfather, Mr. Patrick Dore or Durie, was afterwards Principal of Marischal College, and one of the same set of learned
men who gave such impulse to the pure scholarship of the times, and
imparted to Aberdeen that air of culture so strongly characteristic of it.
He wrote, but less voluminously than Dr. Baron.   William Gordon was
a mediciner at King's College.   The other names are unknown to us.

The occasion was one that justified a baptismal feast as rich and
plentiful as the law would permit.   Excess on such occasions was a
social feature of the times, and one that the authorities found it necessary to regulate by enactment.   Under date 18th February, 1624 :—

" The town-council in view of the great abuse ' laitlie croppin in ' of
superfluous and costlie banquetting at baptizeing of bairnes ; ordained
' that no inhabitant within this burghe quhatsoeuir rank, qualitie, or
degrie they be of, sall at any tyme heireftir invite any mae persones to
be gossippis or cummeris to any of thair bairnes, bot four gossippis and
four cummeris at the maist, and that thair sal be bot sex wemen at the
maist invited, or employed to convoy the bairne to and fra the Kirk,
nather yit sall thairbe any mae persones invited to any denner, supper,
or eftirnoones drink at a baptisme bot sex men and sex wemen at the
most ; and withall ordains, that nane presume to have at thair ban-
quettis any kynd of succouris, spyceries, droggis, or confectiones brocht

from pairtis beyond sea, nather yit any kynd of wyld meat or bakin meat at thair baptismes, &c., &c., under a penalty of £40 to be paid to the Dean of Guild.' "

Exactly fifteen months after Jamesone's son, William, was baptised, he presents his son, Paul, for the same purpose. The entry runs :—

" October 1630 yeeris.—George Jamesone and Issobell toche, ane sone baptized the 27 day, callet paull ; paull menyzeis of kenmundie, prowost, Mr. alexr. Jaffray balzie, Mr. david wedderburne, Mr. robert patrie, patrick Jack, patrick fergusone, androw straquhen, god-fathers."

The majority of Jamesone's friends, godfathers to his son, Paul, are known to us as men of standing and of learning. Such a glimpse of the private life, so to speak, through the personal friendships of the artist, is invaluable. It affords a double proof of his own position and of the cast of his mind, inasmuch as a man is known by the company he keeps.

There is the Provost of the town, (afterwards Sir) Paul Menzies, who seems to give or to get the honour of the child's name. The Chief Magistrate acted as sponsor at the baptisms of the children of very influential citizens only. Sir Paul was a man of much note, and now, in the seventh year of his Provostship, a popular, enterprising, and public-spirited man. Jamesone had already painted his portrait, which, in the course of time, has become the property of Marischal College, in the great hall of which it hangs among many other worthy citizens painted by the same fertile hand.

Then there is the prudent Baillie Jaffray gradually qualifying himself for the highest civic honours, and the graver responsibilities which befel the holder of them and the city he governed during " The Trubles." He was reckoned a very wealthy man, remarkable in many ways, and the father of a still more remarkable son, Alexander, junior, then a boy of sixteen. The Baillie was a quiet, worthy citizen, whose diligent pursuit of business had raised him from the ranks, to the position of a " wealthy merchant." His elevation to the Chief Magistracy was an occasion when some of the citizens pretended that the dignity of the office would suffer detriment in the person of " the oy of a baxter." It was a post usually filled by the best blood of the town, and one so honourable in

8

itself that, less than a century before, the all-powerful Earl of Huntly did not disdain to fill.   Jaffray was, of course, raised to the position of first citizen by his fellow-Councillors, who, in their more intimate association with him at their Board, had come to recognise qualities in him somewhat superior to those of a mere pawky wadsetter.   The citizens were piqued, however, but they mingled with their envy a vein of grim humour, and when Provost Jaffray was at Church hearing sermon, they several times placed a "baken pye" before him to considerately remind him of his plebeian origin.   Spalding, who relates this pleasantry, quaintly adds that the Provost "miskenned all, and never quarrelled the samen"—a discreetness that must have gone far to convince the practical jokers, of his possession of one quality at least, that is an element of dignity and success in any sphere of life—perfect self-command —a quality that during "The Trubles" was admittedly of vast service to his derisive fellow-citizens.

Mr. David Wedderburn was a "Preacher of the Evangel," but better known for his long connection with the Grammar School, of which he was the Rector.   He believed that his strength lay more in the way of teaching than preaching.   He was, however, too strict a disciplinarian to be very popular with his pupils.   He was a great Latinist, and became a Professor of Humanity at Marischal College, of which he was amongst the first *alumni*.   He did very much to promote the advancement and proper teaching of English Grammar by publishing school books on that subject.   He possessed the habit of the pen in the composition of Latin poems, especially of elegiac verses, of a graceful kind, on the death of his friends.

Another of the sponsors is Andrew Strachan, who was also a man of learning, and Professor of Divinity at King's College.   He was the author of various works bearing more or less on subjects connected with the University.   The Professor, in his capacity of public orator, at a capping (*Panegyricus Inauguralis* spoken 26th July of this same year), sought to inspire a feeling of emulation in the students' minds by referring to the many distinguished men either bred by the University, or connected with it, as examples worthy of imitation ; among others, he speaks of Bishop Patrick Forbes, the brothers William and Arthur

Johnston, Professors Sandilands, Baron, and Sibbald, and could point with pride to their portraits adorning the auditorium where they were assembled, and for the most part painted by his friend, George Jamesone. The oration referred to was printed at the Raban press in 1631.

The remaining godfathers are strangers to us, although they were probably relatives of the artist or his wife. Excepting the Provost's portrait, we do not possess a likeness of any of the other guests, although it is scarcely to be supposed that either Jaffray, Wedderburn, or Strachan, such intimate friends and such prominent men, should not have been painted by Jamesone. It is on an occasion like this that we greatly miss the possession of a reliable presentment of the features of men that we can only partly know otherwise.

The conversation among such a congenial group would certainly embrace "random influences from art, from nature, and the schools." Town and gown were worthily represented, and not the least entertaining might be some of those guests who are, unfortunately to us, silent. Jamesone would, of course, be a host in himself. The true portrait painter is almost necessarily a pleasant, social man. He knows the give and take of conversation, when to speak, and how to beget speech. It is an essential part of his art to create that "heart affluence in discursive talk" which lightens and transfigures into happiest mood the features he delineates. He learns insensibly when drawing the face to draw the mind as well, and to read the heart. The art thus used for a specific purpose becomes eventually, by a reflex action, the painter's own prevailing mood. Add to all Jamesone's acquirements in this way the facts that he was a man of education, of culture, one who was mixing with the best society, a travelled man, a man of information, and you have one whose society it is alway a luxury to enjoy.

On an occasion like the present, does the conversation give any sign of flagging? What more grateful withdrawing-room for the gentlemen to step into than the artist's adjoining studio? There, to the uninitiated, would be much that was novel and interesting—curios of various kinds, artists' properties, "effects" (such stuff as pictures are made of), works in various stages of progress, from the "just rubbed in" features of some well-known face, whose likeness stands the revealed result of a single sitting, to the finished painting in all the glory of a "double-gilt muller." It is gratuitous to accuse the painter of having a "touch of the trader" in thus exhibiting his wares, although an almost certain result will be that more than one of his guests at this private view is secretly resolving to give the painter a commission. Such an opportunity of having one's face immortalised must not be lost, be the "terms" what they may.

By this time, Jamesone may justly be suspected to be wholly given to portrait painting. Importunate clients too often become the arbiters of an artist's fate, and, unless he takes strong measures, determine for him his *rôle* in the artists' guild. Many a man has kicked against this form of social tyranny, this compulsion to paint portraits, his ambitions and abilities to do other work meanwhile becoming abort by neglect. Let us charitably suppose that in Jamesone's case a discerning public rescued an excellent portrait painter from the limbo of landscape mediocrity. The doubtful author of "A Description of Aberdeenshire," in referring to the artist, states :—"There are pieces of Jamesone's painting of great value, some carried over to France and Italy and esteem'd there." The superior taste of these countries may have proved more appreciative of any efforts of Jamesone's in the direction of landscape or historical painting than that of his native land. Be that as it may, they are now either lost or difficult to authenticate.   ·

In this same year, another transient glimpse of Jamesone is obtained at the baptism of the child of James Toche, probably his wife's brother. This time the artist is godfather to a little niece. The entry runs :—

"1630 James toche and agnes gordone, ane dochter baptized be Mr
    william forbes the 2nd day of Januar called elspait, patrick
    forbes, alexander Ramsay, george jamesone, gilbert anderson, Mr
    Alexander gordon, god-fathers."

The decade from 1620 to 1630, so full of important activities and progress to Jamesone, was a remarkable one to his native city. His establishment there as an efficient and fruitful artist was enough to signalise it. There was, however, another circumstance that distinguished it as an era of remarkable interest, pointing it out as the birthday not only of art but of literature. This was the advent of Edward

Raban, the self-styled "Laird of Letters, Master Printer, the first in Aberdene," who, in 1622, set up his printing press in the town. Previous to this he had worked both in Edinburgh and St. Andrews, but, encouraged by Bishop Patrick Forbes and the Magistrates of Aberdeen, he transferred himself there with all the apparatus of his craft. His place of business was " on the north side of the Castle-gate, in a new house belonging to the Council, of which the lower part was used as a meal market." Powerfully supported by the Universities, to whom his services were found to be of much advantage, and by that band of learned divines and literary men by which Aberdeen was then so distinguished, Raban's "founts" flowed out in unbroken streams of College Theses, Almanacs, volumes of Poetry, Funeral Orations, Sermons, Theological and Ecclesiastical Discussions, and Versions of the Psalms. He even ventured on the responsibility of authorship, committing himself as well as his customers to the eternity of type. Contemporary with Raban, one David Melville was the first to engage in the distinct business of bookseller and publisher. The dawn of the local literature of Aberdeen is heralded by both these names as printer and publisher respectively, of the earliest Aberdeen books, and with them a new departure is made in the intellectual progress of the people.

1625 was marked by an event of national importance. This was the death of King James and the accession of Charles. In that year, Raban issued from his press a little work by David Wedderburn, entitled, " Aberdonia Atrata Sub obitum Serenissimi, & Potentissimi, Monarchæ Jacobii VI." It is one of his graceful contributions to the memory of illustrious dead.

Up to this point Jamesone's career has been one of unbroken success. Nothing has occurred to mar his prosperity. There were early struggles, as have been seen, of no ordinary kind, but struggles that in the retrospect become transformed into a series of victories, because eventually crowned with success. He was master of his art, and had received not only the approval and patronage of a host of friends, but the *imprimatur* of the greatest living master of the art, whose "tempestuous brush" he had been privileged to see him handle. He had worked hard, had given his best energies to his profession, and had reaped its most legitimate rewards, and was satisfied to feel that he had not been decoyed by an *ignis fatuis*, but that he had achieved for himself eminence and respect, and had implanted in the minds of his countrymen a taste for art and a love of the beautiful. The happiness resulting from unimpeded energies in a direction thus useful and so much after his liking, the satisfaction of living in the kindliest intercourse with all men, the joy of those who not only possess the faculty of making new friends, but that of the deeper natures who possess the power to retain all the old ones, the unalloyed felicity of his domestic life, were now to be brought into contrast with a different set of feelings. The year 1631 dawned darkly for Jamesone and his wife and their little household, for within the first few days of it two of their number were snatched away by the hand of death. The following brief extracts from the account of the Master of Kirk and Bridge Works, to whom certain fees were payable for funerals, briefly record what must have been a long sorrow to the artist and his wife :—

" 6 Januar 1631 Ane barne of George Jamesone's bureit, iij lib."
And again :—

" 20 Januar 1631 Ane uther barne of George Jamesone bureit, iij lib."
In the all too meagre information of these entries we can only suspect that some epidemic had cut off the artist's two sons. The word "*uther*" indicates, with perhaps no intervening entry, that it might have been supposed to be a duplicate of that entered only a fortnight before. It may have been the clerk's mode of expressing his sympathy with the parents—" ane *uther* barne." The names of the children are not recorded, but there can be no doubt that they were Jamesone's two sons, William, a child of eighteen months, and Paul, the infant, three months old, at whose baptisms there were the influential and gladsome gatherings narrated in the preceding chapter.

It is probable that before the year closed Jamesone was called on to suffer another bereavement in the death of his brother William. He was a writer in Edinburgh, and on the 10th of February the artist, who is designated " Georgius Jamesoun, pictor, burgensis de Aberdein," is served his heir general. From this circumstance it may be inferred that William was an unmarried man. Younger than the artist, he had enjoyed the advantage of a similar education to have followed his profession.   By a will executed some time before his death, probably in 1628, he bequeathed to Marischal College his mathematical instruments and library.   In making final delivery of these legacies, George obtained, on the 28th January, 1633, the following discharge from the Town Council :—

"The said day in presence of the prouest baillies and councell compeirit George Jamesone, painter, burgess of Aberdeine, ar, and executor to umquhill Williame Jamesone, writtar in Edinburghe, his brother germane, and exponet and declairit that the said umquhill Williame, befoir his deceas, left his haill mathematicall instrumentis and bookes in legacie to the toune for the use of the professor of mathimaticques within the colledge of the said burghe, and studentis in that professioun present and to come : And conforme thairto the said George delyuerit instantlie the saidis haill instrumentis and bookes at the directioun of the magistrattis and counsall, to Mr Williame Johnstoun, doctour in phisik and present professor of mathimaticques, within the said colledge, be ane speciall inventar writtin and subscryveit be the said Mr Williame on the end of the catalogue of umquhill secretarie Reidis librarie."

From the circumstance that the only portrait dated with the year 1631 is that of Dr. Patrick Dun, there is reason to believe that Jamesone did not leave home much during that sorrowful period.   In the following year he had resumed his peregrinations through the country, working as was his wont.

Availing ourselves of every glimpse, however transient, that in any way reveals to us the man George Jamesone and gives roundness to his life, we are pleased to note his action in a local enterprise of this period. In 1631-1632, there was made a "voluntar contribution of the nichtbores and toun burgesses of the burgh of Aberdeen for maintenance of ane of the ministers of the said burghe to serve the cure at the kirk of futtie within the freedom of the same burghe and parochine of Sanct Nicolas." Here Jamesone displayed not only a very laudable desire to further this church extension scheme, but gives evidence of his wish to act in thorough concert with his fellow-citizens in a public enterprise.   In the artist there was no aloofness nor burrowing in his groove.   To his own particular calling he was devoted and loyal, but, when the occasion served, his sympathies were easily stirred—he was all for " bonaccord."

The contributors were "ordainit to be registrat ad futuram rei memoriam," and they are accordingly preserved on a leaf prefixed to the fifty-second volume of the Council Register. Among the names of fifty or sixty citizens occur these :—

Mr alex Jaffray, baillie . .	vj hundreth lx pundis iij merkis.
Gilbert menzies of Petfoddells .	tua hundreth pundis.
Doctor williame forbes . .	tua hundreth fyve pundis.
Doctor Patrik deun . . .	ane hundreth pundis.
Mr williame guild, minister .	ane hundreth pundis.
George Jamesone . . .	Thriescoir ten pundis.
Mr James Ross, minister .	Thriescoir pundis xiij sh iiij d.
Mr Alexander Ross, minister .	Thriescoir pundis xiij sh iiij d.
Mr William Ogstoune, minister .	Thriescoir & vj pundis xiij sh iiijd.
David Melvill	Threttie-three pundis six shillings iij pence.

A subscription list does not always indicate the means and ability to give of the contributors. We hardly think that Jamesone, in putting down his name for £70, wished to vie with the well-known and wealthy men who gave such large sums, or that the mere vanity of posing as a liberal man influenced him. He approved of the object, and, according to his means, gave conscientiously.

The year 1633 was a red letter year for Jamesone and also for Scotland. Charles, who had reigned seven years, made 'his first Royal visit to his ancient kingdom in that year. The immediate occasion of it was his wish to be crowned King of Scotland, in the land of his nativity. It is matter of history that he would have been content to undergo the ceremony at Westminster if he had succeeded in obtaining the Scottish regalia for the purpose. With this view he made overtures to the Scottish Parliament, who parried the request with the plea that it was contrary to the laws and the Constitution of the realm to suffer the Crown of Scotland to be carried out of the Kingdom; but that if His Majesty would be pleased to receive it in the seat of his ancestors, he should find his subjects of that nation as loyal as those of the southern portion of his dominion. The consent of Charles to this arrangement filled the people of Scotland with the liveliest excitement and joy. Every effort was made by the assembly in Edinburgh of the notables of the Kingdom to render the utmost service to the King that loyalty could exact. The Scottish capital charged itself to leave no stone unturned that could lend any *eclât* to the cherished visit, in arranging for which they did the work very systematically. A committee of "the gravest and most understanding citizens" was appointed for organising all the many details. William Drummond of Hawthornden took a leading part, along with Adamson, Principal of Edinburgh College, and probably Jamesone acted on the committee. Drummond was great on the occasion, writing almost fulsome "panegyrickes" both in prose and verse, even to the extent of compromising posterity in their estimate of Charles, with whom he pleads to "accept the homage of their humble minds, accept that great good-will which they have ever carried to the high deserts of your ancestors and shall ever to your own and your Royal race, whilst these rocks shall be over-shadowed with buildings, these buildings inhabited by men, and while men shall be endued either with counsel or courage, or enjoy any piece of reason, sense, or life."

The eyes of the whole kingdom were on the event. On his progress north the King spent some time at Welbeck, in Nottinghamshire, the seat of the Earl of Newcastle, where a masque was presented for his entertainment, entitled "Love's Welcome," written by Ben Jonson in his capacity of Poet Laureate. He thus refers to the object of the King's journey in lines far from worthy of his powerful pen :—

> Our King is going now to a great work
> Of highest love, affection, and example.
> To see his native country and his cradle
> And find those manners there, which he sucked in
> With nurse's milk and parents' piety.
> O sister Scotland ! what hast thou deserved
> Of joyful England, giving us this King.
>   &c., &c.

With his brave cavalcade, therefore, Charles crossed the Border on the 12th of June, and on the 15th, Saturday, he made his triumphal entry into his Scottish capital amidst such an unbounded display of magnificences that Bishop Burnet avers "the country suffered much by it."

Every place of any importance throughout Scotland sent commissioners to take part in the proceedings, besides whom there was a great influx to the metropolis of people, in their private capacity, urged by patriotism or curiosity.

Jamesone's visit to Edinburgh is said to have been prompted by the Magistrates of that city, who commissioned him to add to the other entertainments of this joyous entrance by painting a series of portraits of all the Scottish monarchs from Fergus I. onwards. That some such collection of portraits was displayed on each side of the Netherbow as the Royal procession passed is pretty certain, but it is ludicrous to imagine Jamesone doing more in the matter of such an exhibition than the arranging of such portraits as could be gathered together. To have done what is implied by the tradition, Jamesone would have outstripped Giordano, whom Philip II. declared to be a "painter for princes," because he could paint three portraits a-day ; or David Beck, who had such a facility in the composition of his pictures that Charles I. used to say, "Faith, Beck, I believe you cou'd paint riding post." Yet David Wedderburn seems to be influenced by the popular belief that Jamesone played a not irresponsible part in connection with the graphic deduction of the King's ancestry—

> Ecce Iamesoni tabulam pictoris ! ab alto
> Sanguine Fergusi proavos per stemmata pictos.
>
> [vide Vivat Rex, 1633.]

Jamesone knew better than to hazard his own reputation and affront the King's discernment by any such display. Charles is well known to have had a very cultivated taste in things artistic, and he is even credited with some practical acquaintance with painting, and with having received lessons from Rubens. "In painting," says an eulogist, "he had so excellent a fancy that he would supply the defect of art in the workman, and suddenly draw those lines, give those airs and lights which experience and practice had not taught the painter."

Vandyck, induced by Sir Kinelm Digby, also a great promoter of the fine arts, had come to England, and Jamesone knew that his work had been under the King's eye for a year, and that that was in itself an education sufficient to deter any man with a regard to his reputation, from hazarding it by any careless venture. The more likely theory is that Jamesone was invited to Edinburgh by its Magistrates with the view of his painting the King's own portrait, if opportunity offered. They desired a portrait of His Majesty, but, with a pardonable pride, they wished the work to be by a native artist.

Another Aberdeen man was brought prominently forward at this time, Dr. William Forbes, whose brilliant eloquence and widely-known abilities pointed him out as a proper man to preach before the King. Forbes had before this captivated the people of Edinburgh themselves, but their ecclesiastical bias and his did not go together, as did that of the folks in the far north.

Aberdeen was strongly represented at the Coronation ceremonies. Besides Dr. William Forbes and Dr. Robert Baron, there was Provost Menzies, Patrick Leslie, Dr. Arthur Johnston, young Alexander Jaffray, and Jamesone himself. Bishop Patrick Forbes should have gone, but was detained by illness. Both he and the Provost had seats at the Convention of Estates, summoned to sit during the King's visit. From the minute detail of all the circumstances attending the King's visit to Edinburgh given by John Spalding, it would seem as if he had been an eye-witness of what passed. It was on this occasion that Arthur Johnston was introduced to Archbishop Laud, who became his patron. Jaffray in his diary mentions his visit to Edinburgh, but refers it to the month of January—probably a mistake of his editor. Here, then, was a group of at least six gentlemen who, with some servants, travelled together to Edinburgh. They made a picturesque cavalcade as they wended their way from the Town-House, where they had doubtless met to drink a *bonaille* with the Council before their departure on that early day in June. Friendly convoys would see them through the town, across the Bow Brig, past the Dovecot Hill, and the Langstane, by the Hardgate, as far as the Bridge of Dee. There they would part and, the travellers putting spurs to their horses, clattering hoofs and jangling swords would soon cease to be heard.

With such poor roads as then existed, a ride of at least three or four days was before them, even with the days at the longest. If an early start had been made their first rest would be Stonehaven. After having passed the most sterile tract of the route, striking inland, their first sleep would probably be at the ancient town of Brechin, thus covering a distance of some forty-five miles—a very good day's work. Their destination the second day would be Perth or Dundee—in either case they would dine at Forfar. If, to save the ferry, Perth was chosen, the ride, though longer, would be through a richer and more interesting portion of Scotland, seeing it in a prime season. From Perth, the mid-day halt would be the village of Kinross, leaving an easy ride to Dunfermline by the evening. If they had preferred the Dundee route, then they traversed the rich and enterprising kingdom of Fife, *via* Cupar, probably reaching the coast at Kirkcaldy by night-fall. The fourth, and shortest day's ride, with the inevitable ferry across the Forth, and with a company increased by numbers, flocking to the capital, bent on a like errand with themselves, would bring them to their journey's end by mid-day.

The city was all astir, bent on giving adequate expression to the excitement which prevailed all over Scotland. When James and his Court quitted his Scottish capital for ever, the kingdom, and especially Edinburgh, sunk into provincial conditions. Now all was joyance that Charles Stuart was come to his own again. The sun of Royalty shone upon Scotland once more. The eclipse had been but partial after all, and by many expedients the lieges tried and probably succeeded to convince His Majesty, that whatever had suffered diminution and loss among them in his absence, it was not their loyalty.

After the King's triumphal entry on the 15th of June, he took up his abode in his ancestral palace of Holyrood. He was crowned in the Abbey there on the 18th, opened Parliament on the 20th, and remained in the city, entertained and entertaining till the end of the month. On Tuesday, the 25th of the month, Dr. William Forbes had the honour of fulfilling his commission by preaching before Charles. This he did from the text—"My peace I leave with you," and with such persuasive eloquence that the King was captivated, and declared that if Edinburgh became a Bishoprick, no one was so fit for the See as Dr. Forbes. In

the following January this forecast was fulfilled. Forbes occupied the
position during a brief incumbency of but three months, when he died.

A great deal of more or less important business was crowded into
the period of the King's visit. Opportunity was, however, found to
introduce Jamesone at Court, and, occupied as His Majesty was,
Charles, with that graciousness which was a characteristic, consented to
sit to him for his portrait. Few monarchs have sat so often for the same
purpose as he, and certainly no Royal features are more familiar,
except those of our present gracious Sovereign's, than are those of
Charles the First. When it is considered that there are about a hundred
distinct paintings of him, without speaking of sculptures, it is clear that
Charles must have spent no inconsiderable portion of his time in sitting
for his portrait. Sitting to Jamesone, the only native Scottish artist,
must have been an interesting engagement. Vandyck had frequently
ere this delineated the King, and Jamesone's intimacy with that artist
would at least form one topic of mutual interest. Tradition has always
said that Jamesone was permitted by the King to wear his hat whilst
engaged in his work, and when it was finished he was pleased to present
the artist with such a conspicuous mark of approval as a diamond ring
from his own hand. Whatever may have been the freedom with which
Jamesone executed his work, the King's portrait was a crucial task.
Charles had highly cultivated tastes, critical of the mediocre in art, but
correspondingly indulgent towards real merit. The eye that was
familiar with the best works of Rubens and Vandyck was not ill pleased
with that of Jamesone, a fact that must have greatly extended the
interest in the portrait and the painter. Hung in a good light, fresh and
glowing from the master's hand, the likeness of the King would be seen
and appreciated by all who, at that stirring time, had the *entrée* of the
Royal apartments. Old friends, and many whom Jamesone had already
painted, were there, ready to speak in encouraging terms of his success.
New friendships were made on the strength of it. Indeed, 1633 marks
a distinct era in Jamesone's career. Hitherto his assiduity had secured
for him a steadily-growing popularity. Warranted by this, Edinburgh
had honourably stood sponsor for the artist, and shared in his success,
which amounted to a public recognition of his merits. The picture of

the King is said to have been a full-length figure, now, unfortunately, to be classed among the lost pictures, although it is probably the original from which at least three replicas were taken, only one of which can now be traced—that in Marischal College.   Respecting one portrait of King Charles, a not well-authenticated tradition has found currency.   It is said that Jamesone, desirous that his native town should possess the King's picture, offered it to the Magistrates, hoping that it might find a place in the Town-Hall.   He was, however, so piqued at the poor price they agreed to pay for it, that he sold it to a stranger.   There were really three to the making such a bargain—the Magistrates, the painter, and the King, and it is impossible now to say where the discredit lay, supposing the story true.   Did the Magistrates cheapen the artist or the Sovereign?   Did the painter exact two prices—one for his art and one for the subject of it ?   Whichever was the case, Jamesone, who was never unreasonable in his prices, and who painted many a portrait for friendship's sake, cannot be chargeable with avarice until we know how much or rather how little he refused.   To give it for nothing would have been far easier than to huxter over the painting, since accepting the price offered implied acquiescence in the valuation of the buyers. The tradition has been, with reason, disallowed on the ground that " the Corporation in that day was no niggard patron of learning or the arts," and with such friends as Jamesone possessed in the Town Council of his native city, it is very unlikely any such proposed bargain should have fallen through.

Among the many noblemen and gentlemen whose acquaintance Jamesone formed during his memorable visit to Edinburgh, that of Sir Colin Campbell, the Eighth Laird of Glenorchy, ancestor of the noble house of Breadalbane, was, without doubt, the most important.   Their intimacy grew to an attachment and a personal friendship ; and, considering Sir Colin's character and attainments, may be taken as a high tribute to Jamesone's.   Sir Colin was a man far in advance of his times. On scholarly pursuits, so much admired by his contemporaries, he engrafted artistic tastes but little understood by them.   He was learned not only in the classic tongues of Greece and Rome, but in the modern languages of France and Italy, and had travelled on the Continent to good purpose. An admirer of the more elegant furniture and upholstery of the Continent, he was the first to import them and to introduce them into domestic use in his own country. He was great in textile fabrics, buying largely in the particular districts famed for their manufacture— silks and tapestries in France, and linen, damask, and napery in Holland. Contemporary portraits exist of his father, Sir Duncan, who was a great favourite with James VI. and his Queen, but to Sir Colin belongs the honour of being the first of the family who ornamented his house with pictures, which he had employed artists to paint for him.

The meeting of two such men as Sir Colin and Jamesone was a happy circumstance. The first intelligent native patron of the fine arts in Scotland and the first trained and excellent Scottish artist were not only contemporary, but intimate and congenial friends, having very perfect correspondences, each exercising on the other an influence for good, and extending a sympathy fostered by community of education, taste, and aim.

After a fortnight spent in Edinburgh, King Charles went as far north as Perth, where he held something like a review of the Glenorchy Highlanders, from the wild glens of mid-Scotland. He also paid a visit to Dunfermline, his birth-place, Stirling, and Falkland, and finally left Edinburgh on the 12th of July. Not till then would the deputies feel at liberty to leave the capital, and when they did so, it was to carry away with them a load of honours, chiefly droppings of that shower of titles which, with lavish hand, Charles repaid the sincerely loyal attentions of his Scottish subjects.

The little party of Aberdonians had every reason to be gratified with the result of their mission. They had worthily upheld the credit of the town, whose loyalty was expressed in their presence. Both Forbes and Jamesone had figured conspicuously, and enhanced their reputation as preacher and painter respectively. Any fears that Jamesone might modestly have had to moderate the pleasure of his waygoing were dispelled, and the journey homeward brightened with his future prospects. The success of his Royal commission, engagements formed among a widened circle of friends, and more especially his alliance with such an appreciative patron and friend as Sir Colin Campbell, were great rewards.

Dr. Forbes, too, having discharged his sacred duties with fidelity and without self-seeking, returns home with grateful satisfaction at being able to speak a word in season. Both had done their duty. The preaching of the saintly Forbes was but a reflex of his blameless life, and exhibited the beauty of holiness. The labours of Jamesone was but an expression of the artist's innate idea of the holiness of beauty.

Worthy Provost Menzies carried home with him one of the half hundred knighthoods dispensed by His Majesty, and was henceforth to be known as Sir Paul. His father, Sir Thomas, had received a similar honour from King James on the occasion of his having gone to London to present to His Majesty an unusually large pearl, found in the River Ythan, now said to be the top pearl of the English Crown. Sir Thomas did not long enjoy his new title, for he died on his journey home. It has been already mentioned that Dr. Arthur Johnston's journey had not been without its fruits. And young Jaffray, a lad of nineteen, if he did not bring honours home with him he found them waiting him on his return, in the birth of his first-born, Alexander, *tertius*. Married at eighteen, the early responsibilities of fatherhood deepened that gravity which accompanied him creditably through so many onerous duties of life, and prepared him to be the persecuted pioneer of that most deeply religious sect, the Quakers, in the north.

The merest outline of Jaffray's singular and eventful career may not be out of place here. Well schooled and educated by his sagacious father, who had well-meant, if somewhat worldly aims in life for his son, the boy's mind had from his earliest a serious bent. Referring to his College career in his diary, "unhappily relating," laments Carlyle, "almost all to the inner life of Jaffray," he complains that his professors, Mr. Gordon, Regent, and Dr. Dun, the Principal—afterwards his own father-in-law—"were both of them unfit for training up youths, so that I had no good example from them." His prudential and managing father sought out a wife for the lad, who admits her to have been "a meek and quiet yoke-fellow. . . . very comfortable and pleasing to me." In order to acquire experience of life, he was immediately sent on his travels, first to Edinburgh, then to London, and afterwards to the

Continent. On returning home, "The Trubles" shortly after broke out, and Jaffray had his share. He was admitted to the Council, and rose eventually to the Provostship. He was captured several times during the civil war, and several times narrowly escaped a violent death. He fought in the disastrous battle known as the Sack of Aberdeen by Montrose, in 1644, where, being "evilly horsed," he nearly fell a victim to the "no-quarter" Irishes. He more than once represented the city in Parliament. In 1649, he was sent as a Commissioner to Holland to bring home King Charles. In 1650, he fought, was wounded, and taken prisoner at the battle of Dunbar. Cromwell, with a true apprehension of his capacity and probity for high State duties, appointed Jaffray Director of the Chancery of Scotland. He was also one of those who negotiated the Restoration of Charles II. It is obvious that Jaffray led a distinguished life, and, had his diary possessed a little more of the spirit of Pepys', we should have had a less pious book, but one, from Jaffray's knowledge of affairs and personal experiences, that would have been an invaluable historic treasure house. His contact with the Cromwellian party led first to his adoption of their religious principles, and then, by an easy transition, to those of the Society of Friends. He died, in 1673, at his house of Kingswells, and lies buried in the trim little Quaker graveyard, on the brae-side beyond it.

CHAPTER VII.

Foreign Travel, &c.

IT is extremely unlikely that Jamesone seriously started work on his return, as he shortly thereafter set out for London and the Continent. With that in immediate prospect, he would not commence any series of engagements lest they should interfere with his travelling arrangements. Except the King's portrait, the only other well-authenticated work of the year is that of his own family group already described, and which may have been painted by way of pastime in the holiday between his two journeys. Travelling then was a tiresome task, and the interval, between efforts past and to come, would also have afforded a happy breathing time in Jamesone's busy life for the enjoyment of the society of his wife and daughters. The peculiar nature of his profession had a tendency to estrange him from his own domestic circle. Besides, a prolonged journey through the Continent in those days involved many preparations and arrangements, requiring time and careful forecasting of various contingencies.

The prolonged tour on this occasion was one of the first fruits of the kindly interest taken in Jamesone by Sir Colin Campbell. Having witnessed much excellent art in the various Continental schools, he foresaw the advantage to Jamesone of a wider acquaintance with their varying styles. He judged rightly that an artist of one model is apt to become unduly mannered. Every true artist will have an individuality of his own, which embodies the truth as known to him. A pupil may appreciate that truth to distraction, may copy it, and feel inspired by it for a time, but not being an emanation of his own mind, cannot live by it. He exhausts it, and often only the husk remains. It is not the truth of one master or of one school, but the truths of many, passed through the alembic of the artist's own mind, issuing therefrom in some concrete form, all his own, which in its embodiment differentiates

him from all others, and gives a charm to his works distinct from all
mere mimetic productions.   Herein he is the creator of new pleasures
in ever new forms of artistic beauty and expression, brought about, if
not by new methods and novel principles, at least by fresh combinations
of the old.

The details of this Continental tour are disappointingly meagre.   So
far as London at least, Jamesone was once more accompanied by
Alexander Jaffray, junior, bent on widening the area of his knowledge
and observation of men and business, preparatory to his entering on an
extended sphere of public usefulness designed for him by his father.   It
is an indication of the esteem entertained for Jamesone by the elder
Jaffray, and his entire confidence in him, that he should, in a measure,
be charged with the care of his son in these journeyings.   Two other
citizens, Robert Skene and Andrew Birnie, completed the little party
who set out together on this occasion, to be augmented at Perth,
Edinburgh, or London, by Sir Colin Campbell.

It is doubtful at what point in the journey Sir Colin joined Jamesone.   Young Jaffray relates that after returning in July from the
Coronation ceremonies he "shortly thereafter" went to London,
accompanied by Jamesone and other two Aberdeen friends, Robert
Skene and Andrew Birnie.   From the circumstance that he makes no
mention of Sir Colin Campbell as a fellow-traveller, it may be inferred
that London had been arranged as the place of *rendezvous*.   The party
made a rest at Edinburgh on the way, and whilst there, Jamesone
entered himself as a burgess of that city.   He foresaw that in future
much of his time would be spent there to overtake the work he had in
prospect.   The following record of his entry is extracted from the
Edinburgh Guild Register :—

"Vigesimo octauo Augusti Jm vjc xxxiijo

" The said day in presens forsaid [Joseph Marjoribanks deyne of gild
and the gild counsell] George Jamesone paynter comperand is maid
Burges and gild brothir of this burgh conforme to ane act of counsell of
the dait of thir presentis and hes gevin his aith in maner above writtin,
and hes payit for his dewtie to the deyne of gild the soume of ane
hundrethe thriescoir sex punds threttene schillings four pennyes—ooo."

Although Jamesone was a burgess of his native town, no record of his entrance there has as yet been discovered.

London at the period contained something under a quarter of a million souls, the entire population of England being under five millions. At that time, as now, London was the centre of attraction to men of eminence in every walk of life. Its great wealth could employ and reward with affluence whatever was deemed worthy, by whomsoever purveyed. Under the direction and patronage of Charles, a taste for the fine arts was making rapid progress. One eulogist says that—" Already had set in that passion for possessing the best that art could produce or that money could buy, and already the nucleus had been made in many a palace and mansion of those priceless collections, now deservedly the pride of their owners."

Eminent artists found a hearty welcome in London. Rubens had paid a temporary working visit, but, although he was handsomely treated, dubbed Master of Arts by Cambridge, and knighted by Charles, he could not be prevailed on to quit his princely home at " An t' werf " for the banks of the Thames. Vandyck, however, had settled down in London, and Jamesone was to renew acquaintanceship with his former fellow-pupil, now become " ' *Sir* Anthony,' principal Paynter in ordinary to their Majesties at St James's." Than Jamesone no one would rejoice more sincerely at the growing powers and popularity of his friend ; but no one would more sincerely lament him as a spoiled man, still person- ally fascinating, but frivolous and fast, environed by difficulties of his own making. He was at the very zenith of his genius ; rivalry had hid its diminished head before his rising talents—he had the ball of success at his foot.

Jamesone is said to have painted a portrait of Queen Henrietta to match his picture of the King, done at Holyrood, and there was no more convenient occasion than this same visit to London. Under such favouring conditions as the artistic society of his old friend Vandyck, and his new friend Sir Colin Campbell, not to speak of the King him- self, we must believe that Jamesone painted his best, and received in the effort some fresh impulses. Supported and introduced by such friends, Jamesone would find ready admission into that society where the best was to be seen and heard.

In letters, London, notwithstanding the loss of some notable men, still bristled with literary activities. This very year Massinger's play, " A New Way to Pay Old Debts," appeared. The light of Ben Jonson's strong genius was becoming dim, and the hand of the " Lime and Mortar " Poet was palsied. Still Jamesone might see the Laureate at " The Mermaid," or hear him at his own hospitable board boast to a Scotchman of his own Scottish extraction, and of his long walk from London to Hawthornden to see his friend William Drummond, with whom Jamesone had been so lately associated. John Taylor, too, the Water Poet, was to be found plying his double craft of Thames boatman and poet this same year, which may be further identified as that in which the immortal Pepys was born. Nine and twenty years later Samuel, having the *entrée* of the London studios and greenrooms, was chattering about art and pictures like a connoisseur. Under date 18th June, 1662, we find him passing an adverse criticism on Michael Wright, who was a pupil of Jamesone's. Pepys had been seeing some portraits at Sir Peter Lely's. " Thence," says he, " to Wright's, the painter's, but Lord ! the difference that is between their two works."

There are no other data respecting this memorable visit to the Continent than that Sir Colin accompanied Jamesone to Italy, and in a general way acted as his cicerone. One circumstance in this connection may be here alluded to, and that is Walpole's statement of the existence of Jamesone's own portrait in the Gallery of Painters at Florence. Sir Horace has a very graceful way of putting in an " effect," and for this one he remains responsible. There is no such portrait acknowledged in the catalogue of that Valhalla of artists, nor is it enshrouded as an " incogna ritratto," whose name there is legion. Had such a portrait ever been there, the probability is that it would be there still. At the author's special request, Mr. George Reid, R.S.A., in 1882, kindly made a searching inspection of the Gallery, and is thoroughly convinced that no portrait of George Jamesone is there now. Without doubt, Florence would be visited, although Rome would be the traveller's goal and the great centre of attraction. It was the shrine to which art pilgrims bent their steps, and it held in its churches and palaces the masterpieces of the greatest painters and sculptors. Besides the works of men who had passed away, Jamesone might see such men as Claude and Poussin plying their busy pencils in Rome at that very time.   To men like Sir Colin Campbell and Jamesone, possessed of rich stores of classic lore, the historic interest alone of the Eternal City would invest their visit with immense value.   In this respect it will be easy to imagine many objects of surpassing interest suggestive of the history of that world of the Roman Empire with whose rise, decline, and fall they were both familiar.   In Jamesone's own special department of art—portraiture—he would find an *embarras de riches*, which, to a naturally modest man like himself, might possibly have a humbling quite as much as a stimulating effect.

Tradition asserts that Jamesone has long been represented by certain works of his in the Eternal City.   In the small chapel attached to the Scots College there, there are four pictures, which were presented to the establishment by a Marchioness of Huntly.   They are supposed to represent, among others, scenes of historic interest from the life of Queen Margaret of Scotland and Malcolm Canmore.   The College authorities show these pictures, and share the freely-expressed belief that they are the work of George Jamesone, the Scottish Vandyck.   It is very difficult to know what to make of this tradition, which, at least, has its doubtful side.   It finds, perhaps, some support in that already quoted local tradition, that, at a certain stage of Jamesone's career, he painted pictures which, presumably not being appreciated at home, were " carried over to France and Italy, and esteem'd there."   The case is one to be decided solely by the internal evidence of the paintings themselves, and, as yet, we are unaware that they have ever been critically examined by any one claiming to be sufficiently conversant with Jamesone's manner to give a reliable verdict on the subject.   There is evidence that Jamesone indulged both in classic subjects, landscape, and even sea pieces, but absolutely none that he ever ventured on the field of such purely historical compositions as are the subjects of the pictures in the Scots College at Rome.   So far as we know, Jamesone's intimacy with the noble house of Huntly led only to his executing portrait commissions for them.   From the mutual good offices of the Right Reverend Bishop Macdonald, Aberdeen, and Monsignore Campbell,

Principal of the Scots College at Rome, a minute description of the pictures there has been furnished, and will be found in the detailed catalogue in the latter part of this volume.

Unless any particular reason existed for revisiting London, the probability is that, after a flying visit to Antwerp, where his respects might be tendered, and his friend Sir Colin Campbell introduced to Rubens, Jamesone would take ship either for Leith or Aberdeen. Such a tour had certainly occupied several months, in the slow-pacing first half of the seventeenth century. Begun in the month of August, it is scarcely likely that the travellers could have been at their own firesides much, if at all, before the close of the year.

The earlier months of 1634 were spent by Jamesone at home. At that time the whole city was stirred by no less an event than the translation of Dr. William Forbes to Edinburgh. The subject mooted at the Coronation ceremonies in the previous year took shape in his formal nomination to the See in January of this year. At his departure shortly thereafter, the Town Council, in order to give suitable expression to the wide-spread feeling of respect and affection entertained by the community for this truly estimable and pious prelate, celebrated the occasion by a farewell banquet in his honour. It was held in Skipper Anderson's house in the Castlegate, and whether Jamesone was present or not, the event was one to excite his interest and sympathy. As these valedictory entertainments possessed some features of novelty, we are induced to extract the following references :—

" Item, disbursit for ane supper in Gilbert Anderson's hous, made to Doctor William Forbes minister of this burghe, befoir he went south to be inaugurat bishop of Edinburgh the magistrattis and remanent of tounes ministers being present thereat. 32 lib. 18s."

" Item, to the violers that nicht. 12s."

" Item, for wyne careit to the Craibstane at the said Doctour Forbes departure. 2 lib. 8s."

Encouraging as were these proofs of the goodwill of his flock and fellow-citizens, and sincere as were their parting good wishes for his future welfare, it certainly was not anticipated that before three months were over, the Bishop's useful career would be closed for ever. It is not unlikely that as Jamesone had partially established himself in Edinburgh in the course of the year, he, in the middle of April, followed regretfully the remains of his friend to the grave. There existed a not dissimilar purpose in the lives of these two men. The life and labours of the Bishop spoke for the beauty of holiness, those of the artist, without straining a point, made for the holiness of beauty.

The chief works of the year were Jamesone's fulfilment of numerous painting engagements for his patron, Sir Colin Campbell, with a sprinkling of commissions from his other friends. Among other portraits painted in Edinburgh was one of Lord Frendraught, from the far north. For his supposed complicity in the well-known and awful tragedy of the burning of his castle, he dared not leave Edinburgh that year for fear of the Gordons, who diligently harried his lands in his absence.

In the charter-room of Taymouth Castle there are two letters written by Jamesone to his patron Sir Colin. The first of these is dated from Edinburgh, 13 October [1634]. It is to the following effect :—

"To the Richt honorable the Laird of Glenvrquhie thes.

"Richt honorable,—I receawed the hundreth merkis fra this berar for the quhilk I shall indewor to do yowr worship better service heirefter ; and as for the picturis quhilk I am yeit to maik I shall do all diligens to get theam with the first occasione, bot it will be in Janvarij befoir I can begin theam, except that I hawe the occasione to meit with the pairties in the North quhair I mynd to stay for tuo monethes ; and if ether ther or heir I can be able to do yowr worship service, I shall be moist willing, and ewer to remane your worships servand.

"GEORGE JAMESONE.

"Edinburgh, 13 October [1634]."

That Sir Colin was a man of strong historical as well as artistic instincts, this of perpetuating his friends and relations in portraiture is a clear evidence, but he seems to have carried the matter too far by employing a German artist to paint "*portraits from fancy*," some of which still cover the Taymouth walls. He "bestowit and gave to ane German artist whom he entereinit in his house aucht moneth. . . the soume of ane thousand poundis," getting in return "*threttie brods*" and the said fancy portraits, and on whose account Jamesone's reputation has suffered some criticism. Altogether, it is a very curious spectacle this of Sir Colin persistently endeavouring to embellish his baronial halls in the mountain fastnesses of Perthshire with works of art by a foreigner, until he could procure a home artist to be his coadjutor in this praiseworthy ambition and forward step in civilisation and refinement. Sir Colin was a child-like lover of pictures, and in these days of the enormous increase, more especially of artistic portraiture, we shall be slow to throw the first stone at his preference. Such art needs no apologist, and it will become growingly popular and humanising in its influence. Employed to embody the beautiful and the lovable, it converts mere personality into heritable property. And whoever the artist and whatever his materials and mode of working, provided only he has worked with a pure mind and loyal to the truth, he is a public benefactor.

Sir Colin's passion for collecting the portraits of his friends was impelled by strong affectional as well as artistic motives. It was his tribute to those qualities that he admired in his friends. Besides the money cost of the gallery thus gathered together, it seems he had to pay another penalty for the privilege, in having to present some of his friends with a "double" of his own portrait. But this had its compensations. It was more work to his artistic *protégés*, an opportunity for testing their dexterity, and a means of diffusing a knowledge and love of art so dear to himself. The portrait which Sir Colin possessed of himself was among Jamesone's early efforts on his behalf, "more careful than the rest, and evidently a characteristic likeness."

The mode of address adopted in Jamesone's letter is perfectly courteous, and bespeaks the manners of a gentleman. The hundred merks acknowledged seem to have been more than full payment of the charge made. Not mercenary, Jamesone asks a modest price; not ungenerous, his appreciative patron gives him more than he asks, although, probably, not more than the real value of the work done. Sir Colin was satisfied, and pays accordingly; Jamesone was grateful, and promises even better service in the future.

The letter indicates that Jamesone's hands are so full of work that he

11

cannot undertake Sir Colin's new commissions till the new year (1635), but, as he intends going home for a couple of months, he may have an opportunity of obtaining sittings from some of the north country friends. It may be conjectured that Jamesone's desire, expressed in his letter to Sir Colin, to be at home towards the end of the year, was one founded on family reasons—probably its increase by the birth of another child. We have no record of its birth, but we have of its burial, in the first month of the new year, 1635, the month that was fatal to his two sons two years before.   It was buried on the 30th of January "in the Auld Kirk" (of St. Nicholas).

The early deaths of the artist's children seem to argue a constitutional delicacy, whether derived from the mother or the father cannot now be discovered.   It is certain, however, that about this time Jamesone conceived the idea of building himself a pleasure house with a garden in the outskirts of the town, as a means of recreation and of promoting the health of himself and family.   Parents who have had half their family swept away by death naturally grow anxious for the safety of the survivors.   Jamesone's ideas about a *Lust Haus* had been derived from his acquaintance with Continental usage.   Rubens had a passion for planting and building.

The spot he pitched upon was in every way suitable for his purpose. It lay at the upper end of the then lovely valley of the Denburn, down which the eye might pleasantly wander, unarrested by anything but its picturesquely-wooded banks until it reached the purpled Grampians beyond the Dee.   The patch of ground referred to was known as the playfield, being, in point of fact, the site on which formerly plays used to be enacted.   It was but five or six minutes' walk from Jamesone's own door, but sufficiently far to be considered in the country.   A great interest attaches to this spot, considered as the theatre of the town, an institution, however, which the growing strictness of morals had abolished.   The dramatic representations took place, of course, in the open air, and every accessory was of the most primitive character.   The stage was the said playfield, a level patch at the foot of the westmost end of the Woolmanhill, on which the spectators ranged themselves and overlooked the actors below.   Companies of peripatetic actors visited

the town from time to time and entertained the lieges. Tradition saith
not what comedy was enacted, where the box plan of the *house* lay for
consultation, what was the scale of prices charged for *admission*, whether
the gods were as autocratic as in a modern playhouse, or at what hour
carriages might be ordered.

A star company visited the town on the 9th October, 1601, having
performed at Edinburgh on their way north before James, who passes
them on with a recommendatory letter, all which the following extract
from the Council records :—

" The samen day, the prouest bailleis, and counsall ordanis the soume
of threttie-tua merkis to be gevin to the Kingis serwandis presentlie in
this burght, quha playes comedeis and staige playes. Be reasoun thay
ar recommendit be his majesties speciall letter, and hes played sum of
thair comedies in this burght and ordainis the said soume to be
payit to tham be the dean of gild whilke salbe allowed in his comptes."

Charles Knight will have it in his somewhat supposititious biography
of Shakespeare that the great dramatist made one of the company
referred to on this occasion. It is very obvious that Lawrence Fletcher,
" Comediane to his majestie," and otherwise very closely associated with
Shakespeare, was one of the band, for thirteen days after he was
admitted a burgess of the Guild of Aberdeen, along with a number of
other gentlemen. " The people of Aberdeen," says Knight, " were a
loyal people, and we are not surprised that they welcomed the King's
players with rewards and honours." It scarcely concerns this narrative
whether or not Shakespeare figured on the playfield along with
Fletcher, in 1601 ; but now, in 1635, it may have been that Jamesone
had a very pleasant reminiscence of himself as a boy of fourteen, an
interested spectator of the play enacted by the " Kingis serwandis " on
the spot he had chosen for his recreative retreat.

Besides its naturally beautiful situation and its early associations in
the painter's mind, another motive still, led him to make an overture to
the Town Council for a lease of the playfield. These attractions were
likely to suffer prejudice, from the fact that the field was fast lapsing by
neglect and disuse into a waste, unsightly place. His proposal was, in
brief, to put the field into thorough repair, with a view to its permanent

reclamation for the future good of the town, and all at his own expense, provided he obtained a life-rent of it for his own use as a pleasure garden.

On the 13th of May, 1635, the matter was brought before a special meeting of the Town Council, and the following extract from the day's record gives us the *ipsissima verba* of Jamesone's most respectful petition, and the decision thereupon :—

> "Apud Aberdēn decimo tertio die mensis Maij anno dominum milesimo sextentesimo trigesimo quinto.

"THE QUHILK day the prouest, baillies and counsall of the burght of Abirdeine wnderwreittin thay ar to say, Sir Paull Mengzeis of Kynmundy, Knight, prouest, Gilbert Collisoun, Maister Thomas Gray, Maister Mathow Lumysden, Maister Robert Farquhar, baillies ; Walter Robertsoun, deane of gild ; Robert Cruikschank, Thesaurar ; Robert Johnstoun, Thomas Mortymer, George Mengzeis, Robert Alexander, Dauid Aedye, Alexander Burnett, Thomas Paipi, Paull Mengzeis, Hew Andersoun, goldsmith, and George Pyper wricht, being conveinit in the tounes counsall house anent the petitioun gewin in to thame be George Jamesoun indweller in the said burght, makand mentioun that for sameikle as a greate pairt of the playfeild belongeing to the Toune whair comedies were wont to be actit of auld besyde the well of Spay, is spoilled, brocken, and cariet away be speat and inundation of watter and is lyabill to the same danger and inconvenient heireftir, so that unles some course be tackin to withstand suche speattis and invndatiounes, the whole playfeild within a short space of tyme will allutterlie decay and serwe for no vse ; and the said George, tacking notice of the Tounes prejudice heirin, and withall havand consideratioun how this litle plott of ground may be vsefull to the Toune heirefter out of his naturall affectioun to this his native citie, he is content wpoun his awin chairges ; not onlie to mak some fortificatioun to withstand the violence of speattis in tyme coming, bot lykewayes to mak some policie and planting within and about the said playfeild for the publiet vse and benefitt of the Toune, wherof he hes takin occasion, be this his petitioun to acquaint thair wisdomes of the counsall, humblie desyiring, for this effect that thair wisdomes wil be pleased to graunt him frie libertie, licience and tolerance,

to mak sic building, policie, and planting within and about the said plott
of ground, as he sall think most fitting and convenient both to wyth-
stand the violence of the watter fra doinge forder harme thairwnto. And
to the effect the same may redound to the publict use and benefitt of
the Toun; onlie this muche he desyiris for his trawellis cost and expenss
to be bestowit on this work, that he may hawe a lease of this plott of
ground, and the wse thairof to his awin behowe during his lyftyme
allanerlie ; And efter his deceas, he is content that the magistrattis and
councell of this burght for the tyme intromett thairwith, and apply
the same in all tyme thaireftir to the publict wse and benefitt of the
Toune, as they sall find most convenient, without any recompense to be
sought be him his aires, executoris, assignayes, or successoris, for any
chairges that he sal happen to bestow thairwpoun, as at mair length wes
conteint in the said petitioun : Quhilk being red, hard, and consid̃erit
be the saids prouest baillies and counsall and thay thairwith being
ryplie advysed thay find the desyir thairof to be most reasonable as
being a motioun tending to the publict gude and benefitt of the toune,
acknowledging thairby the petitionar to expres himselff as a weill
affected citizen towards the furtherance and incres of policie in this his
native toune, AND THAIRFOIR be thir presentis thay giwe, grant, and sett
to the said George Jamesoun a lease and tack of the said plott of ground
callit the Playfeild during all the dayes of his lyftyme allanerlie, his
entrie thairto to be and begin the day and date heirof, with full power,
libertie and priuiledge to him to build and mack sic policie and planting
in and about the said plott of ground in all pairts, and throughout the haill
bounds and limites thairof as he sall think most convenient, PAYAND
thairfoir yeirelie during his lyftyme to the thesaurar of the said burght
for the tyme in name of the toune thric shillings foure penneis vsuall
Scottes money at the feist of Witsonday yeirlie if the same be asked
allanerlie, for all vther maill or dewtie that may be requyred thairfore
during the space foirsaid WITH THIS alwayes condit̃õ and prowisioun,
that immediatlie eftir the deceis of the said George the magistrattis and
counsall of the said burght for the tyme, in name of the Toune, or thair
Thesaurar in thair name, sall hawe full and frie power to mell and intromett with the said Playfeild, haill policie, building and planting within

and about the same *brevi manu*, without any proces of law or declara-
tor, and to apply the same to the public; vse and benefitt of the haill
toune in all tyme thaireftir, without any recompense to be gewine be
the Toune to the aires or executoris of the said George, for any cost or
charges he sall happin to mak and deburse in planting and building
thairvpon, quhairunto the said George Jameson consentit and agriet
and accepted of his lywerent tak aboue writtin wpoun the condition
foirsaid."

Such are the bald business minutes of the Council Registers, but
what of all the eulogistic speeches of the Provost who moved, and the
First Baillie who seconded, the acceptance of Jamesone's proposals, as
well as the rest of their "wisdomes of the counsall" who had a right to
speak and a claim to be heard on this important occasion ?   There is
no newspaper file which can be referred to for reports of what passed at
the meeting.   Jamesone's public spirit had been made a topic of remark,
the personal worth of this "weill affected citizen" would be adverted to,
and very much made of the professional honours that had been awarded.
There would not be wanting the inevitable bit of humour from some
baillie body who deemed it his function to be funny.   Of course it
cannot now be seen where the laugh had come in, but, no doubt, the
"chaumer" echoed to the peal, and so with hearts elate they voted
with unanimity for the motion, which transmogrified the "playfield"
into the "four neukit garden," by which name it has ever since been
known.   The "Garden Neuk Close" names a lane which skirts
the eastern, and probably original wall of the garden to this day.
The completed transaction is alike creditable to both parties.
There cannot be a doubt of the strong vein of good feeling which
prompted Jamesone's action.   His warm heart, informed by an artist's
eye for the beautiful, conspired to preserve at least one of the amenities
of his native town.   Nor were his motives misinterpreted by his fellow-
citizens who, while they felt in duty bound to impose a small yearly
grassum, only to be paid if asked for, were evidently flattered by the
painter's patriotism.   For a few years past he had been moving freely
about the country, making at times prolonged stays in Edinburgh, and
had probably anticipated his permanent removal before long to some

enlarged sphere of activity. They were all proud of him. He had acquired fame and reflected it on them, and his action about the play-field was received as a grateful pledge that he meant to remain an honoured citizen amongst them. The current of popular favour set strong towards him at this time. Indeed, public opinion can always be concurrently more favourable to an artist than to most men, and in greater sympathy with his fame than perhaps with any other kind of fame. He contributes to the stock, knowledge, and appreciation of the beautiful by an art which of itself belongs to no party, and therefore does nothing to arouse in us any polemic or combative feeling. He pleases to instruct and instructs to please—his works are a permanent heritage and his fame a popular trust.

Numerous references exist to the said garden. Parson Gordon does not omit to delineate its site on his map of the town, nor to in-dicate the painter's little summer-house situated in the middle of it, still apparently existing, in 1661, when the map was published. Sir Robert Sibbald, too, in his MS. in the Advocates' Library, refers to it in these terms :—" In vicina fontis [Well of Spa] est hortus suburbanus celebris pictoris, Georgii Jamesonii, ubi Museum ejus manu depictum est visendum." Dr. Arthur Johnston also takes up a similar strain, but in epigrammatic form. It was just such an occasion as to excite Johnston's muse :—

> Hanc quoque Lanaris Mons ornat amœnior illis,
> Hinc ferrugina Spada colorat aquis,
> Inde suburbanum Jamesoni despicis Hortum,
> Quem Domini pictum suspicor esse manu ;

which in its turn is quaintly " Englished " by John Barclay :—*

> The Woolmanhill which all the rest outvies,
> In pleasantness this City beautifies,
> There is the Well of Spa, that healthful Font,
> Whose Yr'ned hewed Water, colloureth the Mount.
> Not far from thence a Garden's to be seen,
> Which unto Jameson did appertain,
> Wherein a little pleasant House doth stand
> Painted (as I guess) with its Master's hand.

* Succinct Survey of the famous City of Aberdeen, 1685.

In what manner Jamesone humoured his fancy in the embellishment of his garden-house is, of course, unknown. The structure was probably of wood, admitting of decorations without and within, and it is easy to imagine that he spent many a pleasant leisure hour in beautifying its walls, or in cultivating the fruits and flowers of the garden itself. Alone, or in the company of his wife and daughters, or in the entertainment of a garden party of his friends, it is to be hoped that the painter enjoyed many delightful days in the healthful resort he had rescued from the ruinous "speattis and invndatiounes" which threatened it.

The Well of Spa was one of the attractions to the locality. From its mineral waters the painter is said to have received from time to time considerable relief from his sufferings, caused by calculus in the bladder, a disease which has for long been peculiarly common to the north-east of Scotland. In addition to the expense Jamesone was at in reclaiming the playfield and enclosing his garden, with a grateful generosity he thoroughly rebuilt the well and protected it with a vault of hewn stone. This action, in the matter of the well, speaks volumes for Jamesone's goodness of disposition in his desire to perpetuate its benefits to those coming after him, who might have the misfortune to be similarly afflicted with himself. Dr. William Barclay wrote in praise of the virtues to the water, which he says was carried as far as France for the relief of the sick. He mentions that the well being "verie old and worne, a virtuous citizen, George Jamesone, the celebrated painter, did build it of new . . . because of the many proofs he had of it in his own person in curing him of the stone." The fountain was again repaired, in 1670, at the private charges of another eminent citizen, Baillie Alexander Skene. Byron, when a boy at the Grammar School, took, it is said, a daily draught at the Well of Spa. The last thorough repair of the fabric took place about forty years ago ; but there is now no special virtue in the water. The course of the spring seems to have been disturbed by some operations at the adjoining Royal Infirmary, and River Dee water has been introduced.

It may be mentioned that Jamesone's name has been identified with another suburban spot about a quarter of a mile to the west, and still on the course of the Denburn, in the vicinity of Cherry Vale. Judging from the conformation of the ground, it had been a very attractive valley, and was long known as Jamesone's Garden, but with what good reason does not now appear. Within the memory of persons not very old, a number of composition statues adorned the locality, and probably that circumstance has something to do with the tradition.

These improvement schemes being arranged, as well as a good deal of local portrait-painting, Jamesone returned to Edinburgh. In June he writes again from there to Sir Colin Campbell, making arrangements for a long list of sixteen portraits. Interesting information may be gleaned from his letter, both as to his scale of prices and the rate of speed at which he worked. His usual price for a half-length was twenty merks, but, if he provided a gold frame, the price became twenty pounds. Modernising these values, the cost of the painting alone was £1 2s. 6d., and with a gold frame, £1 13s. 4d. Roundly, the artist charged twice as much as the carver and gilder. These apparently very low prices must be viewed relatively to the poor remuneration given for all labour at the period, and to low prices which ruled for all materials. The country was poor and money scarce, but above all, Jamesone's own circumstances, partly from his industry and partly from his heirships, were sufficiently easy to content him with very moderate prices. The letter makes it quite clear that he is no huxter at least. He appraises his work at what he considers to be its value, and it is the same to all comers, whether peer or peasant. " Thus I deal with all alike." An equitable man—one to whom the love of the work was of more importance than its money payment. The postscript to the letter furnishes an idea of the rate of production. It obviously means that in eight clear weeks he expects to execute sixteen portraits—two every week. This was doubtless his most prolific period, and it forms a useful base by which an estimate may be formed as to the quantity of work which must have passed through his hands during the course of his long painting career of nearly forty years. Making due allowance for an early want of dexterity, to the paucity of sitters, and to his pursuit of other works than portraiture, as well as to the inevitable interruptions which occur in the busiest of lives, it is not unlikely that at least a thousand portraits left his easel from first to last. The letter runs :—

"Richt Honorable,—I receawed yowr worships letter with ane measure concerning the maiking of soume picturis, quhairof sextine of theam ar set doune in not. I will werie willinglie serwe yowr worship, and my pryce shall be bot the ordinarie since the measure is just the ordinarie. The pryce quhilk ewerie one payes to me, abowe the west, is twentie merkis, I furnishing claith and coulleris ; bot iff I furniss ane double gilt muller, then it is twentie poundis. Thes I deall with all alyk ; bot I am moir bound to hawe ane gryte cair of your worships serwice, becaus of my gouid payment for my laist imployment. Onlie thus your worship wold resolwe at quhois charges I mist go throwe the countrey to maik thir picturis, for all that are heir in town neidis onlie yowr worships letter to theam to causs theam sitt, and for theam quhois picturis I hawe allreadie, I shall double theam, or then giwe yowr worship the principall. So, leawing this to yowr worships consideration and ansuer, I shall ewer remaine, your woirships willing servand,

GEORGE JAMESONE.

"Edinburgh, 23 Junii [1635]."

"Iff I begin the picturs in Julii, I will hawe the sixtine redie about the laist of September."

Interesting collateral proof of these transactions with Jamesone's most munificent patron is given in the Black Book of Taymouth—a perfect repertory of information of the family history :—

"Item, the said Sir Coline Campbell gave unto George Jamesone, painter in Edinburgh, for King Robert and King David Bruysses, Kings of Scotland, and Charles 1st, King of Great Brittane France and Ireland, and his majesties Quein, and for nine more of the Queins of Scotland their portraits, quhilks are set up in the halls of Balloch the sum of tua hundreth thrie scor pundis."

Here are thirteen portraits detailed for a total amount of £260, and :—

"Mair, the said Sir Coline gave to the said George Jamesone for the Knight of Lochow's Lady, and the first Countess of Argylle, and six of the Ladys of Glenurquhay their portraits, and the said Sir Coline his own portrait, quhilks are set up in the Chalmer of Deass of Balloch, ane hundreth four scoire punds."

Another batch of nine portraits for £180, being at Jamesone's rate of £20 each.*

In full employment, and at his own prices, Jamesone was making a very good annual income of not less than £1000 or £1500 a year. This must be considered very handsome for poor Scotland, which could only afford King James £5000 a year, before he ascended the throne of England, where princes and painters were much better paid. James was twitted with this—

> Bonnie Scot, witness can
> England's made you a gentleman.

At that time as much as £30 or £40 sterling was paid in England for a painted signboard. Michael Wright, Jamesone's pupil, is said to have got as high as £60 sterling for portraits he painted.

In addition to the many single portraits painted by desire of Sir Colin Campbell, he further gratified the worthy knight this year, by executing "ane greit genealogie brod pantit of all the Lairds of Glenurchy and of those that ar come of the house of Glenurchy." This interesting work still adorns the walls of Taymouth, and is referred to in connection with Jamesone's other works there.

It is quite apparent from the portraits that Jamesone produced during the ensuing five years that a good deal of his time was spent from home. He was among the Carnegys, in Forfarshire, where he painted three of the brothers, now in Kinnaird Castle. He also did the Stirlings of Keir; and in Fifeshire he did Alexander Lesley, the Earl of

---

* To reduce Scots money to its sterling equivalent, it is necessary for the period to divide by 12. Hence—

£1 or 20s. Scots	= 20d.	sterling.	
1 merk	„	= 13½d.	„
1 shilling	„	= 1 penny	„
1 plack	„	= ⅓ of a penny	„
1 bodle	„	= ⅙ „	„
1 doit	„	= 1/12 „	„

Leven, and the Lindsays of Wormistone, as well as Captain Erskine of Cambuskenneth, and the full-mailed figure of Lord Cardross.

During these years Jamesone lived much in Edinburgh, although there is no evidence that he removed his family there. Indeed, he can scarcely be said to have had any settled place of abode, for he travelled through the country to suit his sitters, not a few of whom were ladies, to whom at that time of day travelling long distances was not a convenient thing. Jamesone ever painted female heads the best ; his thinness of manner being better adapted for delineating the greater grace and delicacy of a woman's face. Sir Colin Campbell soon detected the artist's forte, and hence the large proportion of female portraits by Jamesone in the Taymouth collection.. A few other of Jamesone's more notable sitters about this time were the Marquis of Hamilton, cousin of the King, whom he accompanied to Scotland on his Coronation tour ; David Beaton of Balfour, Lord Haddington, the Earls of Kinghorn, Mar, and Loudon, the Chancellor of Scotland. Sir Thomas Hope, the Lord Advocate, yet professed champion of the Covenanters, and one of that small but invaluable race of diarists, makes an interesting note respecting the painting of his own portrait. He evidently sat with the grudge of a man whose hands were too full of graver matters. And, in 1638, his time and attention were claimed by very weighty affairs, both of Church and State. The following are the brief entries of Sir Thomas :—

"20 July, 1638, Friday. This day William Jamesoun painter (at the earnest desyr of my sone Mr. Alexander) was sufferit to draw my pictur."

Then, on the following Friday :—

" Item, a second draught be William Jamesoun."

In impatient haste to have the ordeal over, the old gentleman was too pre-occupied to catch accurately the artist's Christian name, and confuses it with that of Jamesone's brother, William, the Edinburgh writer, whom Sir Thomas in all probability remembered. The great lawyer lived in a spacious mansion in the Cowgate, and there, in obedience to the hortative motto over his own door (*Tecum habita*—keep at home) he would give Jamesone sittings. If the two entries in the diary indicate all the times he sat, which is very likely, it was scarcely doing the artist justice, unless, indeed, they were more prolonged than is customary. We know that Jamesone worked with great speed, using whatever means would facilitate the work. Hence the meaning of the traditional proverb, that "George Jamesone's thumb was worth the five fingers of some." Indeed, it must be frankly admitted that the portraits of the last and most hurried decade of Jamesone's work do not, as a rule, contrast favourably with those painted in the preceding ten years. There is only so much that one can accomplish well.

CHAPTER VIII

Ibis Closing]Oears.

ECCLESIASTICALLY the period was fast becoming charged with elements of grave anxiety. Public opinion and events were ripening into civil commotion and warfare. From the stool-projecting episode in St. Giles' Cathedral, in 1637, affairs acquired gathered force during the remaining years of Jamesone's life.

He was moving freely among the principal actors in the great events of these stirring times, yet it is extremely unlikely that he took any active share in them. Conversant with every phase of the burning questions of the day, he seems to have rigidly abstained from entering the arena of controversy. His temperament and profession alike forbade his doing so. A momentary doubt on this point has been created by the occurrence of the name of a George Jamesone on one of the most important and numerous committees of the General Assembly of Glasgow, in 1638, namely, that "to consider the complaint against the Prelates." The doubt has been completely dispelled by the dis-covery that the said George Jamesone was a "merchand burgesse of Cowper." It was scarcely in *our* Jamesone's way to make such a clean sweep of the Bishops as did this influential but strongly partisan com-mittee. It was not like him to be a "green book" for the recording of any man's besetting sins, such as "Sabbath breaking," "common carding," and the like. He was more willing to hand down the prelates' portraits than their peccadilloes to posterity.

Aberdeen has been termed the "northern fastness of prelacy" of that period ; yet Jamesone has been usually adjudged a Presbyterian in principle. Up to 1638, Episcopacy had succeeded in quashing the opposition of that party. Among others, Samuel Rutherford was silenced and banished "with his logick syllogismes" to Aberdeen, as to an ecclesiastical Siberia, where his doctrines, even if allowed to express them, were little likely to influence such trusty upholders of the Episcopal order as were the inhabitants of the Granite City. The temper of the General Assembly of 1638 gave most unequivocal proof of the dominance of the Presbyterians, with whom, after the expulsion of the Bishops, it became a first duty in the following year to coerce the Aberdonians into subscription of the Covenant. With this view, and to over-awe Huntly, who, as King's Lieutenant in the north, was fanning the flame of Episcopal contumacy, a Covenanting army took the field, under the leadership of the young Earl of Montrose, who possessed all the zeal of a convert to the cause.

Never had such a well-appointed, numerous army menaced the brave burgh of Aberdeen. Past Jamesone's very door (Saturday, 30th March, 1639) trooped 9000 men, officered by many of his personal friends, among others, David Lesley, Marischal, Kinghorn, Erskine, and Carnegy. Horse and foot, they streamed through the town, bannered " For Religion, the Covenant, and the Country." They entered by the Upperkirkgate port, passed through the Broadgate and Castlegate, out at the Justice port, to the Links. The inhabitants were variously affected by this parade of military power.

It was the opening act of that tragic period for Aberdeen, best known as " The Trubles." As such, it did not last long, nor mean very much. Before three months were over, Montrose was again thundering at the gates, and had to fight a two days' battle at the Bridge of Dee before they were opened to him. From this period onward the plot thickened, and the town was like a camp, till, in 1644, Montrose, who had schooled it into the adoption of Covenanting principles, now returned, and cruelly beat it with scorpions for leaving its first love. Five wretched years of military exactions, organised pillage, fines, sur- prises, skirmishes, changing masters, were at last crowned by a cruel *tableau* of a successful attack, followed by an unmitigated sack of the town. How for the best part of a week the defenceless town was left to the tender mercies of the " Irishes," how its peaceful dwellings were ransacked, and its merchants' booths plundered, and how its streets ran red with the blood of its unburied citizens, must all be referred to the course of general history.

So far as George Jamesone was concerned, that long spell of political quiet following the Union of the Crowns, affording a breathing space to the nation at large, and to himself the most favourable conditions for a successful prosecution of his life work, was now broken.   Now a time of unsettling and of bloodshed had supervened, which, notwithstanding the position he had reached, must have interfered with him in his profession.   With what composure could he work at home, or with what peace of mind could he remain for any length of time absent from it, knowing it to be so constantly menaced with disturbance and danger? These and other circumstances pressed on his mind and led him to ponder.   True, his personal fame was secured in that wealth of honest work done whilst the times served.   He had become a rich man and a landed proprietor, with a reasonable prospect in the event of his death of leaving those he loved in competent circumstances, but his own essentially pacific disposition was perplexed at the untoward course that public events had taken.

His friend Vandyck died this year.   Rubens, too, their mighty master, as well as Sir Colin Campbell, had passed away a year before. These warnings of mortality, along with an access of the constitutional infirmity under which Jamesone laboured, were not lost upon him, now a man of fifty-two, and, before the year was out, he prudently began to set his house in order, and devised his last will and testament.   It was a holograph.   In it he provided for his wife and their three daughters.   It is also very creditable to him that by the same instrument he provided for a natural daughter, whose existence had not before been surmised. She is made to share in her father's property equally with her otherwise more fortunate sisters, affording additional proof, if it were needed, of Jamesone's good sense and right feeling.   Besides leaving legacies to some other relatives and friends, he remembers the poor.   To Lord Rothes he bequeathes a picture of "Martha and Mary in one piece," and also a full length portrait of the King—probably the one for which the Town Council would not give him his price.   To William Murray he leaves a coffer full of medals—the treasured collection of a lifetime.

Jamesone had a literary and pictorial curio on which he set a high value.   It was a MS. of "200 leaves of parchment of excellent write adorned with divers historys of our Saviour curiously limned." Mr. Jamesone, of Leith, a descendant of the painter, and who furnished Walpole with many details, possessed a memorandum, written and signed by the painter, in which this highly prized MS. is referred to, and which he values at £200. What it really was, by whom it was executed, or whether it is still in existence, cannot now be determined.

Whatever solemnity of feeling may have touched the artist in making these dutiful settlements of his affairs, it did not diminish his activities. He continued to follow his usual pursuits, working sometimes at home in the midst of his family, sometimes at a nobleman's seat in the country, making prolonged visits to Edinburgh and its vicinity.

In 1640, he was a good deal in the far north painting members of the Duff family and connections. One of the finest female heads he ever painted adorns the walls of Duff House, the seat of the Earl of Fife. It is that of a Mrs. Duff, and forms a choice specimen of Jamesone's skill. He has painted her young and beautiful face with a mastery of art sufficient to secure him a high place among artists. He continued to work for the Duff family every year thereafter till his death.

In the veracious pages of Commissary Spalding there is a reference to Jamesone which cannot be overlooked. In proof of how the Covenant was lengthening its stakes and strengthening its bands, in the enforcement of its claims, he details with some *minutiæ* the names of many persons who, in June, 1640, were seized for their refusal to subscribe the Covenant. At a council of war, held by Earl Marischal and General Munro in the Tolbooth of Aberdeen, the recusants, consisting of several Aberdeenshire lairds and burgesses of the town, were examined. Not answering satisfactorily, some thirteen of them were remitted for trial to Edinburgh, "leaving their friends with sorry hearts." At their re-examination at Edinburgh the situation was not altered, and the verdict held them as "outstanders of the good cause." Several of the party were imprisoned to their great displeasure and loss of health, and on others heavy fines were imposed. Thomas Nicolson was fined 2000 merks, David Rickart, William Petrie, and George Gordon, were each fined 1000 merks ; and George Johnston and Robert Forbes were each fined 1000 pounds.

13

Two of the prisoners, " George Mòresoune and George Jamesoune,"
although not exonerated from guilt, " be moyan wan frie, and paid no
fine."   The George Moresoune mentioned as at both the Aberdeen and
Edinburgh trials, was a somewhat prominent citizen, and an ex-Dean of
Guild of Aberdeen.   It is noticeable that George Jamesone's name
occurs only at the Edinburgh trial, and, although unhappily without any
identifying mark, refers in all probability to none other than the artist,
as he occurs in the group designed by Spalding as " our townsmen."
The explanation may be found in the suggestion that Jamesone, working in Edinburgh at the time, underwent only the Edinburgh trial.   But
what need was there, it may be asked, for a trial at all in Jamesone's case
if he was a Presbyterian?   The reply probably tendered by his friends
in Court was, that being an *Episcopalian* in principle he could not subscribe, but that he had not strongly identified himself with either party,
and might with safety be allowed immunity from fine or imprisonment.
Montrose, Rothes, and Sir Thomas Hope would have no great difficulty
in satisfying the Tables as to the artist's views.

The year 1640 was otherwise sufficiently and sadly notable to
Jamesone.   It marked the death of two of his very oldest and warmest
friends—Dr. Arthur Johnston and Sir Paul Menzies.   Approaching the
grand climacteric himself, gaps in his large circle of friends would now
occur with admonitory frequency, although few would be so touching to
him as those just mentioned.   The former, with whom he was associated
from their boyhood in the kindliest intercourse, and the latter, with an
almost fatherly interest in the rising artist, filled niches in the artist's life
that could not be re-occupied.   The painter and the poet have ever been
identified in their lives and pursuits :—

> The first in painting, Jamesone will shine,
> As Johnston does in poetry divine.

From this point forward, the memorial incidents in Jamesone's life
are very scanty.   In 1641, death struck perhaps the saddest blow of all
at the artist's diminished and afflicted household.   On the 5th of
October of that year, with the last of his four sons was buried any
remaining hope (a very natural one) that Jamesone may have entertained of the survival of his name in his family.   In the male line, it was

now for ever extinct. This circumstance, coupled probably with his own somewhat impaired health and the growingly disturbed state of the country, probably curtailed his activities. There is reason to believe that, to a certain extent, he continued his usual migratory habits—suiting the convenience of his clients by visiting them at their own homes. He was working for the Haddington family in 1644, the year that he died. An unknown portrait at Yester bears that date, and may have been the very last from his hand. It is pleasant to find him so near his end in the society of those with whom he had long been good friends.

Of the particular circumstances of the artist's death nothing is known, beyond the bald facts that he was seized with a serious illness, of which he died at Edinburgh in the year just mentioned, and that he was buried, where so many of his eminent countrymen lie, in the historic Churchyard of Greyfriars. All else is conjecture and questionings. Did he succumb to some fresh access of the distressing malady from which he had so long suffered? What friends surrounded him in his last hours and took their good-night of him? It is not unlikely that his daughter, Marjory, was married by this time, and living with her husband in Edinburgh. If so, we cannot doubt that affectionate hands were about him, with all the ministeries that love knows to apply.

Thus, let us hope, the gentle spirit of the painter passed away. The blank to his family circle is not conjectural, nor is it doubtful that it would be felt by perhaps a wider circle, where he was more favourably known than many of the public personages of his day. The news that the hand of the master had lost its cunning would be borne regretfully not only to his native town for his attractive social qualities, but in countless mansions of the land would the news be received with unfeigned sorrow. In that year, 1644, the national crises of religious and civil warfare were becoming more bitter every day. The men whom Jamesone had painted were now fighting for and against each other, and displaying more passionate characteristics than could be supposed to reside under the placid features on his canvases. He happily died before the worst came to the worst. It is, perhaps, a proof of the strained relations of society at the time that Scotland was deprived of its first artistic genius, that his remains were allowed to sink into an unknown and unvisited tomb. The exact spot where he lies has never been discovered.

> Sweet be thy sleep ! where'er thy dust
> Is laid,—in earth or ocean's cave ;
> Thy soul is now in peace, we trust ;
> A nation's heart shall be thy grave.
> Enough ! thy spell is o'er us cast ;
> Thy work remains, thy toil is past.

Jamesone's death had occurred late in the year, and just at its close, " 11th December Mary, Issobella and Marjorie Jamesone " were served heirs portioners in general to their father, Mrs. Jamesone during her lifetime being secured in the free revenue of the property, which was not inconsiderable.

Jamesone, however, was not without a sincere panegyrist. The kindly and more facile pen, perhaps, of Arthur Johnston was at rest, but that of David Wedderburn remained. The old man, now retired from his long accustomed dominie duties and living on the grateful bounty of his fellow-citizens, occupies his learned leisure in turning a few verses in memory of his old friend. These, though printed as a broadsheet by Edward Raban, and probably widely circulated, have gone the way of so much fugitive literature, so that we are now indebted for their repro-duction to perhaps a unique copy of a reprint of them, now in the pos-session of Alexander Kemlo, Esq., Aberdeen :—

SUB OBITUM VIRI SPECTATISSIMI,
GEORGII JAMESONI,
ABREDONENSIS
PICTORIS EMINENTISSIMI,

Lachrymæ.

Gentis Apollo suæ fuit ut Buchananus, Apelles
    Solus eras Patriæ sic, JAMESONE, tuæ.
Rara avis in nostris oris : Tibi mille colores,
    Ora tibi soli pingere viva datum.
At Te nulla manus poterit sat pingere ; nempe
    Lampada cui tradas nulla reperta manus.

Quin si forte tuas vatum quis carmine laudes
Tentet, id ingenii vim superabit opus.
Quicquid erit, salve pictorum gloria, salve :
Æternumque vale Phosphore Scotigenum :
Phosphore, namque tua ars tenebris prius obsita cæcis,
Fors nitidum cernet Te præunte diem.

Tumulus Ejusdem.

Conditur hic tumulo JAMESONUS pictor, & una
Cum Domino jacet hic Ars quoque tecta suo.
Hujus ni renovent cineres Phœnicis Apellem ;
Inque urna hac coeant Ortus & Interitus.

Ejusdem Encomium meritissimum.

Si pietas prudens, pia si prudentia, vitæ
Si probitas, omni si sine labe fides ;
Partaque si graphio Magnatum gratia, dotes
Nobilis ingenii siquid honoris habent ;
Si nitor in pretio est morum cultusque decori,
Et tenuem prompta sæpe levasse manu ;
Æmula si Belgis Italisve peritia dextrae
Artifici laudem conciliare queat :
Omne tulit punctum Jamesonus, Zeuxe vel ipso
Teste ; vel hoc majus Græcia si quid habet.

Amoris indissolubilis ergo

DAVID WEDDERBURNUS.

Ad Exemplar ABREDONIÆ Impressum per *Edwardum Rabanum*, 1644.

Humanly speaking, many more years of good work might have been
looked for. He died in full artistic powers at the comparatively early
age of 57, died, it is to be feared, from an over-application to the work
for whose popularity he was responsible—to his credit be it said. Never
a strong man, his early struggles, ardent pursuit of the profession of his
choice, much travelling in the exercise of it, he became a susceptible
victim to attacks of disease, but not before he had left numberless
memorials of his skill in the interesting portraits of his contemporaries,

and established a school of native artists, who, having bettered by his instructions, take at this day a distinguished place in the ranks of art.

Although Jamesone left behind him no son to hand his name down to posterity, his descendants in the female line are very numerous, and move in the most respectable ranks of life. His daughter, Marjory, was married to Mr. John Alexander, a native of Aberdeen, but who became an advocate in Edinburgh. Turning again to Sir Thomas Hope's diary, the Lord Advocate, with a little more detail than that in a former reference to his interesting pages, records the admission of Alexander, Jamesone's son-in-law, to the Edinburgh bar. The greater circumstantiality of Sir Thomas is due to a little vanity excited by the adroit young lawyer, who made him a complimentary speech on the occasion :—

"22 Decr 1642. Mr John Alexander admittat advocat, quho being vnknawin to me befoir that present moment, expressit his respect in geiving me publiklie thanks." Thus flattered by an unusual public recognition of his personal merits, the great legal adviser of the Covenanters could not do less than make a note of it.

In the year following Jamesone's death this gentleman, anxious to secure to the artist's family his interest in the garden at the reclaimed playfield, petitioned successfully the Aberdeen Town Council to that import. (See Appendix.)

At Jamesone's death the houschold consisted of his widow and two unmarried daughters, Isabella and Mary. In the records of the Burghal Sasines of Aberdeen (detailed in the Appendix) there is one under date, 6th of January, 1645, in favour of Elizabeth, Isabella, and Mary Jamesone, of lands belonging to their late father, George Jamesone. Elizabeth is doubtless the love child—one of his beneficiaries by his will. Of her, nothing more is known. Marjory's name is absent, which may be accounted for by the supposition that her marriage portion and settlement in life precluded her sharing in this property. It is probable that Isabella survived her father but a few years, and died unmarried. The widow apparently survived her husband about nine years, for at the end of that time, 1653, the Sheriff Records of Aberdeen give evidence of the family property being divided between the two surviving sisters,

Marjory (Mrs. Alexander) and Mary, still a single woman. At this stage there is no mention of the natural child :—

"1653 20th May Who being solemnlie sworne upon their great oathes, affirmit that the deceast George Jamesone, painter, burgher of Aberdeen, and father to Marjorie Jamesone, spous to Mr John Alexr, Advocat, and to Marie Jamesone, bearers heirof, died last . . . . . vest and sast as of fee, in all and haill the Mayns of Eslemont, with the manour-place tour fortalice yardes and pertinents of the same ; in all the halfe toune and lands of Cowhills, with the pertinents, lyand within the barrony of Esslemonth and Sheriffdome of Abdn and that the said Marjorie and Marie Jamesones are the nearest and lawful heirs portioners of their said deceast father in the lands and others foresaid."

Mary Jamesone inherited her father's artistic tastes. These found expression in such womanly ways as in her time were deemed admissible. Like her father, she produced pictures and on canvas, but with needle and thread. Four large specimens of her technical skill as an industrious sewer of tapestry have found fitting use as part of the adornments of the West Church of Aberdeen: They consist of representations of certain Scripture subjects—the Finding of Moses, Ahasuerus presenting the golden sceptre to Esther, Jephthah's rash vow, and the Apocryphal incident of Susanna and the elders. Together they form a series of the most interesting objects in the Church. The probability is that it was in the West Church where Jamesone and his family worshipped, and was thus selected as an appropriate home for Mary's embroideries. They are still in an excellent state of preservation, and were, in all probability, wrought from Jamesone's designs. It has been shrewdly suspected by the late Mr. Andrew Gibb that the engraved portrait on the monumental brass of Dr. Duncan Liddell, in the same edifice, was from a sketch furnished by Jamesone. From the circumstance that Jamesone's artistic daughter has by tradition been designated "Bonnie Mary Jamesone," it is apparent that she had derived her good looks from her comely mother. Her personal attractions secured for her no fewer than three husbands, by all of whom she had children. Her first husband was Mr. Peter Burnett of Elrick, the owner of a small property in what is now New Machar Parish. She then, in· 1669, married her second cousin, the famous Professor James Gregory, who, Newton excepted, was perhaps the greatest philosopher of his age, and the progenitor of a remarkable race of men of inherited genius. His own great merit is his discovery of the reflecting telescope. Professor Gregory died, in 1675, at Edinburgh, in the University of which he filled the Chair of Mathematics. The circumstances of his death were peculiar. In the act of examining the satellites of Jupiter through a telescope, he was struck totally blind, and only survived a few days, leaving Mary Jamesone a widow for the second time, with a young family—a boy and two girls.

Much sympathy was shown to Mrs. Gregory in the calamity that left her a second time a widow. To mark the high esteem in which her distinguished husband was held, the King (Charles II.) graciously extended the Royal bounty of 800 merks as an annuity until the youngest child, the boy, should reach the age of sixteen. Janet, one of the daughters, married the Reverend William Forbes, a younger son of Sir John Forbes, of Waterton. Helen, the other daughter, married, in 1690, Mr. Alexander Thomson, of Portlethen, Town-Clerk of Aberdeen, as was his son after him. Their daughter, Mary, married Mr. James Carnegie, the first of three generations of Town-Clerks of Aberdeen. It is through Helen Carnegie, a daughter of this branch, that Major John Ross, of Kincorth, becomes the lineal descendant of George Jamesone, being the artist's great, great, great, great grandson.

To return to Mary Jamesone, it falls to be noted that for her third husband she married Baillie George Ædie, a magistrate of the town and a cadet of an influential merchant family.

It is well known that Mr. John Phillip, himself a distinguished artist, had it in his generous mind to erect some fitting memorial of Jamesone in their native town. His own comparatively early death hindered the execution of this purpose, and the only thing specially commemorative of Jamesone is a stained window which was put into Saint Machar Cathedral, in 1874, which had just then undergone a species of restoration. A number of gentlemen, prominent among whom were Mr. J. F. White, Mr. George Reid, R.S.A., and Mr. Alexander Walker, Dean of Guild, rightly conceived the occasion a very suitable one on which to effect the double duty of beautifying the Cathedral and of honouring the memories of three distinguished artists, all natives of Aberdeen—George Jamesone, William Dyce, R.A., and John Phillip, R.A.—by the insertion of a memorial window. The execution of the work was intrusted to Mr. Cottier, of Glasgow, who fulfilled the commission with his accustomed good taste. The Painters' Window is divided into three lancet compartments, in which are represented emblematical figures of Faith, Hope, and Charity, and within the intersections of the mullions are portraits of Phillip, Dyce, with Jamesone in the centre space. Running along the breadth of the window, at the foot, in two lines is the motto :—

IN . HONOREM . GRATAMQUE . MEMORIAM . TRIUM . PICTORUM .
ABERDONENSUM

FAUTORES . ARTIUM . NONULLI . HANC . FENESTRAM . ORNANDUM
CURARUNT . ANNO . SALUTIS . MDCCCLXXIV.

Between these lines are three separate, distinctive inscriptions. Under the Phillip compartment (" FIDES" holding a chalice), to the spectator's left there is—

JOANNIS . PHILLIP . ACAD . REG . SOC .
COLORUM . SPLENDORE . ILLUSTRISSIMI

Under the Dyce compartment, to the right ("SPES" resting on an anchor), is inscribed—

GULLIELMI . DYCE . ACAD . REG . SOC .
DOCTRINA . ET . SCIENTIA . CLARISSIMI

Under the central, Jamesone, compartment ("CARITAS" with children), is inscribed—

GEORGII . JAMESONE . PICTORIS
SCOTORUM . PRIMI
BRITANNORUM
SÆCULO . SUO . LUMINIS . UNICI

14

CHAPTER IX.

General Remarks.

THE following general remarks on Jamesone's style and pictures are intended as a connecting link between the preceding biographical notices of the artist and the detailed catalogue of his particular works. England has been called " The land of liberty and the land of portraits," and in Scotland how fertile of the latter the field has been since Jamesone's day the recent interesting Loan Exhibitions of Historical Portraits must be sufficiently convincing. From George Jamesone to George Reid the artistic succession of native talent has been at once unbroken and richly varied, including such names as Alexander, a lineal descendant of Jamesone's, Scougal, Allan Ramsay, Nasmyth, Dyce, Phillip, Watson Gordon, Raeburn, Macnee, Wilkie, and Herdman, all more or less notable portrait painters.

Jamesone has been spoken of as having founded a school. This can only be taken in the modified sense of having preceded the men whose names have just been mentioned. Excepting Michael Wright, who is vaguely reported to have been a pupil of Jamesone's, it is very unlikely that Jamesone, strictly speaking, trained any one to his art.

Jamesone's portraits were widely known, but whatever influence they may have possessed on the rising artists after him, no one has slavishly copied him, and where his works are seen in their native condition his style is sufficiently marked and characteristic to distinguish him from all other artists. That there should be a considerable amount of ignorance on this point is not to be wondered at, for until recent years that groups of Jamesone's portraits, numerous enough for due comparison, have been brought together, very few have had the opportunity of schooling themselves to the peculiar manner of his work. Jamesone was in his grave more than a century before anything like a study of his works was made, or before the facts of his life were sought to be collected. Horace Walpole, in his "Anecdotes of Painting" (1762), was amongst the first to give anything like a succinct sketch of Jamesone's life, and to furnish an estimate of his style. Both are wonderfully accurate, and reflect credit not only on the noble author, but also on his informant, who must have characterised Jamesone's style for Walpole, who probably never in his life saw a genuine Jamesone.

The late Earl of Buchan rendered considerable service to the subject by making out a more complete list of Jamesone's works than had appeared. His lordship had a very decided taste for what was of any antiquarian or artistic value, and, having the *entrée* of so many mansions where Jamesone's works had a place, was able to do a good deal in the way of noting them. I have been privileged to peruse his MS. in the library of the Society of Antiquaries, and, although it is not complete or infallible, is an intelligent attempt to rescue Jamesone's memory from the semi-mystic condition into which it had fallen. He even went the length of having some of the portraits copied for his own gallery at Almondell. At the very close of last century, the old "Statistical Account of Scotland" followed with a pretty comprehensive *resumé* of the subject. Pinkerton gave added interest to the subject by reproducing several of Jamesone's portraits. Besides these, Pennant, Allan Cunningham, Chambers ("Lives of Eminent Scotsmen"), Dr. Joseph Robertson, and Bruce, have all more or less traversed the same ground. The valuable labours of the Spalding Club should not be forgotten, important side lights from general history, as well as actual references to Jamesone, having helped to clarify and amplify the subject.

Jamesone's pictures may be classed as to their condition under three divisions. *First*—Those that remain untouched and are, except as altered by age, in the condition in which Jamesone left them, and these, unfortunately, are not very numerous. *Second*—The pictures that have been tampered with, euphemised under the term *cleaned.* Under hands more or less skilful, the pictures have been worked on, and the original bloom and character injured. This is infallibly the case, even where the artist so working on the pictures was superior to Jamesone himself. This is by far the most numerous class. The temptation to improve the appearance of a portrait is no doubt very great, especially if it has, in the course of generations, been subjected to any evil treatment from exposure to damp, or heat, or gaslight, or sunlight, or accident, or, as in some cases, to the too-officious cleansing operations of ignorant domestics. *Third*—The pictures that have been restored, that is, ruined. It is very lamentable to think of the large numbers so dealt with, pictures whose historical authenticity and artistic genuineness have been destroyed at one blow. A general semblance of the person represented *may* be retained by a skilful artist, but that subtle something of the original artist's manner is lost beyond recovery, and what one instinctively says in such a case is that the picture may have been once a Jamesone, but that it is now no longer one. This iniquity has arisen from the ignorance or indifference of the possessors or the so-called restorers, sometimes of both ; but, however brought about, the disappointment is very great to all true lovers of art and historic value on viewing brand new-painted portraits gleaming from walls where one expected to see the well-preserved and mellowed visages of men and women painted two or three centuries ago, and exhibiting a series of tints that our artist never had on his palette. The reply that ought in most cases to be given to all but the most judicious cleaners of pictures is, "Hands off." Otherwise evil, and that continually, will be wrought on those priceless art treasures that human art cannot replace when once subjected to the seldom necessary treatment in question. If even partial decay is threatened, very much better is it to make as faithful a replica of the original as it is possible to execute. Thus, with the pattern before the eye, and not under the hand of the artist, there is a reasonable hope of reproducing the desired work in a more satisfactory way than by burying it under fresh coatings of paint. The gain will be great. In the one case the original will be destroyed without replacing it with a reliable substitute. In the other the original will be *preserved* along with its *alter ego*, a desirable and fresh replica. The power we now possess to produce what is artistically excellent and worthy of preservation is unprecedentedly great, but closely on the heels of this productiveness there treads by devious paths a ruthless destroyer, who, by natural decay and accident, is constantly robbing us of much that is valuable, and there is the less need that his work of spoliation should be aided and abetted by following the mistaken practices here indicated.

It must be confessed by all unprejudiced critics that, notwithstanding what has been said regarding the thinness and transparency of Jamesone's style of painting, his best preserved and untouched works were so painted that with fair play they require, as a rule, no so-called cleaning, far less restoration, and after two hundred and fifty years nothing but simple Vandalism dare lift a brush at them. There is a romantic charm about these fine old portraits by Jamesone where one admires not only

> A grave, calm, firm-fleshed, oval face,
> Of strong unwavering lines and curves, ..

but the very dress, so redolent of Caroline times, is beautiful and picturesque in its very simplicity of cut, yet so susceptible of ornamentation.

Jamesone only occasionally signed his pictures, adding the word *Pinxit,* but he usually dated them in one of the upper corners, along with the age of his sitter—as, for example, " ANNO 1633 Ætatis 35." To the expert his works require no signature—being, so to speak, signed all over with his well-defined characteristics. In the course of long-continued inspections, many pictures attributed to Jamesone were found to be by another hand, whilst, in the same residence, perhaps, pictures, appraised by their possessors as of little value, and consigned to obscurity, were discovered to be his genuine works—their very neglect having happily saved them from the mutilations of the restorer. Next to the pleasure of recovering a lost Jamesone is that of disallowing the claims of a spurious picture to be his handiwork. This last is, of course, no pleasure to the mistaken owner, even although the disappointment should be softened by the honest assurance that the picture is by a superior hand. Mr. Mark Napier's graphic story of his discovery of Jamesone's " Montrose," quoted in the Catalogue, will be read with interest. It is a romance of a picture, albeit his joy was not on account of a recovered Jamesone, but over a revived Montrose.

What is true of Jamesone's pictures is true of many more. The possession of pictures, like that of other property, seems to entail responsibilities, one of which is the careful identification both of the subject and the artist. This does not diminish their value or pleasure to the owner, but the reverse, whilst their historical value is enhanced. Pictures not so identified are tantalising, but not misleading, but the neglect is apt to lead to a subsequent erroneous naming of which there are many well known and absurd examples. It is not difficult to account for, or excuse this neglect by a glance at the road by which it has travelled.

In the case of a portrait it does appear unnecessary to label it before the very eyes of the subject of it and the artist. In courteous deference to the latter, at least, it needs no such kenmark. And so, though in a somewhat less degree, to the succeeding generation. To those who follow and who come to possess but a traditional knowledge of the facts, how soon do such heirlooms as the portraits of a line of ancestors, if not identified in some way, become the effigies of the dead, wrapped about with the cerements of uncertainty and confusion? True, the trained eye readily detects the Vandycks, the Jamesones, the Lelys, and the Raeburns, and in a distant way, so helped, guesses at the persons represented, but history need not go on such crutches. To obviate this, a model "house" catalogues, with full particulars, each picture when it is acquired. Each entry has a consecutive number corresponding with one on the picture. In the course of time, when the pictures have passed beyond the stage of contemporary history, the name of the subject, the artist, and the date are published on the picture by being neatly painted on the canvas or on a gilt label on the frame. To be thus "troubled with a pride of accuracy" is to satisfy the historic *manes* and to have a care of posterity worthy of high commendation. It might be gratuitous did the gallery consist simply of the portraits of the successive heads of the house. But, happily, such is not the case. Distinguished branches of the house, marriage alliances, political and literary connections, all contribute their share in the enrichment and variety of the art treasures grouped together under one roof, and render positively necessary in some form or other the desired identification.

In collating existing lists of paintings attributed to Jamesone, some have had to be rejected, on internal evidence or other grounds, as not the work of that artist. Others are omitted because they do not now exist. Among these is Archibald, the first Marquis of Argyll. It is doubtless this picture to which his Grace, the present Duke of Argyll, refers in a courteous note, as "having been found in a cottage near Castle Campbell, which, on being cleaned, turned out to be a very fine portrait of about that date, and may have been by Jamesone or a pupil. But this valuable picture was lost in the fire which burned part of my house in 1877." A like fate overtook the picture of "Martha and Mary in one piece," bequeathed in the artist's will to his friend the Earl of Rothes. It is believed to have perished in a fire which occurred at Leslie House. The Earl of Buchan refers to a portrait of the artist himself, no trace of which has been found. It is said to have been done closet size (twelve by ten inches), and to have then been in the posses- sion of a Mr. Jamieson, a wine merchant in Leith. With far less regret, reference may be made to such works as Jamesone may have painted by way of decorations at the Coronation ceremonies of 1633. David Wedderburn confirms the tradition that he did employ his pencil so idly, as painting the portraits of the dead from the faces of the living for that pageant.

> Ecce Iamesoni tabulam pictoris ! ab alto
> Sanguine Fergusi proavos per stemmata pictos.

The possession of Wedderburn's own portrait would have been worth a gallery of such. And this naturally leads to the suggestion how many notable names are absent from all lists of Jamesone's works—men whom he might have been expected to have painted, and the possession of which would gladden the hearts of all lovers of historic veracity. Among his more prominent fellow-citizens, how we miss the Jaffrays, Edward Raban, the Laird of Letters ; worthy John Spalding, Doctor Baron, and many others !

If they ever were painted, their preservation is less likely to be secured than are those pictures in the possession of landed families, whose more enduring roof-tree shelters for long ages the contents gathered under it.

George Jamesone

Through the kindness of Mr. Alexander M. Munro, by whose industry several
important facts of Jamesone's history have been gleaned, we are able to present
the above *fac-simile* of Jamesone's signature.   It occurs on a discharge given
on the repayment of a loan of money granted by Jamesone.   The document
itself is in another hand.

CATALOGUE

OF THE WORKS OF

GEORGE JAMESONE,

SO FAR AS WELL AUTHENTICATED.

1885.

IN preparing the following Catalogue of Jamesone's works, the main object has been to verify each one as genuine. In the few cases where this has not been personally done, the author has had such trust-worthy evidence as to justify their admission to the list. And although every reasonable clue has been followed to the discovery and recognition of Jamesone's works, the Catalogue will probably err in its omission of un-reported pictures—portraits as yet un-noted in the mansions of the Scottish nobility and gentry or else carried out of the country.

The lesson of Jamesone's style is soon learnt. It has its varieties and gradations of merit, but his *modus operandi* has been very uniform, and the general result is a pronounced individuality. With few excep-tions, his portraits are half lengths—"to the waist"—as he himself expresses it. The face is a three-quarters, looking to the sitter's left. The head is usually slightly smaller than life size, and this, with an ample development of the bust, somewhat detracts from the dignity of the portraits. His treatment of the details of costume, and especially of the beautiful lace collars and trimmings worn then both by ladies and

18

gentlemen of distinction, is very artistic. It approximates the manner of the great masters, and is to be clearly distinguished from the hard details wrought out with such painful, mechanical minuteness by Zucchero, or the poor, unfeeling workmanship of Jamesone's restorers. The drawing of the face is, as a rule, mannered ; with, however, an easy naturalness not devoid of expression. The eyes are well formed, soft and restful. The nose is long, and not particularly well modelled. The mouth is a characteristic feature, the corners being usually turned up. This is, of course, more observable in the case of smooth-faced lady sitters, and the object was doubtless to impart a pleased or smiling expression. It had, however, the effect of giving a rather rounded character to the lower part of the face. The lips are closed, with usually the only bit of positive colour in the whole face. In Jamesone's best pictures pleasant grey tones prevail, and the shadows, to use Walpole's perfectly accurate description, have been "helped with varnish." When first applied this varnish was a medium which gave a desired *chiaroscura*, but in the course of ages the chemical character of the impaste has changed to a yellowish but not unpleasant pigment characteristic of the school to which Jamesone owed some instruction. Hands are not often introduced, and where they are they are not so shapely as those of Vandyck, which they are said to resemble. Draperies are never introduced, and but rarely any other accessories. As a whole, the portraits possess much repose, and have the true artistic merit of growing in one's admiration. In describing the pictures, the directions *right* and *left* are used in relation to the picture and not the spectator.

ABERDEEN UNIVERSITY—KING'S COLLEGE.

THE EVANGELISTS.

There were originally, and until a few years ago, four separate paintings of these, but that of Saint Matthew has now disappeared. As already conjectured, they were probably copies made by Jamesone either from Rubens or from some other great master while abroad. They have, unfortunately, all been tampered with, and unfeeling backgrounds painted in by some rude hand. They hang in the staircase leading to the Senatus Room.

1. SAINT MARK—on a Panel.

A venerable, grey-bearded man, with his left hand on a book and his right on his breast. There is pen and ink beside him, and at his feet a lion couchant, being his own proper emblem.

2. SAINT LUKE—on a Panel.

A venerable man with the nimbus, his right hand on a book, and the left uplifted. His peculiar emblem, an ox, is just indicated over his right shoulder.

3. SAINT JOHN—on a Panel.

A youthful figure in a rapture, with raised right hand. He has the usual nimbus, and wears a picturesque red gown. On a table are writing materials, and at his left hand in the shadow an eagle is suggested, his emblem of sublimity.

REPRESENTATIONS OF THE TEN SIBYLS.

These have always been attributed to Jamesone. It has been found impossible to trace the history or to identify Jamesone's hand on these canvases. The probability is that along with the four Evangelists, the Sibyls were copied by Jamesone from originals he had seen on the Continent—possibly passing through the *atelier* of his master Rubens, and thus the two series of pictures may be regarded as a practical outcome of his residence at Antwerp. This theory of the pictures being simply copies will sufficiently account for the fact that they do not conspicuously show the treatment peculiar to Jamesone. Still another reason for this may be found in the fact that in some instances, at least, the pictures have been tampered with, and have been renewed by another hand.

Jamesone's classical knowledge must have given the Sibyls some interest in his eyes, and furnished some inducement to the labour of making a complete copy of the set.

They have been spoken of as portraits of the reigning beauties in Aberdeen, and tradition has been so definite as to name some of the families to which these ladies belonged. One family alone is said to have furnished four sisters who figure in this galaxy of beauty. Unfortunately for this theory, one of the ladies is black, and if adjudged a beauty it must be by a different standard and from another latitude than ours. Neither the names nor the emblems of Jamesone's Sibyls quite tally with the usual lists, but artists who cared to delineate these subjects were not strict to accord their productions with classical prototypes.

One can now scarcely pass judgment on these pictures as works of art, as they have endured some ill-usage in various ways, for which it would be unfair to cause the artist to suffer criticism. Although the Sibyls have been painted over, and apparently with a house painter's brush, yet the rough process has not been effectual in dispelling the Jamesone feeling from them. Both the drawing and colour are more suggestive of him than the pictures of the Evangelists, beside whom they hang on the walls of the staircase.

4. THE SIBYL " ÆGYPTIACA."

Is represented reading a book. The painting is at present in rather bad condition, although that fact may be taken as a proof that the original has not been tampered with.

5. THE SIBYL " CVMŒA."

Is a very delicate painting. She wears, as a symbol, in her breast a red rose.

6. SIBYLLA " ERYTHRŒA."

Is represented with an emblematical lamb in her arm.

7. THE EUROPEAN SIBYL.

Is a very graceful figure, and wears a broad-brimmed hat, shading her forehead. She reads a book, and holds a sceptre, which rests on her right shoulder. It is inscribed " Evropœa."

8. THE HELLESPONTIC SIBYL.

She holds a shut volume in her left hand, and in her right three corn stalks, with the ears rising above her shoulder, and probably symbolical of the Cross, the peculiar emblem of " HELLE," as the picture is designated.

9. " ITHICA."

Is probably a mistake for Ithaca, and is represented by a graceful figure with downcast expression. She holds three ears of corn in her right hand.

10. THE LYDIAN SIBYL.

Is represented by a swarthy, not to say jet, daughter of Ham, with upturned gaze and crossed hands on her breast—all indicating an ecstatic condition of a prophetess or a most devout worshipper. A white scarf round her neck, falling in front, contrasts very strongly with the tawny complexion of S[ibylla] LYBICA, as the picture is inscribed.

11. THE PHRYGIAN SIBYL.

This is a very bold, well-drawn subject. She holds a sword in her right hand, and she has a hopeful aspect.

12. THE SAMIAN SIBYL.

Is a striking figure with a fur hat of peculiar shape. She appears to be reading an open volume in front of her, and holds in her hand, between her and the book, a crown of thorns.

13. THE TIBURTINE SIBYL.

Is a turbaned figure in a very graceful attitude, poising a chalice in her left hand. The picture is inscribed TIBURTINA.

14. Dr. ARTHUR JOHNSTON, M.D. (1587-1641.)

This "fine head," according to Granger, is on a panel, and inscribed, "Anno 1623 . Ætatis 36 . *Nasce te ipsum.*" The picture is as it left the painter's hand, and bears evidence of his most careful manner. The result is a refined and thoughtful countenance, originally done with much delicacy of treatment and now still farther mellowed by time. The poet has an expansive forehead.

> " Long visaged, strong chinned, high of nose,
>   Large eyed, with gaze stern, sweet, sublime,
> Well bearded, grand of chest and arm,
> Browed as if brain to heaven would climb."

An ample piped linen collar covers his shoulders. The picture has been repeatedly engraved, and is one of those copied in oil by Wales for the Earl of Buchan.

Referring to Benson, who procured the erection of a monument to Milton's memory in Westminster Abbey, and edited an edition of Johnston's poems, a couplet of the Dunciad runs:—

> " On two unequal crutches propt he came,
>   Milton's on this, on that one Johnston's name."

Before 1628, Johnston was appointed Physician-in-Ordinary to Charles I., and, in 1637, was appointed Rector of King's College. He died four years later, whilst on a visit to his son-in-law at Oxford, where he was buried. In a biographical note of Johnston in the "Funerals of Patrick Forbes," Edinr., 1845, p. 20, it is said :—"There is no portrait of the poet preserved in King's College, as has sometimes been erroneously stated." So the above picture must have been placed there since that date.

He was the fifth son of George Johnston, of that ilk and Caskieben (now

Keith-hall). After being schooled in the neighbouring burgh of Kintore, he ran the curriculum of Marischal College, probably in the class with Jamesone, who was exactly the same age. He graduated in medicine at Padua, and was laureated at Paris in the same year, before he was three-and-twenty. He continued his travels in Germany, the Netherlands, Denmark, and England; and before his return to Aberdeen was justly reckoned a distinguished physician, scholar, and poet. His muse, a Latin one, was facile and easily stirred, as his many minor pieces, written on a great variety of occasions, amply attest. His most sustained and important effort is his metrical version of the Psalms, referred to in the rather disparaging couplet by Pope, who it is suspected knew as little of the theme as of the translation.

15. Professor JAMES SANDILANDS, of Craibstone. (B. 1587.)

The portrait is inscribed, "1624 Æt. 37 Splendente vivo Secedente Pereo." A very fine, untouched specimen, but not in very good keeping. He has a round bullet head, high brow, small keen eyes, and short crisp beard. He wears a ruff, and holds in his right hand a closed book. In the upper left corner is painted a flower, with a symbolical sun shining on it.

Professor Sandilands was descended from the Barons of Middlerig, in Lanark, and settled in Aberdeen about 1606. He was a doctor of law, an advocate before the Court of Session, and Commissionary of Aberdeen. By virtue of this office he was Vice-Chancellor of King's College, where he was likewise Rector and Professor of Canon Law by the nomination of Bishop Patrick Forbes. He was for many years clerk to the General Assembly of the Church of Scotland, and appears to have been the first who was deprived of office for adhering to the measures of the King.

16. A VIEW OF THE BUILDINGS OF KING'S COLLEGE, with Figures in the Foreground.

This is probably the only known specimen extant of landscape or architectural painting by Jamesone. Were it not that the perspective has not been carried out as if he quite understood the laws of it, the picture is, on the whole, a very interesting production, as showing structural features long since passed away or modified. There is much spirit in the manner in which the figures have been put in—the artist having evidently some Dutch master before him.

The costumes are those of the period, and are worth studying. The picture is on panel, and measures 33 inches by 21 inches. It has been engraved for Orem's "Description of Old Aberdeen," but with an entirely new foreground.

MARISCHAL COLLEGE.

17. Reverend PETER BLACKBURN, Minister at Aberdeen.

A fine, venerable head, on which Jamesone's original tints have been fairly matched by Giles. There is a becoming skull cap, a flowing old man's beard. The eyes are very small, and an awkward right hand holds a closed book.

Peter Blackburn was "an honest Glasgow merchant's son"; and, according to Robert Melville, was himself "a precise, honest minister to a bishop."

18. Sir THOMAS BURNETT, of Leys. ("Anno 1624, Ætatis 33.")

A characteristic portrait representing a ruddy-bronzed country gentleman, with crisp, auburn hair, wearing the conventional, stiff, white linen ruff, with lace edging. In the upper right corner is a shield, emblazoned with a saltier, crenated, gules, between a bugle horn, a rake (or Y-shaped figure), a trident, and a *fleur-de-lis.*

Sir Thomas was created a Baronet of Nova Scotia in 1626. He was the son of Lord Crimond, a senator of the College of Justice, and his mother was sister to Sir Archibald Johnston, Lord Warriston. His younger brother was the celebrated Dr. Gilbert Burnet, Bishop of Gloucester, the historian of "His own Times." Both brothers were *alumni* of Marischal College, and Sir Thomas became an eminent physician in Edinburgh. Spalding describes him as "A faithful follower of the House of Huntly, and a great Covenanter also." In conjunction with the Marquis of Montrose, he threw himself with ardour into the political controversies of the day, and strenuously opposed the measures of the Court. He at last withdrew into private life, unmolested by both parties.

19. Reverend ANDREW CANT. (D. 1664.)

In very bad preservation, if not past remedy. It is in Jamesone's style, but has been tampered with. The face is remarkably sharp and attenuated, bearing

"Stamp of fleshly waste
Through heat of intellectual flame."

His thin lips, firm set mouth, and keen eye, bespeak the incisive polemic he was. He wears the skull cap and gown of the divine, with a ruffed collar. His hair is advanced grey.

Cant cut a very prominent figure in his stirring times. He was an active, fearless, uncompromising, but unpopular advocate of the Covenant.

Somewhat acid in manner, he was one, says Baillie, "in whom was some
things evidentlie wanting." He was great in his opposition to Episcopacy, and still greater in his opposition to Popery, although Pennant admits
that he " Canted no more than the rest of his brethren, for he lived in a
whining age." Cant has incurred some ridicule from his extreme views.
Having on one occasion to sleep in a room in which was hung a portrait of
Saint Peter, he requested that it might be removed. His host did so, and
hung up in its place Mr. Cant's own portrait, with the lines written beneath—

> " Come down, Saint Peter, ye superstitious saint,
> And let up your better, Mr. Andrew Cant."

He was probably brought into contact with Jamesone whilst in Aberdeen as
one of its ministers. A good life of Cant is still a desideratum. It is
understood that the late Mr. Andrew Gibb was well advanced with Cant's
biography when his own untimely death occurred.

20. ROBERT GORDON, of Straloch. (1580-1661.)

A characteristic specimen, but has suffered renewal. He has a fine dome-
like, bald head, with only a fringe of hair on the lower parts. His
features are marked, and the whole countenance instinct with intelligence.
An ample linen collar surrounds his neck, with a rich lace edge of two or
three inches deep. His doublet is dark and of brocaded stuff. His right
hand is displayed, with a deep, lace-edged cuff carefully painted. The
picture has been engraved for Chambers' "Lives of Eminent Scotsmen."

Robert Gordon was the son of Sir John Gordon, of Pitlurg; and, after
being educated at the Grammar School of Aberdeen, is believed to have
been the first *alumnus* of Marischal College, after which he underwent the
usual course of study on the Continent. On succeeding to his father's estates
he settled down at Straloch to his favourite pursuits of history, antiquities,
and geography. It was in the last named branch that he achieved his
greatest successes. He applied himself with ardour to the study of the
geographical conformation of Scotland, which he was the first to delineate
on the basis of actual mensuration.

This led the way to his engagement by Charles I. to assist the Bleaus of
Amsterdam with one of their atlases. He took little part in the civic com-
motions of his times, and was exempted by Act of Parliament from the new
taxes levied, and he and his tenants were relieved from the exactions incident
to a condition of civil war. He was not unobservant of what was going on,
and left historical memoranda afterwards published by his son James
Gordon, the well known parson of Rothiemay, who inherited much of his
father's peculiar talent.

21. ARTHUR JOHNSTON, M.D. (See No. 14.)

The poet is represented as a youngish man of perhaps thirty, and has the same *spirituelle* expression as the portrait in King's College. He holds in his left hand a rose, which surmounts his shoulder. His dress is of a brocaded stuff. The picture is on panel, and is a very fine and but slightly-touched specimen of Jamesone's work.

22. WILLIAM JOHNSTON, M.D., of the Family of Caskieben.

A fair specimen. The figure is enveloped in a cloak, with the right hand emerging at the breast. Very singularly, a bright carnation is worn in front of the right ear, with what object it is difficult to say. He is represented as a ruddy man of full habit, perfectly answering to the word portrait of him by the Parson of Rothiemay :—" He dyed June fourteenth [1640] before the sixtieth yeare of his age, suffocate with a squinance, a disease to which he was much subjecte, being a corpulent man, and a sanguinean ; he was tackne awaye to the greate greefe of his freends and acquaintance."

Dr. William Johnston was a younger brother of Dr. Arthur Johnston, whom he much resembled in his abilities and career. He was educated at Marischal College. He went abroad, and was appointed Professor of Philosophy at Sedan. From 1626 to 1640 he acted as the first Professor of Mathematics in Marischal College on Duncan Liddel's foundation. Though less eminent than his brother Arthur, William also was a good Latin poet.

23. Sir PAUL MENZIES, of Kinmundy. (1553-1640.)

A fine portrait of a handsome subject, and, notwithstanding the manifest touch of another hand, is substantially what Jamesone left it. Under a bald dome there is a set of fine, regular features, and the whole expression and dress bespeak the gentleman. A rich lace collar, reaching from the ears to a point half way down the breast, forms a suitable background to the flowing, pointed beard. His arms are painted in the upper right hand corner, with *S. P. M.* of Kinmundy Vive vt Vivas Anno 1620 Ætatis 67.

Sir Paul was a prominent member of a family which for many generations had taken a leading part in Aberdeen affairs. From the beginning of the fifteenth century the Provost's chair was never for long without a Menzies. Sir Paul had the honour of knighthood conferred on him by Charles II. at the Coronation ceremonies, which he attended as Provost of Aberdeen, in 1633. He seems to have been an attached personal friend of Jamesone's, and lent him his powerful support.

24. GEORGE KEITH, 5th Earl Marischal. (1553-1623.)

Enclosed within an oval border, inscribed " Nobiliss Georgius Comes Mariscal

Acad. Mariscallanæ Fvndator." The Earl wears a moustache and short-
pointed beard, and is attired in a short sloped hat and ruff. Round his
shoulders are folds of a gold chain with a pendant badge with miniature.
The portrait is not in very good preservation, and has been engraved both
for Pinkerton's and Smith's " Iconographia Scotica." This picture is not an
original, but a *Copy* by Jamesone's descendant, Alexander, who with his
accustomed care has inscribed the back of it :—"A Protoypr [sic] Georg
Jameson, Depict Cosmus Ioano Alex' Pinxit A D 1742 Ætatis suæ 18."

This nobleman, the heir of large estates in Kincardineshire and
Aberdeenshire, was educated at King's College, and subsequently spent
several years at the Universities on the Continent and at Geneva, where he
came under the influence and instructions of Theodore Beza. He further
increased his knowledge of life and of diplomacy by visiting most of the
Courts of Europe. On returning home, he became implicated in various
turbulent proceedings of those days, including the Raid of Ruthven, but was
able to vindicate his innocence. Recognised as a man of experience and
ability, he was intrusted with various commissions by the King, who held his
character and judgment in high esteem. He negotiated the King's marriage
with Anne of Denmark, and, in 1609, he was appointed Royal Commissioner
to the Scots Parliament. He was a cultivated man, and his founding of
Marischal College is a lasting proof of his advanced views on the subject of
education. Pennant, in an appreciative notice of the Earl, suggests that " a
full and authentic life would be a pleasing tribute of gratitude from some
member of his foundation." He died at his picturesque Castle of Dunnottar,
2nd April, 1623.

ABERDEEN FREE CHURCH COLLEGE.

25. ALEXANDER THOMSON, of Portlethen.

Inscribed Ætatis 65 [?] under a coat of arms, consisting of a mantled shield
bearing a deer's head caboshed, and in chef three stars. The portrait is a
fair specimen, but it has been (judiciously) refreshed, probably by Giles. He
wears a skull cap, and a short, chequered scarf appears below the chin beard.
A considerable bush of iron-grey hair falls on the plain linen collar. A
rather graceful hand, wearing a ring, holds a pen.

This picture was bequeathed to the College by the late Mr. Thomson,
of Banchory, a descendant, and probably represents the father of the
Alexander Thomson, of Portlethen, Town-Clerk of Aberdeen, who married,
in 1690, Jamesone's grand-daughter, Helen Gregory.

ABERDEEN GRAMMAR SCHOOL.

26. PATRICK DUN, M.D.   On panel, 27 by 22 inches, in the Rector's Room.

This portrait has evidently suffered a slight degree of restoration sufficient to remove the original bloom and some of the Jamesone expression. Dr. Dun is represented as a man between fifty and sixty years of age, and he wears a skull cap, the token of a professional man. He also has the fluted linen collar of the period. The hair of moustache and chin beard is a light brown. The frame is inscribed—" MDCXXXI Patrik Dune ÆD Presented (1864) by Lessendrum."

Dr. Dun was a native of Aberdeen, and after graduating at Marischal College, went abroad and studied medicine under his fellow-townsman, Dr. Duncan Liddell, then professor at Helmstädt. Dun returned to Aberdeen, where he pursued a successful career as a physician. He was Principal of Marischal College for twenty-eight years, 1621-1649. During that period it suffered from fire, and Dun contributed the handsome sum of 2000 merks " for the reparatione of the edifice of the said College." Besides this, he contributed in his lifetime his lands of Ferryhill for the support of four masters in the Grammar School of Aberdeen, which constitutes him "the founder" of that institution. The portrait of Dr. Dun in the Aberdeen Town Hall is a copy of the above by a later hand.

ABERDEEN TRADES' (OR TRINITY) HALL.

27. MATTHEW GUILD, Armourer.   (1542-1603.)

This picture is reputed to be a copy of Jamesone's portrait of Guild. It is much more likely to be a copy by Jamesone for the Hammermen, of which Guild was a prominent member, from an earlier picture. The pose, looking to the sitter's right, is not such as Jamesone, without good reason, adopted ; and the date forbids the idea that Jamesone could have painted Guild from the life. It is inscribed in the upper right corner with a shield between Guild's initials, and on the left, Ætatis 61, Died August Anno 1603, and crown and hammer. Guild wears a sugar-loaf hat, close ruff, and cloak. The original, no doubt of foreign workmanship, had been solidly painted, and so is the copy.

Matthew Guild was the father of Dr. William Guild and of Jean Guild, Jamesone's aunt by marriage with David Anderson. He was an armourer or "swerd slippar," and cut a very prominent figure in town and trade affairs.

As the doctrines of the Reformation began to spread in Scotland, one of
the fruits they bore was the prohibition in Aberdeen of such recreations and
pageants as Robin Hood, Abbot of Reason, and Queen of the May. As these
had their beginnings in Papistry, and their endings in certain irregularities of
conduct, the Magistrates laid such gatherings under ban. And it is in connection with this that Matthew Guild comes to the front as a conservator of
the ancient customs. How he defied the Town Council and how he was
punished will be best seen from the following quotation from the Burgh
Records :—

" The said day James Masar, Lourens Masar, Methow Guild, Thomas
Huntayr, and Androw Wysman wer convickit for the cumyng throw the
toune upon Sunday last wes, eftir none, with ane menstrall playand befor
thaim throch the Gallowgett, in contemptioune of the townis actis and
proclamaciouns maid obefoir, and breaking of the actis of parliament, and
contravening of the same ; quherfor thai wer put in amerciament of court,
and wer ordanit to remane in the tollbuth, quhill thai find sourtie for fulfilling and satisfeing of the emends to be modifyt be the consel."

28. Dr. WILLIAM GUILD. (1586-1657.)

This portrait is a *Copy* by Mossman from a now lost original by Jamesone. It
is a large, knee picture, and represents Guild seated in a chair and habited
in his gown. It deservedly occupies the place of honour of the fine Trinity
Hall, and has been engraved in Mezzotint, prints of which have been popular
and are well known.

He was the son of No. 27, and was one of the most wisely beneficent of
Aberdonians. He was educated for the Church, which he entered at a very
early age. Possessing a facile pen, he at once employed it in the then
favourite pastime of religious polemics, in which he met with a flattering
success. His first charge was that of the parish of King-Edward, and he was
afterwards translated to the diocese of Aberdeen, where his preaching was
highly esteemed. Possessed of ample means, and the same beneficent senti-
ments as his sister, he made to the town various substantial bequests, the
greatest of all his donations being to the Incorporated Trades, of which his
father, Matthew Guild, was a member. To this day, at the annual gatherings
of the Trades, the loving cup circulates in solemn silence to his grateful
memory.

Although the Episcopal side of the ecclesiastical squabbles of his day
had his warmer sympathies, yet, "for the peace of the Church and other
reasons," he signed the Covenant under certain limitations. Principal Leslie,
of King's College, declining to accept the Covenant on any terms whatever,

was replaced in his post by Dr. Guild, who resigned his pastoral charge to fulfil its duties. From this position he was ultimately ousted on a suspicion that his bias towards Royalty was strong. He would gladly have resumed his ministerial functions, for his heart was in the work, but his wish was un-gratified, and he spent the remainder of his days in a beneficent retirement. A handsome monument in St. Nicholas Churchyard marks his burial place.

LADY KATHERINE BANNERMAN, OF CRIMONMOGATE.

29. DAVID ANDERSON, of Finzeauch. (D. 1629.)

In excellent preservation. It has probably undergone a very slight restoration, and is on an oak panel. He looks a stalwart man of purpose and in the prime of life. His hair is very dark and thick, and comes far down on his brow. His moustache and short beard are lighter in colour. He wears a high ruffed collar, with a plain close-buttoned coat. In his right hand he holds a roll of paper. On the background is delineated a standard globe, with a compass resting on the top of it.

David Anderson, of Finzeauch, was the artist's maternal uncle, and pretty fully described in pp. 26-28. Philopolitæius, in his "Succinct Survey," refers to "the renowned Art and Industrie of that ingenious and Vertuous Citizen, David Anderson." This was not a solitary opinion, and in appreciation of his many public services to the community, at a head court held in 1598, they voted him exempt from the payment of all taxes. The service rendered by men of this type, in the directions they may choose, cannot be over-rated. Not satisfied with things as they are, they leave their mark in the improvements and ameliorations they are able to effect. The son of a wealthy merchant, he became himself a man of considerable means, and acquired the landed estate of Finzeauch in the parishes of Keig and Tough, Aberdeenshire. At his death he bequeathed "the soume of Thrie hundreth marks Scots money for the benefit of the decayed Gild brethern," by the hands of his son, "Mathew who compeired personallie before the Provost Baillies and Counsell."

Following her husband's example, and with even a more liberal hand, his widow, Jean Guild, sister to Dr. Guild, four years later mortified the sum of 500 merks Scots "to widowes that hes bein the wyffes of burgesses of Aberdeine, merchands or craftsmen, livand both in the time of ther widow-heide, and in the time of ther mariage and cohabitatione with ther husbandes, of good lyfe and conversatione frie of any publict scandell or offence and to aiged virgines who are borne bairnes in Aberdeine and who haue lived in the state of virginitie and continowes in that estate to ther lyves end, frie of publict Scandell." And, not content with these benefactions, in 1649, in conjunction with some of her relatives, she mortified the handsome sum of 4700 merks Scots, besides "all and haill the tenement of land callit the blakfriars manse with the yeards barnes and pertinents belonging thereto lying at the Schoolhill of the burgh for the use of ten poor orphanes of both sexes who are to be educat and trayned up in the knowledge of the ground of Christian religion and also in reading wreiting Schewing and all such as may fitt them for anie vertuous calling or trade of lyfe according to their sex."

These extracts speak for themselves, testifying not only to the wealth, but to the wise benevolence and character of these good folks.

David Anderson was succeeded in his estate by his son, David, whose representatives are the Bannermans, Baronets of Elsick. There were two daughters, Christian, of whom nothing is known, and Janet, who married the Rev. John Gregory, Minister of Drumoak, and became the mother of that remarkable race—the Gregorys—so conspicuous for their inherited scientific and literary genius. Mrs. Gregory is credited with possessing the mathematical bias of her busy-brained father.

THE RIGHT HON. THE EARL OF BREADALBANE, TAYMOUTH CASTLE.

Time and family changes have somewhat diminished the total number of pictures by Jamesone in this ancient castle-palace, but it still maintains its supremacy in possessing the largest collection of any other house.

30. MARIA DUCESSA DE LONGUEVILLE, Regina Scotorum.

A rather doubtful picture, on account of the solid painting and general treatment. A crown, studded with pearls, rests on the back of the head. The face is round and plump, the neck and bosom are treated precisely as the Countess of Wigton's is (No. 71). She wears a yellowish silk bodice, with a shawl thrown round the shoulders. Her hand is well drawn, and she holds a trinket between the forefinger and thumb. The work is good, but scarcely the goodness of Jamesone. The probability is that the work has been much tampered with. The portrait is surrounded by an oval such as Jamesone used occasionally to paint.

31. DOMINA MARIOTA EDMESTOUN.

A characteristic work of Jamesone's, and remains as he left it. She wears a widow's head-dress or bonnet of the Queen Mary style, and has a standing frill which rises almost to her ears. Engraved in Pinkerton.

32. ANNABELLA DRUMMOND, Queen of Robert III. about 1390.

An untouched characteristic specimen, but in the rare attitude—looking to the right. She is "naked necked," with long bare bosom. This lady was the daughter of Sir John Drummond, of Stobhall, progenitor of the Drummonds of Hawthornden and of the Earls of Perth.

The picture is engraved in Pinkerton, who conjectures "that Jamesone had some archetype from her tomb at Dunfermline, or some old limning." In any case the picture retains the undoubted merit of being an untampered-with work of Jamesone's.

Round an oval border he has inscribed it :—Annabella Drvmond filia militis de Stobhall Regina, Scotorum Anno dom. MCCCXC. She was the mother of James I. as well as of three daughters, one of whom, Margaret, married Sir Colin Campbell, of Lochow—hence her presence here as a progenitor of the house.

33. MARIA MAGNE, Britannæ Regina.

Smaller than life, with a crown, and looking from left to right. Long black hair hanging down over the white neck and bosom imparts a corpse-like appearance, increased by a cold blue silk dress trimmed with lace. An unmistakeable work of Jamesone's.

34. "DOMINA JONETA STEWART, filia Willielmi Domini Lorne. Eivs Sponsa, Anno Dom MCDXL."

Such is the inscription round the picture, but Douglas, in his "Peerage," calls her Margaret, daughter of *John*, Lord of Lorne, and wife to Sir Colin Campbell. There never was a William, Lord of Lorne.

A fine careful portrait of a stately lady in what looks like mourning costume. She has marked features, and the aquiline nose is well modelled. Over her reddish hair she wears a black velvet head-dress. She also wears a pearl necklace, and a suspended locket is gracefully held between her fingers. Her dress is cut square across the breast, and is trimmed with insertion lace. The picture is engraved in Pinkerton.

35. MARGARET OF DENMARK, Regina Scotorum, wife of James III.

She ascended the Scottish Throne, in 1469, in her 13th year.

An attractive portrait, but with characteristics that render it a somewhat doubtful Jamesone. The solid painting, especially for a lady's portrait ; the pose, looking to the right ; and the colour, all suggest another hand. She displays a broad fair bosom with square shoulders, round which is gracefully thrown a richly brocaded cloak. Engraved in Pinkerton.

36. DAVID II., Rex Scotorum.

This represents the King as about middle age, looking to the right. He wears a dark velvet jewelled cap over a bushy head of hair. A short thick beard rests on a highly ornamented dress, bordered with ermine. He holds in his hand a medal suspended by a gold chain. This fine portrait is engraved by Pinkerton, who suspects that Jamesone had some ancient limning before him when he painted it. He thinks that being an antiquary, possessing collections of medals and coins, the authenticity of his ancient portraits is strengthened. There can be little doubt, however, if through them we seek to find

> "How far our [Scottish] portraiture
> Illustrates [Scottish] history,"

they are comparatively valueless.

These seven paintings are properly described as "fancy pictures," that is, representations of persons long dead painted probably from living subjects. Jamesone had some notable exemplars for this absurd practice.

37. Sir ROBERT CAMPBELL. (1641.)

A fair complexioned middle-aged man, with flowing hair and peaked beard. It has been much repainted, and Jamesone's thinnish painting has been quite overlaid by colour much more solid. A replica (No. 40) of this gentleman, by Jamesone, is set over one of the four doorways in the same apartment.

38. Sir JOHN CAMPBELL. (1642.)

This is a genuine, untouched Jamesone. The colour is good, and the pose and general treatment characteristic of the artist. The kenmark of this picture is a purple jerkin partly covered by an ample linen collar. Another portrait (No. 41) of Sir John, by Jamesone, on panel in a floriated frame-work, is let into the wall over one of the doorways in the same apartment. Engraved in Pinkerton.

39. ARCHIBALD, Lord of Lorne.

This is a genuine, untouched work of Jamesone's, and represents a man in middle life, with a tangled mass of dark hair fringed down his brow and flowing over an enormous linen collar. It is a stiff uncomfortable looking picture. Probably the idea that it could not be improved has protected it from the restorer.

In the splendid Baron's Hall, where the whole of Jamesone's portraits are hung, the following eight, arranged in pairs, are set over the four doorways. They are on panels and surrounded by floriated, carved, and gilt framework. As they have been all subjected to restoration they do not all merit minute description :—

40. Sir ROBERT CAMPBELL. (1641.)

An old man with fair, flowing hair. (See No. 37.)

41. Sir JOHN CAMPBELL. (1642.)

A youngish man dressed in a red jerkin. (See No. 38.)

42. WILLIAM GRAHAM, 7th Earl of Menteith, Strathearn, and Airth. (1637.)

An excellent specimen, notwithstanding its having been to a certain extent restored. It is engraved in Pinkerton, and represents the Earl as an oldish man with a face full of character.

It has a place at Taymouth because the remarkable subject of it was by his mother connected with the Campbells of Glenurchy. She was Mary, the daughter of Sir Colin. The Earl took a prominent part in State service, being a Privy Councillor, Justice-General of Scotland, and President of the Council under Charles I. Tracing back his pedigree, the Earl fancied himself to have a possible claim to the Crown. This, however, he solemnly renounced, although with vanity declaring his blood to be the reddest in Scotland.

The bare suggestion that he was "sib to the King" raised such a public ferment and a prejudice in the mind of Charles that he quashed the titles of Strathearn and Menteith and bestowed the meaner and more obscure one of Earl of Airth. He was driven from office and, it is said, imprisoned besides.

43. JOHN, Lord Neper. (1637.)

A fine specimen, but little handled. He wears a beautiful lace collar, and the whole expression of the picture is attractive. The subject of it was the son of the great Napier, the inventor of logarithms.

These two pairs of portraits flank the great window. The following two pairs are at the opposite end of the hall :—

44. ANNE CUNNINGHAM, Marchioness of Hamilton.

She was the daughter of James, 7th Earl of Glencairn, and wife of James, 2nd Marquis of Hamilton. She was a lady of a very masculine spirit, and, sprung from a family of strong Presbyterian leanings, she ranged herself with the

17

Covenanters and gave them a powerful support.   Her husband's early death
threw her largely on her own resources and gave her prominence.   Both her
sons joined the Royal interest, and when James, the eldest, entered the
Forth, in 1639, with a fleet intended to overawe the Covenanters, "she
appeared among them on the shore at the head of a company of horse,
and drawing a pistol from her saddle bow declared she would be the first to
shoot her son should he presume to land and attack his countrymen and
country." This spirited conduct of this mother in Israel is supposed to have
been one cause why the Duke did not land.

The portrait answers precisely to the masculine character of the
Marchioness, even to a *soupçon* of a moustache.   Her dress is severely plain
and her head is enveloped in an ample hood, whilst a man's ruff surrounds
the neck.   The picture was painted in 1636, and is engraved in Pinkerton.

45. JAMES, 2nd Marquis of Hamilton. (1636.)

A bearded middle-aged man, with a blue ribbon.   In every respect a doubtful
picture.   It is not suggestive of Jamesone's work.   The Marquis died in 1625,
and the picture must have been by another hand at some prior date.   If it is
a restored Jamesone, originally painted in 1636, then the picture is more
probably of the third Marquis, afterwards the first Duke of Hamilton.

46. CHANCELLOR LOUDON. "Lord of Lowden 1637."

This portrait is engraved in Pinkerton.   It has been considerably tampered with.
Loudon took an active interest in public affairs, and is said to have been the
most eloquent man of his time.

47. JOHN, Earl of Mar. (1637.)

An interesting picture.   He is habited in a fine rich collar, and the blue ribbon
of Councillor of State and Treasurer.   His public career is too well known to
need comment.

48. THE GENEALOGICAL TREE OF THE HOUSE OF GLENORCHY.

This is a very interesting piece of work, and has lately been put into the most
perfect state of repair and relined.   It is about 5 ft. in height and about 2½ ft.
broad.   It is very elaborately and carefully painted.   The tree is stiff enough,
and bears about 150 discs, which give a record of the family history.   There
are, at the foot, nine medallion portraits—rather primitive—including
Archibald, 1st Lord of Argyll.

The picture is inscribed, "The Genealogie of the house of Glenorquhie quhairof is descendid Sundrie Nobill houses." 1635 ⧈ame/one *faciebat.* This date proves the work to be one of Jamesone's very earliest efforts at Taymouth, for his other portraits are mostly dated from 1636 to 1642.

THE RIGHT HON. THE EARL OF BUCHAN, ALMONDELL.

49. JAMES ERSKINE, 1st Earl of Buchan, son of the Lord Treasurer Mar.

An undoubted work of Jamesone's, dated 1636. It is rather stiff, and lacks expression. The hair is combed down over his brows, and is long and flowing behind. He wears a grey dress, surmounted by a very rich lace collar, such as Jamesone delighted to paint. The picture is engraved in Smith's "Iconographia Scotica." It was originally one of the Taymouth set, but was considerately presented by Lord Breadalbane to Lord Buchan, the founder of the Society of Antiquaries of Scotland, and the first to take any real interest in Jamesone's paintings.

The Earl of Buchan was the eldest son of John, 7th Earl of Mar (Treasurer Mar), by his second wife, Lady Mary Stewart.

He married Mary Douglas, Countess of Buchan, and thereupon assumed the Earldom of Buchan, on the resignation of which, she being under age, a Royal charter was granted (1617) of the lands forming the Earldom of Buchan. This charter was taken to the Countess and her husband, the said James.

50. HENRY ERSKINE, 1st Lord Cardross of Dryburgh, the second son of the Treasurer Mar. (D. 1636.)

This picture is a characteristic Jamesone, and presents a man of stronglymarked features, high forehead, and altogether a Shakespearian cast of head and face, with a very pleasing expression, peaked beard, stiff linen collar, over a black dress which is striped with brocaded silk. In Pinkerton's "Scottish Gallery of Portraits" there is a fine engraving of it. It was painted in 1626.

Lord Cardross was the companion and bedfellow of Henry, Prince of Wales.

51. DAVID ERSKINE, 2nd Lord Cardross.

A full faced man, with long black hair to his shoulders, and combed down over his brows. The picture is in good preservation, and, like the former two, does not appear to have been tampered with.

This nobleman's first wife was a daughter of Sir Thomas Hope.

52. Sir ALEXANDER ERSKINE.

A full-length mail-clad figure, which the author has not seen. The picture was painted in 1638, and was removed from Almondell to his lordship's London residence two years ago.

MR. JOHN BULLOCH, ABERDEEN.

53. STEWART, of Hisleside.

A capital example of Jamesone's. It is the likeness of a youth, probably under 20. He wears a crimson coat or jacket, with a carefully-painted right hand extended over the breast. He holds his gold-laced hat in his left. In the upper right corner the picture is inscribed—"Stewart of Hisleside," and in the lower left—"Jamesone Pinxt." The picture is in fine preservation, and, excepting the fingers of the right hand, which have been slightly painted on, the rest happily is untouched. It is in its original frame, a double-gilt muller. It was purchased at an auction sale at Edinburgh, in 1883, by D. Bennett Clark, Esq., who, on going abroad, sold it to the author.

Although it has been found impossible to trace the descent of the picture, its historic authenticity is well proved. The estate of Hiselsyde is one of the earliest minor holdings in the parish of Douglas, in Lanarkshire, and is to be found under various aliases—Hazleside, Heisleside, Hezilside, Hessilsyde, Heyslesyde. The earliest known possessors of the lands were the all-powerful family of the Douglases, who bestowed them, according to Blind Harry, on one Dickson, who had rendered assistance to Sir William Douglas and Wallace in some of their efforts to oust an English garrison from a castle in the district. This family remained in it, and apparently changed their name to that of the Barony of Symonton, which they possessed ; and, in 1605, are spoken of as custodiers of the Castle of Douglas, the Castle Dangerous of Sir Walter Scott's romance, in which there is a reference to Hazelside, both in the introduction and in the body of the romance.

The Stewarts appear to have become lairds of Hiselsyde early in the seventeenth century. On the 2nd June, 1647, William Stewart, in all probability the subject of the picture, is retoured as his father's heir—"haeres Archibaldi Stewart de Hissilsyde, patris,—in terris et baronia de Symontoun tam propriete quam tenendris cum advocatione ecclesiarum." In 1674, Griselda Stewart, William's daughter, is retoured as his heir. Subsequent retours find the lands merging, in 1702, into the hands of the Douglases. The Stewarts do not appear in any conspicuous capacity, but as a county family in possession of their estate, which had a "good house and pleasant seat by a wood." The farm of Mains of Hazelside is the modern representative of the property.

SIR ROBERT BURNETT, CRATHES CASTLE,
KINCARDINESHIRE.

54. Sir THOMAS BURNETT, created 1st Baronet of Leys by Charles
II., in 1626.

A very fine portrait of this old gentleman on panel. He wears a black velvet
skull cap and a stiff ruff. He has a rounded beard and moustache. The
features are well moulded, and age has mellowed the whole picture, which
hangs over the great fireplace in the vaulted dining hall, at the hospitable
table at which he so long presided. The fine, old, many-gabled Castle of
Crathes was a rendezvous of the Presbyterian party, and here, in his Covenanting days, came the great Montrose and many other notables on the same
side. Sir Thomas looks a man between sixty and seventy, painted in a solid,
careful manner, and is probably the first done of the Burnett group, which
are the very oldest pictures of this very ancient family.

Jamesone painted another portrait of this worthy man, in 1624, when he
was plain Mr. Thomas Burnett, of Leys. (See No. 18.)

55. A FAMILY PORTRAIT. A son of Sir Thomas Burnett, 1st Baronet
of Leys.

A perfect specimen of Jamesone's work on panel, painted with very great care,
representing a man of perhaps twenty-five, with long auburn hair, moustache,
and peaked beard. There is rather more than usual of the amber-coloured
medium which Jamesone used in his shades. A large Vandycked collar,
with lace edging, surrounds the youth's unusually sloped shoulders.

56. A FAMILY PORTRAIT. A son of Sir Thomas Burnett, 1st Baronet
of Leys.

A youngish man of about 23, on panel. He has a profusion of long black
hair, with slight moustaches, and has a pleased expression. The plain linen
collar and dark dress bespeak Covenanting proclivities. Of all the five
pictures at Crathes this is the only one that suggests having been tampered
with, but, happily, it is only a suggestion, and is insufficient to raise any
serious doubt as to the genuineness of the picture.

57. A FAMILY PORTRAIT. A daughter of Sir Thomas Burnett, 1st
Baronet of Leys.

A most characteristic Jamesone, on panel, almost as fresh as it came from the
painter's easel. She is habited in a suit of deep mourning—a black stuff
dress, the shoulders, breast, and neck being covered, chemoisette fashion,

with fold upon fold of an ample, plain-hemmed linen or white crape collar, apparently tied with three black ribbons of different sizes. A little back from the brows the hair is confined by a black band, but otherwise it flows loosely down her neck and shoulders.

58. JANET BURNETT, daughter of Sir Alexander Burnett, of Leys.

A stately lady, looking to the right. The picture has been much painted over, so as to greatly impair the characteristic colouring of Jamesone. She is richly attired in a low-bodied blue silk, probably bridal dress, trimmed with red bands and bow knots, whilst a broad border of Vandycked lace environs the bosom. It is on panel. A replica, *vis-a-vis*, with her husband, Alexander Skene, 15th laird of that ilk, is at Duff House. (See Nos. 81 and 82).

P. MOIR BYRES, ESQ., OF TONLEY.

59. SANDILANDS, of Coates, near Edinburgh.

A very fine picture, representing Mr. Sandilands as an old man of at least seventy, in a skull cap, trimmed with lace. He has a moustache and long grey beard, which falls on an ample fluted collar. The portrait has been touched in a very slight manner, but in no way to injure its original feeling. The worst that has befallen it is successive films of copal varnish by which the canvas has been rendered as hard as a panel. It was not uncommon when a mansion was under the hands of a house-painter to give the family pictures a coat of varnish, *pour les encourager.*

60. Sir JOHN BYRES, of Coates, East Lothian.

An excellent portrait of a man in middle life, quite characteristic of the artist. A heavy mass of curly hair, cut in the fashion betokening the Cavalier, that is, with the right side cut shorter than the left. The eyes are dreamy and almond-shaped, and the face, as a whole, is grave, with Charles I. beard and moustache. An ample fluted collar surrounds the shoulders. The dress is of rich stuff, with slashed sleeves and trimmed with fine lace. He is an ancestor of the family.

THE RIGHT HON. THE EARL OF CRAWFORD AND BALCARRES, HAIGH HALL, WIGAN.

61. Sir DAVID LINDSAY, 1st Lord Lindsay of Balcarres.

This nobleman was one of the group raised to the peerage by Charles I. during his memorable visit to Scotland in 1633. He died in 1641.

62. ALEXANDER, 2nd Lord Lindsay of Balcarres.

It was probably as such that Jamesone painted the portrait of this nobleman, who was advanced to the Earldom of Balcarres in 1651. He died in 1659. Lending his undoubted abilities to the Royal interests, he was honoured in being trusted with many high offices of State, as, for example, Governor of Edinburgh Castle, Secretary of State, and Commissioner to the General Assembly.

63. Sir ALEXANDER LINDSAY, 1st Lord Spynie.

He was the fourth son of David, 9th Earl of Crawford, and was raised to the peerage by James VI. "Spynie" took an active share in the movements of his day. He was present at the battle of Aberdeen, and, tarrying behind Montrose, to whose army he was attached, he was captured and imprisoned in the tolbooth, and afterwards conveyed to Edinburgh.

The portrait of this interesting person was, until a few years ago, the property of the Stewarts and Drummonds of Grandtully, from whom it was acquired by the late Earl of Crawford to complete his family gallery.

———————

SIR JAMES HENRY GIBSON-CRAIG, OF RICCARTON, BARONET.

64. Sir ARCHIBALD JOHNSTON, Lord Warriston.

This picture presents a well-modelled, massive head, set in Jamesone's characteristic manner. Johnston wears a black velvet skull cap, under which, on either side of the face, flows a profusion of flaxen hair. He has a short neck, and is apparently a man of a portly build. An ample, plain linen collar surrounds his shoulders.

Johnston was an eminent lawyer, and a central figure among his contemporaries, and was deeply engaged on the side of the Covenanting party, with whom he had great influence, although ostensibly their servant in his capacity of Clerk of the General Assembly, a post to which he was unanimously elected in 1638. Baillie has a high opinion of Johnston, and speaks of him as a "nonsuch for a clerk." On the death of Sir Thomas Hope, Johnston succeeded him as Lord-Advocate. Johnston's career is too well known to need dwelling on here. At the final success of the Parliamentary party, Cromwell conferred a peerage on him, giving him a seat in the Upper House. At Cromwell's death, the mere consistency of Johnston's political principles did not save him. He fled, was outlawed, and finally brought to the scaffold, in 1663. Bishop Burnet, whose uncle he was, gives, on the whole, a discriminating view of this extraordinary man.

LORD CLINTON, FETTERCAIRN HOUSE, KINCARDINESHIRE.

65. ALEXANDER FORBES, 1st Lord Pitsligo.

Lord Pitsligo was raised to the peerage in 1633, and was married to Lady Jane Keith, daughter of the Earl Marischal.

SIR R. K. A. DICK-CUNYNGHAM, PRESTONFIELD, EDINBURGH.

66. Sir WILLIAM DICK, Baronet. (1590-1655.)

Represents an oldish man in a lace-trimmed cap. He is habited in a scarlet robe, with a ruff. The picture has been ruined by being wholly repainted.

Sir William was a wealthy Edinburgh banker, who from time to time replenished the Royal Exchequers of James VI. and Charles I. on the security of the State revenues. From the latter he derived the honour of knighthood, evidently intended as a repayment of the sums borrowed, of which he got but a sorry account. He was Provost of Edinburgh, but from the loss of his money, imprisonment, and fines for his supposed disloyalty, he lost status, and ultimately died in prison at Westminster in absolute poverty.

MAJOR GORDON DUFF, OF PARK AND DRUMMUIR, BANFFSHIRE.

67. Sir ADAM GORDON, of Park.

Second son of Gordon of Edinglassie. He was married first to Christian Gordon, daughter of Gordon of Gicht, and afterwards to Helen Tyrie, daughter of the Laird of Drumkelloc.

68. LADY GORDON, wife of Sir Adam Gordon.

These two pictures are undoubted and characteristic examples of Jamesone's, but too long time has elapsed since the author saw them to warrant any description here.

ROBERT DUNDAS, ESQ., OF ARNISTON.

69. Sir JAMES DUNDAS, Lord Arniston. (D. 1679.)

Although restored, this picture retains much of the feeling of Jamesone. The pose is very dignified. He is in armour, and a broad-fringed sash is thrown across the right shoulder. Long dark hair falls on the usual scalloped lace collar.

The Dundases of Arniston have produced several notable members, and not the least was the subject of this portrait. His father was Sir James Dundas, Kt., Governor of Berwick. He sat for Midlothian in the Scottish Parliament, and was for a short time Lord of Session. He was knighted in 1641, a proof of his loyalty to the King. On the question of ecclesiastical polity he sided with the Covenanters in their resistance to Laud's tyranny. This induced him to resign his position rather than compromise his consistency. His place was kept open for him for eighteen months in the vain hope that he would abjure the Covenant. But on this point he remained firm.

CHARLES C. BETHUNE, ESQ., OF BALFOUR.

70. DAVID BEATON, of Balfour. (1574-1636.)

Inscribed, "D.B. Anno 1636 Ætatis 62." It is easy to believe this picture to have been originally painted by Jamesone, but it has been so painted over since, that except in the drawing and general style it has totally lost Jamesone's peculiar handling. The portrait is that of a full faced country gentleman with a grey moustache and beard. He wears a plain cap, stiff ruff, and his dark doublet is marked by a series of still darker diagonal lines.

David Beaton (or Bethune) was a member of an influential Fife family, of Creich and Balfour, who made, it is said, a greater number of matrimonial alliances with the noble and more powerful families of the kingdom than any other family.

SIR W. H. GIBSON CARMICHAEL, OF SKIRLING, BART.,
CASTLE CRAIG, DOLPHINTON.

71. Sir ALEXANDER GIBSON, of Durie. (1570?-1644.)

This is not unlikely to have been by Jamesone or a copy from an original, but from the circumstance that it has been wholly re-painted it is impossible to tell.

Sir Alexander was a very eminent lawyer, and, in 1620, was elected a Lord of Session as Lord Durie, and at length rose to be Lord President of the College of Justice. He was considered an able and upright judge, and left behind him several legal works of value as a tribute to his industry. His unflinching integrity once subjected him to an indignity characteristic of the age when he lived. Traquair, who feared an adverse decision of his lordship

18

in a case in which he was interested, had him forcibly abducted and kept
in solitary imprisonment for three months.   During that period his friends
believed him to be dead and wore mournings for him.

THE RIGHT HON. THE EARL OF DALHOUSIE, BRECHIN CASTLE.

72. UNKNOWN GENTLEMAN.

An undoubted Jamesone, but the picture has suffered some injury in having
been slightly restored.   He has dark hair, moustache and chin beard, and
wears a plain linen collar of a dark doublet.

LORD ELPHINSTONE, CARBERRY TOWER.

73. The EARL OF WIGTON.   (1589-1650.)

A three-quarter-length portrait, inscribed " John, 2nd Earl of Wigton NA. 1589
OB 1650 Ætatis SVE 62."   A very graceful picture, a companion to the
Countess, and very probably painted at the same time, showing a man
approaching forty years of age.   He is dressed in a snuff-brown suit.   His
attitude is easy and graceful.   In one hand he holds a glove, and in the
other his hat.   From his left ear depends an ear-ring, with a red drop resting
on the white ruff.   The hands are well drawn, and the whole work done in
an unusually elaborate manner.   The Jamesone tone has been somewhat
lost in the course of preserving processes, and there is some reason to
doubt its genuineness.

The Earl of Wigton took an active share in public affairs.   In 1640 he
was a member of the Committee of Estates, and, in 1641, was appointed a
Privy Councillor by Parliament.   Nevertheless he entered heartily into the
Association to support the cause of Charles I., framed at his house of
Cumbernauld, in January of the latter year.

74. The COUNTESS OF WIGTON.   (n. 1595.)

This is a three-quarter-length or knee portrait, and is inscribed " Lady M.
Livingston and Countess of Wigton NA. 1595 OB   Ætatis SVE 30.
1625."   The lady is represented in an elaborate dress and with a nimbus of
lace, against which a delicately-painted face and bosom makes a very fine
headpiece to an otherwise stately figure.   This large canvas has been very
carefully covered down to the minutest details, and is altogether such a
picture as to make one hesitate to say that it is not a Vandyck.

MRS. ERRINGTON, MERRYOAK, SOUTHAMPTON.

75. THOMAS FORBES, of Waterton—on a panel 19½ in. by 16½ in.

The sitter is presented in a very dignified and graceful attitude, with long hair and moustache. He is attired in a picturesque, dark red coat, with white slashings, handsome fluted collar, edged with lace.

This gentleman was a son of Forbes, of Tolquhon, and the tragedy attending his death is well known. He was killed in a fray with the Kennedys of Kermucks. Their estates lying in the neighbourhood of Ellon marched, and in a dispute as to boundaries they met and fought in February, 1652. The Sheriff-Clerk had his arm broken, a servant of Forbes' was shot, and Mr. Forbes wounded in the head. He languished till June, when death ended his deep sufferings. A criminal process against the Kennedys led to their flight, forfeiture, and outlawry.

THE RIGHT HON. THE EARL OF ERROLL, SLAINS.

76. AN UNKNOWN LADY.

This is an undoubted and untouched specimen. The lady is somewhat hard-featured, with a low brow, having her light hair combed backward, under a binder at the back. She wears a pearl necklace. The dress is low-bodied, and trimmed with a handsome lace, which tells well on the black fabric underneath.

77. AN UNKNOWN LADY.

Another undoubted and untouched specimen. It represents a young, handsome, oval face, with fine open brow, and large expressive eyes. Yellowish hair falls to her shoulders. Her ear-ring is literally a ring suspended by a minute chain from the ear. Her shoulders slope gracefully, and they are enveloped to her throat in a fine linen collar trimmed with a double row of beautifully delicate lace.

These ladies are probably members of the household of Earl Francis, who, with the other Popish Lords, Huntly and Angus, gave King James so much trouble. The Earl had had three wives and eight daughters, and died in 1631.

THE RIGHT HON. THE EARL OF FIFE, DUFF HOUSE.

78. ADAM (?) DUFF, of Muldavit.

A bust of one of the ancestors of the family encompassed by an oval. A pale-faced man of 30 years, with expressive eyes looking askance. He wears a bright blue sash across his right shoulder. The sash is much better draped than Jamesone was accustomed to do. Indeed the work has been renewed, thereby greatly interfering with its authenticity. A shield of armorial bearings occupies the left corner.

79. JOHN DUFF. (" Ætatis 25—1640.")

This is a very fine and undoubted sample of Jamesone's, notwithstanding that it has been evidently repaired. Raeburn's manner is suggested in the treatment of this subject, but whether the association of ideas is due to Jamesone's treatment of the picture, or (is it possible?) to Raeburn's treatment of Jamesone, will not be easy to determine. This gentleman is distinguished by a white satin dress, Cromwellian collar, and embroidered belt.

80. Mrs. DUFF, of Muldavit. (1643.)

This is a companion picture to the last, and although the restorer has been at work the spirit of Jamesone has not been lost. The lady is the wife of John Duff, whom she faces by looking to the right. She is remarkable for her long swan-like neck. Her dress is of blue, watered silk, and altogether one has little hesitation in accepting the portrait as one of the Jamesone gallery.

81. ALEXANDER SKENE, 15th Laird of Skene.

An undoubted, untouched Jamesone. Its immunity from mis-named restoration is probably due to the fact that, until the other year, it has been in Skene House, where "a little wholesome neglect" has saved it. The subject is a fine-looking man, about fifty, with a high forehead and peaked beard. He wears the customary linen collar with a deep Vandycked lace edging, an embroidered sash under it crosses the right shoulder, displaying the right arm in armour.

82. JANET BURNETT, wife of Alexander Skene, the last mentioned, and daughter of Sir Alexander Burnett, of Leys.

A thinly painted characteristic Jamesone, with the surpassing merit of not having been "improved" in any way. The pose is from left to right, and the head is well set on an ample bust. She is attired in a blue dress trimmed with red bows, and the display of lace over the shoulders and on the breast is magnificent. Replica of No. 58.

83 and 84. JOHN DUFF, of Muldavit, and his SISTER.

These are on one canvas, the boy on the right hand, about 10 or 12 years old, and the girl on the left, about 15. They are hand in hand and exhibit much naturalness of manner, are painted in Jamesone's most careful style, and fortunately have been left untampered with. The sleeves of the girl's dress are nicely puffed. The simplicity of childhood has been very happily caught, and altogether the picture is most charming.

The picture came from the collection of the Bairds, of Auchmeddan, into which family Miss Duff married.

85. VISCOUNTESS FALKLAND.

An interesting picture. The lady wears a graceful, broad-brimmed hat. Her dress exhibits puffed and slashed sleeves, and is trimmed with black rosettes. There is an ample lace collar. It is difficult to make out the date, but it is 1623 or 1628, probably the latter. This fine picture has evidently been much repainted, so that the work of the original artist is obliterated. It is a doubtful Jamesone. The lady was probably the first Viscountess.

86. AN UNKNOWN GENTLEMAN.

This is probably one of the Skene Family, as the picture is one of the set which came from Skene House. It is the portrait of a youngish man, with his hair falling to the shoulders and fringed across his brows. A huge lace Vandycked collar is stretched over his breast from shoulder to shoulder. A genuine Jamesone, sweet and charming in its simplicity of treatment.

COLONEL FRASER, OF CASTLE FRASER.

87. ANDREW FRASER, of Muckills (the former name of Castle Fraser).

During "The Trubles" Fraser was of the Covenanting party, and, as a country laird of some importance, figured in the vicissitudes of the contending factions.

88. Mrs. FRASER, wife of Andrew Fraser, Laird of Muckills.

She was daughter to Robert Douglas, Earl of Buchan.

ALEXANDER GORDON, ESQ., OF PARKHILL.

89. ROBERT GORDON, of Straloch. (See No. 20.)

In excellent condition, although one of the pretty numerous class of north country pictures that passed through the hands of Mr. Giles. The face has been very slightly repainted and the lace collar wholly so. The open hand extended across the breast is painted in a superior manner. Two coats of arms, surmounted by a ribbon and motto, are represented in the upper left corner. One shield bears a saltier with a crown in the centre, and the other, suspended from it, has the Gordon arms, three boars' heads. An excellent engraving of this picture occurs in "Chambers's Lives of Eminent Scotsmen."

THE TRUSTEES OF THE LATE BARRON GRAHAME, ESQ., OF MORPHIE, AT DUNBOG HOUSE, FIFE.

90. Sir ROBERT GRAHAME, of Morphie.

The picture is of the usual nearly-square size, 26 by 23 inches. Sir Robert's portrait is without date or signature. He is dressed in a black doublet, with frill or ruff round his neck.

Sir Robert Grahame figured prominently in the Covenanting times. He was married to Euphemia Carnegie, sister to the 1st Earl of Southesk, who was, therefore, aunt to the wife of the great Montrose. It is conjectured that this portrait had been executed about the same time as that of the Earl of Montrose, to whom he acted as a guardian, namely, in 1629. Sir Robert took the Covenanting side of the questions of his day, and played a very important part in them.

SIR FRANCIS GRANT, OF MONYMUSK, BART.

91. Reverend JOHN LIVINGSTON. (1603-1672.)

A very fine head, but the peculiar modelling of the features renders it a somewhat doubtful Jamesone. If originally his, it has been largely repainted by a modern, distinctive hand, who has also inscribed the picture, "Mr. Iohn Livingstone Person of Ancrum." He wears the divine's skull cap, and in his left hand holds a small book.

Livingston was a cadet of the noble family of the Lords Livingston. His father was a minister at Kilsyth, where young Livingston was born. After some dubiety he chose the ministry as a profession, in which, although of an unusually retiring disposition, he became the Whitfield of his day. One of his earliest engagements was that of private chaplain to the godly Earl and Countess of Wigton (Nos. 73 and 74). He preached with extraordinary fervour, and was, at this period, the instrument of the famous revival at Shotts. On ecclesiastical matters he felt keenly, and was too outspoken to pass un-noticed. Finding but little encouragement to settle at home, he went to Antrim for some years, and all through his life sustained a sympathy with the Irish people. The course of events shortly enabled such ultra-Presbyterians as himself to open their mouths more freely, and he accordingly returned home, and by his splendid oratorical talents and spiritual gifts became a power in promoting the objects of the Covenanting party. He became minister of Stranraer, was a member of the General Assembly of 1638, and, in 1640, was attached to the army. It was not till 1648 that he went to Ancrum, and if it was as the minister of Ancrum that this portrait was painted (and the portrait is that of a man of fifty), then, of course, it is not the work of Jamesone at all. In 1650, Livingston was one of the group who negotiated with Charles at the Hague, and perhaps the only one who saw that historic episode in its hollow and farcical light. After the Restoration he fell under the displeasure of the Government, and was obliged once more to leave his native land. This time he went to the Continent, and died at Rotterdam in 1672.

SIR PETER ARTHUR HALKETT, OF PITFIRRANE, BART., 12 ROTHESAY PLACE, EDINBURGH.

92. WILLIAM DRUMMOND, of Hawthornden.

This may be considered a favourable example of Jamesone's. The poet is represented as a man of at least 35, of a sallow complexion, but with an easy expressiveness, making a very pleasant picture. The silky hair of the head and beard has been carefully done, and the poet holds a book in his right hand. There is a very traceable likeness between this and the other portraits of Drummond.

Was it Jamesone that Drummond had in view as he penned the following eulogy ? :—

" Ye who so curiously do paint your thoughts,
    Enlightening every line in such a guise
    That they seem rather to have fallen from the skies
    Than of a human hand by mortal draughts."

93. PORTRAIT (Unknown).

This is the likeness of a man in middle age, with the moustache and peaked beard of the period. He wears the customary collar, and the work bears ample trace of Jamesone's hand. It is a bust portrait, and is somewhat hard in treatment.

THE RIGHT HON. THE EARL OF HOPETOUN, HOPETOUN HOUSE,
SOUTH QUEENSFERRY.

94. Sir THOMAS HOPE, Lord Craighall, Lord Advocate.

In a scarlet robe, fur-lined, and in a dark wig. It is so completely repainted
that not a suggestion of Jamesone is left but the pose, and it therefore presents a sad example of the restorer's art.

95. Sir JAMES HOPE, son of No. 94.

He is attired in the robes of a Lord of Session, but the picture, whilst retaining
a suggestion of Jamesone, has been completely ruined by being re-painted.

96. COUNTESS OF HADDINGTON.

This picture has not hitherto been attributed to Jamesone, but, although a
slightly doubtful case, is not within the forbidden degrees. Except the
direction of the head (looking to the right), the drawing and colour are
thoroughly after Jamesone's manner. She has a fine head of brown hair,
which falls on her bare shoulders. Her fair skin is otherwise relieved by a
necklace.

She is the celebrated and beautiful Henrietta de Coligny, great grand-
daughter of the celebrated Admiral Coligny, and Countess of the 3rd Earl of
Haddington, who died in his minority, in 1645. The Countess afterwards
married a Huguenot nobleman, from whom she got herself separated, and
turned Catholic in order, it was said, that she might never see him in this
world or the next.

THE RIGHT HON. THE EARL OF HADDINGTON,
TYNINGHAME HOUSE, PRESTONKIRK.

97. FAMILY GROUP OF THOMAS HAMILTON, 2nd Earl of Haddington, his Countess, and Children.

This is an oblong picture, about 3 ft. by 2½ ft., forming a landscape group of
portraits. The Earl himself, surrounded by two boys and a girl, are gracefully grouped on the left beneath a spreading tree. The Countess, Lady
Catherine, a daughter of the Earl of Mar, is seated on the right, on a terrace,
with a child standing at her knee. A dwarfish page enters from the right
bearing a salver with fruit. The two groups are if anything rather detached
by the intervening space which develops into a distant and attractive landscape. It is the introduction of this *paysage* that raises the only doubt as to
the genuineness of this interesting work. In this feature it is unique and

creditable, and may have been introduced in honour of the family, who appreciated Jamesone and freely patronised him.

A certain tragic interest attaches to this portrait of the Earl. He was governor of Dunglass Castle, in Berwickshire ; and, in August, 1640, was there with a number of Covenanting chiefs when, by a sudden accident, the gunpowder in the magazine on the ground-floor exploded and blew the castle with all its inmates into the air. The Earl himself perished, along with his two brothers, his brother-in-law, a son of the Earl of Mar ; Sir John and Sir Alexander Hamilton, and several other gentlemen, besides about fifty-four men and women servants. This sad event occurred within three months after his second marriage with Lady Jean Gordon, daughter of the 1st Marquis of Huntly.

98. LADY CATHERINE ERSKINE, Lady Binning, afterwards Countess of Haddington.

A thinly painted bust, statuesque in colour, with cherry lips. The portrait betrays signs of having been quickly painted.

This lady was fourth daughter of the Earl of Mar, and wife of the 2nd Earl of Haddington (No. 97), whom she predeceased.

99. THOMAS HAMILTON, 3rd Earl of Haddington.

A bust portrait. Good, and quite characteristic of the artist.

This youth was married to the beautiful Henrietta (No. 96), great grand-daughter of " the good Coligny," and died in his minority when but a year in the enjoyment of the earldom.

100. General ALEXANDER HAMILTON. (D. 1649.)

A carefully and solidly painted portrait. The artist's peculiar use of varnish to blend his colours is favourably seen in this example—a luminous, rather reddish, effect being produced, without those hard lines which disfigure some of Jamesone's reputed pictures.

The General was fifth and youngest son of Sir Thomas Hamilton, Lord Priestfield, and brother to the 1st Earl of Haddington. He was a General of Artillery, and held a high command in the army sent to the assistance of the King of Sweden, under the 1st Duke of Hamilton, in 1631.

————————

THE HON. R. BAILLIE HAMILTON, LANGTON HOUSE, DUNSE.

101. THOMAS, Lord of Binning. (D. 1645.)

Inscribed, " Thomas Loird of Bining, 1636." A boy of fourteen, an excellent specimen, very delicately painted. He is looking to the right, a circumstance

which indicates it to be probably a companion picture. His hair is of a
yellow tinge. The nose is, perhaps, rather aquiline for one so young. He is
attired in a buff jerkin, with slashed sleeves and trimmed with braid. Over
it is a rich lace collar.

This nobleman was son of the 2nd Earl of Haddington, and held this
title during his father's lifetime, at whose violent death he succeeded as 3rd
Earl of Haddington, at which time Jamesone again painted his likeness
(No. 99). He died in his minority.

102. WILLIAM, 6th Earl Marischal. (1636.)

A very fine characteristic specimen, in excellent preservation, that is, cleaned but
not restored. The whole treatment is simple to a degree. The face is pale ;
with moustache. The head is surrounded by a mass of lightish hair. A
large, plain linen collar completely covers the shoulders, and the close-
buttoned coat or doublet is unmarked by any ornament, as became the Covenanting party, of which he was an active and distinguished member. He
was the son of George, the 5th Earl (No. 24), and married the lovely Lady
Mary Erskine, daughter of the Earl of Mar, whose beautiful portrait (No.
143) will be found *in loco.*

103. JOHN, 2nd Earl of Kinghorn. (D. 1647.)

This picture has suffered restoration, but not sufficiently to destroy Jamesone's
influence. It represents a fine-looking man in his prime. His hair is parted
in the middle, and flows gracefully to his shoulders. He wears a Charles I.
moustache and beard. A large linen collar, trimmed with a rich lace, rests
on his dress of dark material. The picture is dated 1637.

He is an ancestor of the Strathmore Family, and with the preceding
(Marischal), his brother-in-law, took rank as a conspicuous leader amongst
the Covenanters. He was married to Lady Margaret Erskine, third daughter
of the Earl of Mar.

104. JOHN, Lord Leslie. (D. 1681.)

Represents a young boy of ten or twelve years of age, painted in that happy
manner in which Jamesone delineated young people. He has light blue eyes
and fair hair. He wears a round cap, ornamented with lace, a large, plain
linen collar, over a tunic with slashed sleeves. His waist is confined by an
ornamented band.

He must have been a member of the Rothes Family, probably he who
became the 6th Earl and Duke of Rothes. Unlike his father, he was a
staunch Royalist, and filled in succession the highest offices of State.

105. Lady MARGARET DOUGLAS.

Inscribed, "Domina Margarata Douglas filia ANGVISIE Comitis ejus Sponsa . MCDXCVI." This portrait has a hard outliney, not to say corpse-like appearance. The lady wears a rounded hat with a veil flowing from either side of it. She holds a book in her right hand. This is probably one of the pictures "from fancy" painted for Sir Colin Campbell, at Taymouth, to which collection the whole of this series belonged.

106. Lady MARIOTTA STEWART.

Inscribed, "Domina Mariotta Stewart filia Roberti Comitis de Fyffe et Monteith Ejus Sponsa MCDVI" [sic]. A good specimen, but probably a fancy portrait. The features are well modelled, but corpse-like. The lady is stately, but severe in expression. Fair hair. She wears a red bodice, with a blue scarf thrown round her shoulders.

107. Lady KATHERINE RUTHVEN.

Inscribed, "Domina Katherina Ruthven filia Wilhelm II Domini Ruthven Ejus Sponsa A.D. MDLXXXIII." Enclosed in a painted oval and looking to the right. Dark hair, enclosed behind with a jewelled ceinture. Her features are hard, with a very aquiline nose. A peculiar looking red bodice, bound with a blue material, rises with a collar-like expanse, forming a background to the neck and bare bosom. Her left hand extends across the breast. Probably one of the "fancy" set, and, as so, historically worthless.

108. Lady MARIOTTA STEWART.

Inscribed, "Domina Marriotta Stewart filia de Joannis de Athol." A fair haired lady looking to her right. She wears a graceful hat, displays an open bosom with a pearl necklace, and her left hand extends across her breast. Although the treatment of the whole is flattish, there is not wanting an expression of repose and dignity. The picture is, on the whole, a desirable specimen.

———

SIR ARCHIBALD HOPE, PINKIE HOUSE, EDINBURGHSHIRE.

109. Sir JOHN HOPE, 2nd Baronet of Craighall. (D. 1655).

Massive head of dark hair, eyes, and eyebrows. Wears an easy smiling expression. Attired in a black dress, slashed with white, with a fluted linen collar.

Sir John was the eldest of fourteen children of his father, Sir Thomas Hope. He, with two of his brothers, was a Lord of Session, under the title of Lord Craighall.

110. Lady HOPE, of Craighall, *neé* Margaret Murray of Blackbarony, and wife of Lord Hope, of Craighall (No. 109).

> This lady was still young when painted by Jamesone, and must have been a more patient sitter than her father-in-law, Sir Thomas Hope, for no haste is betrayed in painting her elaborate attire. She has fair hair, slightly reddish ; hazel eyes. Her collar is of transparent cambric, starched out on either side of the bust. She wears a necklace of heart-shaped ornaments, pendant jewel —crossbar and crescent,—pear-shaped pearl hanging by a string from her right ear, besides the ear-ring. The dress is of a rich black, with gold-brocade stripes, slashed in strips, with a crimson bow on the bosom.
>
> Sir Thomas Hope affectionately laments this poor lady's death, under date "3 October 1641 Sounday About 9 of nycht my dear dauchter D. M. Murray spous to my sone Craighall deceissit in childbirth scho and the barne in her womb. God in mercie pitie me and my children for it is a sore straik."

111. Lady WEMYSS, the Honourable Jean Gray, daughter of the 7th Lord Gray, married, in 1610, John, 1st Lord Wemyss.

> A stately lady, with rather marked features, fair hair frizzed out, stiff linen collar, forming a sort of background to the neck and bust. She wears a black dress slashed with white, a black bow in front. On her bosom is suspended a coloured jewel.

THE RIGHT HON. THE EARL OF KINNOULL, DUPPLIN CASTLE.

112. Sir THOMAS NICOLSON.

> Has been entirely repainted, with the necessary effect of at once discrediting the likeness and the original artist, whose influence can only be faintly traced. It is still a fine massive head of a man of sixty. The expansive brow, the large, restful eyes, and the square jaw, indicate a powerful man. He has on a small black velvet skull cap, from which escapes a profusion of grey hair, imparting a leonine aspect.
>
> Sir Thomas was a native of Aberdeen, and the son of a plain burgess. Receiving a University education, he entered the law and rose to high eminence at the bar. He accompanied the Embassy which negotiated the marriage of James VI. with Anne of Denmark. From Sir Thomas are descended the Nicolsons of Glenbervie and of Kemnay.

113. GEORGE HAY, 1st Earl of Kinnoull. (D. 1634.)

> This picture bears evident trace of Jamesone's hand, but it has been largely repainted. He wears a fine cap, richly ornamented with lace, and a common

ruff, over a plain doublet. It is a usual feature of these repainted portraits that the dates of Jamesone's pictures are generally sacrificed by the restorer.

He was the youngest son of Peter Hay, and was appointed a Gentleman of the Bedchamber, and honoured with the dignity of knighthood (1598). He was created Baron of Kinfauns and Viscount Dupplin, in 1627, and, in 1633, was created Earl of Kinnoull. He married Margaret, daughter of Sir James Haliburton, of Pitcur. He died in 1634.

114. GEORGE, 2nd Earl of Kinnoull.

An interesting and curious picture of a youth of eighteen, inscribed, " Ætatis suæ 18," in the upper right corner, and the arms of the Hays in the left, with " 1632" beneath. This picture has received some very shameful treatment, and is now not in good preservation. The face has been worked on by a rude novice, and much injured. The collar is the feature which is noticeable. It stretches straight across the breast with scolloped edges and rounds the back of the neck.

THE RIGHT HON. THE EARL OF KINTORE, KEITH-HALL, ABERDEENSHIRE.

115. Sir JOHN STEWART, 1st Earl of Traquair, Lord Treasurer Deputy of Scotland. (1599-1659.)

This is a bust portrait representing the Earl as a man past mid age and bald. The handling of this picture is not strongly characteristic of Jamesone. It has evidently been worked over by another hand, evidently that of Mr. Giles. His costume is the usual ruff, edged with lace, over which his short, grey, peaked beard falls, though with less luxuriance than would seem to justify the phrase applied to him, " bearded like the pard." From a ribbon round his neck is suspended the badge of his office, which he had so much " moyan" to obtain. When Jamesone painted him he was in the hey-day of his prosperity or climbing towards it, and possesses a complacent, not to say astute, aspect. Clarendon commends his " wisdom and dexterity," and speaks of him as " a man of great parts." Charles I. ennobled and enriched him, and confided to his care his most important interests, although it has been said that Traquair never did his master a good turn. He was an accomplished, scholarly man, and could be eloquent when the occasion served, but we can scarcely read in the placid face, hung on the line in the " Prayers Room" at Keith-Hall, the " highly aristocratic" personage, " hasty and hot in the temper, and full of strange oaths," that Mark Napier pictures. Traquair in his politics was limp, compliant, half-hearted. He had not the courage of his opinions, and his movements were dubious, and only developed a series of false positions, painful to himself, and so hateful to his contemporaries, that some of whom were determined " to sweep his name furth of the land."

Traquair was married to the eldest, and Montrose to the youngest of six daughters of the Earl of Southesk, and both bulked largely in their time, and contrasted sharply in their conduct. Traquair, for whom nature had done much and culture, perhaps, more, had nothing of the nobleness of his illustrious brother-in-law, whose fame only excited his jealousy. The tragic fate of the latter, the result of his singleness of purpose, was much preferable to that of the former, whose vacillations incurred such romantic alternations of fortune, that he was to be seen at last, an oldish man, traversing the streets of the capital, where he is said to have died of hunger, begging an alms of the passers by, and "lost to use and name and fame." His life was a romance of the peerage. It is said that he died whilst smoking a pipe of tobacco, and at his burial had no mortcloth. (See p. 52.)

116. GEORGE KEITH, 5th Earl Marischal—the Founder of Marischal College.

This picture hangs in the "Prayers Room." It is undoubtedly by Jamesone, and bears a striking resemblance to the portrait in Marischal College (No. 24). It has suffered restoration, in which it is not difficult to trace the hand of Mr. Giles, R.S.A.

The Earl was a conspicuous figure in his day, and filled with dignity, ability, and prudence, various high State functions. The title and estates were forfeited, in 1716, on account of the then Earl's share in the Rebellion of that year. The Kintore Family are now the representatives of the Earls Marischal.

117. PORTRAIT (Unknown).

The head of a gentleman of the family. The pose and treatment thoroughly in Jamesone's style. It hangs in the Drawing-Room.

118. PORTRAIT (Unknown).

Another male member of the family, possessing all the marks of a genuine picture by Jamesone. It hangs in the Drawing-Room.

MRS. LEITH, CANAAN LODGE, EDINBURGH.

119. GEORGE JAMESONE, his WIFE, and CHILD.

This deeply interesting picture might be more accurately described as Mrs. Jamesone, her husband, and child, for the artist and little girl, who complete the group, occupy but a subordinate place to the central figure, as described in pp. 56 and 57.   The picture has been handed down through the Gregory line, springing from Mary Jamesone.   When Walpole wrote it was in the possession of Sir George Chalmers, the painter, who married a Gregory—a great grand-daughter of Jamesone's, and a beautiful engraving of it appears in Dallaway's edition of the "Anecdotes of Painting."   It was exhibited, as the property of Mr. Gregory, Edinburgh, along with about forty of Jamesone's other portraits, at the Exhibition of Historical Portraits held at Aberdeen in connection with the meeting there of the British Association.   From his possession it has now passed into that of his cousin, the present owner.   Recalling to memory the picture of 1859 and inspecting the one of to-day the contrast is extreme, and exhibits, perhaps, the most regrettable example of the evils of restoration.   To look at the bright, fresh painting with its clean new canvas at the back, it is most difficult to believe that it is not an entirely new picture, conveying no impression whatever of Jamesone's manner.   Had one to speak of it as a copy, it would be in terms of praise, but of the wanton destruction of the original, which lies between the new canvas and the new paint, very different language must be used.   A well-known engraving of it was executed by Alexander, a descendant of Marjory Jamesone.   It is inscribed, "*Georgius Iameson Scotus Abredonensis* Patriæ, suæ, Apelles, eiusque uxor Isabella Tosh, et Filius . Geo Jameson Pinxit Anno 1623 [1633 ?] Alex! pronepos fecit Aqua forte A.D. 1728."   This plate is becoming very scarce, although there are some five or six impressions in Jamesone's native town of Aberdeen.

120. DAVID GREGORIE, of Kinairdie.

An excellent example, although another hand has worked on it.   It represents a keen-looking man in a cap, dark hair, moustache, and short beard.   The body has more of a side turn than is usual, the right arm only being seen. He holds a shut book, and on the table a skull is laid.   On a little bracket in the left upper corner is a sandglass.

He is a member of the famous Gregory Family, and was librarian at Marischal College (1663-1669), and father of David Gregory, Savilian Professor of Astronomy at Oxford.

THE RIGHT HON. THE EARL OF LINDSAY, KILCONQUHAR.

121. PATRICK and JOHN LINDSAY, of Wormieston.

Inscribed, "1636 Ætatis 5   1636 Ætatis 3."   This picture has unfortunately suffered from the zeal of some servant maid, who has scoured off much of the bloom and delicate work of the original. Happily nothing has been done in the way of *super-imposing* colour. It represents two boys, who look older than the ages recorded on the canvas by something like ten years, and they are fondling a King Charles spaniel. They are dressed alike in scarlet tunics, with large lace-edged linen collars and cuffs. They are both fair-haired and old enough apparently to have pronounced political opinions —the hair on Patrick's right and on John's left side is shortened in the most orthodox cavalier fashion. The picture is in its original black-and-gold frame.

The Lindsays of Wormieston to which these boys belong are a branch of a very ancient, numerous, and influential family in Scotland. Their principal home and holdings seem to have always been in the kingdom of Fife.

122. AN UNKNOWN LADY.

Inscribed, "Anno 1636 Ætatis 25." She is attired in a very ample black felt hat, such as at first sight to suggest its being a male portrait. The chest is covered by a linen scolloped collar up to the neck, showing only a long strip of the bare bosom in front. The face has, unfortunately, been worked on in such a manner as to heighten the suspicion that the portrait is one of the sterner sex. Had Jamesone's tenderly feminine tints and outlines been left alone this would have been found one of his very choicest and most careful works.

ALEXANDER LESLIE, ESQ., C.E., 12 GREENHILL TERRACE, EDINBURGH.

123. JOHN, 7th Earl of Mar, K.G., the Lord Treasurer. (D. 1634.)

This bust portrait formerly belonged to the late William Marjoribanks, Esq., of Balbardie. The subject is a middle-aged person with a bald head. The face is flattish, and the features do not stand out well. There is a notable want of shadow or of the varnish which Jamesone used as a substitute. A blue ribbon surrounds the Earl's neck, with a gold badge of office suspended from it. Jamesone may have painted this picture, but it is far from being a favourable example of his style.

History assigns a prominent place to Treasurer Mar. He was educated, along with James VI., at Stirling Castle. He took part in the Raid of Ruthven, for which he was attainted, but afterwards pardoned and received back into the Royal confidence, and appointed Master of the King's Household, Governor of Edinburgh Castle, and ultimately, in 1615, Lord High Treasurer of Scotland, an office he retained for fifteen years.

THE MOST NOBLE THE MARQUIS OF LOTHIAN,
NEWBATTLE ABBEY, DALKEITH.

124. ARCHIBALD CAMPBELL, 8th Earl and 1st Marquis of Argyll.
(1598-1661.)

This bust bears every token of being Jamesone's work. The posture and treatment are quite characteristic of him, although not, perhaps, what can be
called a very favourable example.

As a staunch Covenanter, and great opponent of Montrose in his
Royalist days, the Marquis figured very conspicuously in the history of his
times, and, in common with his rival and with so many of the principals of
the stirring events of the period, he forfeited his life and was executed
in 1661.

125. Lady ANN DOUGLAS, the Marchioness of Argyll.

Inscribed, "1634." This, at least, is an undoubted example, its excellence but
very slightly impaired by the cleaner. She may be called the White Lady.
She has fair hair, pale, almost corpse-like face and breast, white lace, and a
white satin dress. To the artist it must have been a rather trying task— but
he has contrived to produce a pleasing picture, by relieving the whiteness by
the introduction of a little colour in her hair band, necklace, bow knots, and
waistband.

She was the second daughter of William, 8th Earl of Morton, Lord
Treasurer of Scotland, and wife of the 1st Marquis of Argyll (No. 124).

126. "WILLIAM, Earl of Lothian Æt. 15." (D. 1675.)

This is a very attractive little picture—a full-length figure dressed in a red suit
pleasantly relieved by cross stripes of gold. It is inscribed as above. The
face is somewhat flattish and is wanting in expression. Indeed, the want of
the whole figure, which is well drawn and most conscientiously painted, is
that of shading. This results in a loss of roundness, but the easy grace of
the figure, as a whole, goes far to atone for its other defects. It is considerably less than life size. His right hand rests on his side, and in his left
he holds his hat.

Sir William Kerr, Kt., was created 3rd Earl of Lothian in 1631. He was
a Groom of the Bedchamber to James VI. and Charles I., but joined the
Covenanters in 1638, to whom he did signal service both in a military,
political, and diplomatic capacity. Throughout his career it is to be re-
marked that he never allowed party spirit to over-ride his independence of
opinion.

20

127. Sir THOMAS HAMILTON, Earl of Haddington. (1563-1637.)

An excellent picture.   The Earl is attired in a scarlet tippet, edged with fur.
The work has been attributed to Jamesone, but it is certainly a doubtful
canvas.   If not by Jamesone it is the work of Vandyck, of whom, however,
it is scarcely a worthy specimen.

The Earl, as Sir Thomas Hamilton, was a distinguished member of the
bar, and from the circumstance of residing in the Cowgate of Edinburgh,
King James playfully designated him "Tam o' the Cowgate."   His great
abilities soon raised him to the bench.   In 1592, he was appointed a Lord
of Session, and ultimately Lord President of the Court.   He was greatly
engaged in political affairs, reaching to such high offices as Secretary of State
and Lord Privy Seal.   By his enormous industry, ample emoluments, and
successful enterprises, he amassed such wealth that the credulity of the time
attributed to him the discovery of the long-sought philosopher's stone.

Referring to this picture, and to other doubtful examples, the Marquis of
Lothian expresses himself with much judgment when he says :—" I believe
the picture . . . was painted by Vandyck and not by Jamesone—that is
to say, that if other well known portraits supposed to be painted by Vandyck
are really by that master, then the portrait of the third earl of Lothian is also
his.   If, on the other hand, my picture is by Jamesone, I have no doubt but
that others hitherto attributed to Vandyck are also really by Jamesone."

128. General ALEXANDER LESLIE, Earl of Leven. (D. 1661.)

Attired in an embroidered coat and a magnificent collar.   Attributed to
Jamesone, but is quite worthy of the reputation of Vandyck.

Having early adopted the profession of arms, he pursued an active
soldierly career on the Continent, reaching the high position of "Felt
Marshall" in the Swedish service.   During the Covenanting wars, General
Leslie was recalled to take chief command of the Covenanters.   This he did
with great skill, and he was ultimately raised to the peerage as Earl of Leven.

THE RIGHT HON. THE EARL OF MAR AND KELLIE,
ALLOA PARK.

129. JAMES ERSKINE, 6th Earl of Buchan—first of the Erskines.
(D. 1640.)

This is a favourable example of Jamesone, and does not appear to have been
tampered with.   He is a heavy featured man.   His hair is dark and straight,
and he wears a moustache and pointed chin beard.   He is attired in a large
fluted collar over a slashed doublet.

He is the second son of the Treasurer Mar, by Lady Marie Stewart. Having married Lady Mary Douglas, Countess of Buchan, he assumed the title, afterwards confirmed by a Royal charter dated 1617, of Earl of Buchan.

130. JAMES ERSKINE, 7th Earl of Buchan—second of the Erskines.

Inscribed, " Ætatis 14 . 1627." This is an excellent, untouched specimen. The youth bears some resemblance to his father, the preceding subject. The expression is sweet and thoughtful, not to say melancholy, for one of his age. A large lace-tipped collar is worn over a very carefully painted slashed and embroidered dress.

He married Lady Marjory Ramsay, daughter of William, 1st Earl of Dalhousie.

131. JOHN ERSKINE, 3rd Earl of Mar, K.B. (D. 1654.)

This is a characteristic, not to say powerful, portrait, and we venture to believe that, in the highly arched eyebrows, aquiline nose, and somewhat waggish air of the Earl, Jamesone has succeeded in producing a life-like portrait. The picture is not in good preservation, but has suffered less from the ravages of time than it may have done from Vandal attempts at restoration. The Earl is attired in a brown jerkin, relieved by a plain white collar and a red ribbon thrown across his right shoulder. He died in 1654.

He is the eldest son of the Treasurer Mar, by his first wife, Anne, daughter of Lord Drummond.

132. Lady MARY MACKENZIE, Countess of Mar. (D. about 1660.)

Bears evidence of having been a fine example of Jamesone's work, but the face has been entirely re-painted. She has a luxuriant head of auburn hair, several curls of which are brought over her forehead. Her shoulders slope very much, and she displays a bare bosom, rich discs of lace being employed to trim the surrounding linen.

She was the second wife of John, 4th Earl of Mar.

———————

SIR JOHN MAXWELL STIRLING-MAXWELL, OF POLLOK AND KERR, BART., KEIR HOUSE, PERTHSHIRE.

133. Sir GEORGE STIRLING, of Keir.

The portraits of Sir George and Lady Stirling are both beautifully engraved in the " Life of Montrose " by Mr. Mark Napier, whose description of them we subjoin :—

"This head-sized portrait is in very good preservation and, as well as the companion portrait, Lady Stirling, presents a good specimen of the costume of well-conditioned people in Scotland at that period. It is signed in the lower corner, next the left arm, 'Jamesone,' and dated in the upper and opposite corner, above the head, 'Anno 1637 Aetatis 22.' The first year of 'The Trubles,' most probably, both of these [Nos. 133 and 134], which originally occupied one frame with a slip between, were marriage portraits, and painted in their wedding garb. Jamesone has affixed his signature to each of them, but has only dated the husband's. The deeds of the marriage settlement are preserved in the Napier Charter Chest, and bear the date 2nd January, 1637, the same year as the date on Sir George's portrait. That Laird of Keir thus became the nephew of Montrose by marriage. He was beloved and respected by our hero, and suffered prosecution along with him, although he appears never to have served in arms. Montrose, in corresponding with him, used to address him as '*Mon Frere*,' a style which, through the mistake of a transcriber, we had inadvertently printed 'Honble Sir' in the 'Memorials.'

"Sir George Stirling was twice married. Young as he was in the year 1637, Margaret Napier was his second wife. There is a melancholy story attached to Sir George in early life. The following affecting inscription, in date four years earlier than his second marriage, in 1637, when he was but 22 years of age, is preserved in 'Monteith's Theater of Mortality,' p. 54 :—

"'Here lyeth Dame Margaret Ross daughter to James Lord Ross and Dame Margaret Scot (daughter to Walter Lord Buccleugh and sister to Walter Scot Earl of Buccleugh) She was married to Sir George Sterline of Keir Knight, and chief of his name, and having lived a pattern and paragon for piety, and debonaritie beyond her sex and age, when she had accomplished seventeen years she was called from this transitory life to that eternal ; 10th March 1633. She left behind her only one daughter Margaret : who in her pure inno-cency soon followed her mother the 11th day of May thereafter, when she had been 12 months showen to this world, and here lyeth near unto her, interred.

"'Dominus Georgius Sterline, de Keir, Eques auratus, familiae princeps conjugi dulcissimæ poni curavit . M.D.C.XXXIII.'

"Thus heavily had the hand of God visited this chief of 'Ancient Keir' when he was but eighteen years of age. The above date is immediately prior to the advent of Charles I., to his Coronation in Scotland, and to Montrose's departure upon his travels abroad three years after his own boyish marriage."

134. MARGARET NAPIER, Lady Stirling, of Keir.

"This is the companion portrait to the one just mentioned, and in former days used to be framed along with it, as arms matrimonial are sometimes impaled in the same shield. We demur to the propriety of separating such ancient couples for the sake of separate modern establishments. The dress of this portrait is very perfect, and displays the delicate and accurate pencillings by Jamesone. But the fair complexion and the details and texture of the golden hair have suffered much, and probably more from modern attention than from ancient neglect. The hair is dressed, doubtless, after the fashion of the day, in a very unbecoming manner."

HIS GRACE THE DUKE OF MONTROSE, BUCHANAN HOUSE.

135. The MARQUIS OF MONTROSE. (Dated 1640.)

Apart from the internal evidence, which is conclusive that Montrose is the subject and Jamesone the painter, few pictures come before us so carefully authenticated. Mr. Mark Napier, in his "Memorials of Montrose," gives a very succinct and interesting narrative of its history, first quoting the following legend, which appears on the back of it, and then describing it in his own masterly fashion :—

"The great Marquis of Montrose when in England, in the year 1640, took refuge in the house of Mr. Colquhoun, a clergyman, second son of the Camstraddan Family, where he remained for a considerable time. When about to depart he thanked Mr. C. for the respect and tenderness with which he had been treated and the fidelity with which he had been concealed, regretting that he had not something more substantial than words by which to express his gratitude. Mr. C. replied—' You now have it in your power to repay an hundred-fold any little service we have done you ; a likeness of your Highness would be inestimable ;—that if he would condescend so far, Jamesone, the Scotch painter, was in the house, a man of honour, a friend that might be trusted.' The Marquis agreed, and the picture now in our possession was the likeness taken. About the year 1775, my father, Robert Colquhoun, of Camstraddan, became possessed of the portrait, and, in 1776, Lord Frederick Campbell carried it to London and had it cleaned. On bringing it back to Camstraddan, he told my father it had been greatly admired by Sir Joshua Reynolds and other judges of painting. No copy was ever allowed to be taken, as far as my memory serves me. Such is the account I have often heard from my father, who died, 1787, aged seventy-one.

"MARGT. HALDANE COLQUHOUN."

" Melville Place, Stirling, 2. March, 1833."

"The attitude in this half-length portrait is precisely the same as that painted in 1629. But the costume is very different. The sleeves only of a pink and white satin doublet appear, and these not puffed or slashed. The rest of the person is covered by a military buff coat, which imparts a fine tone and colour to the picture. A broadsword belt, richly embroidered, crosses the breast, and these warlike signs are relieved by a falling collar of costly lace, and true Vandyck pattern, such as a countess might covet in these degenerate days of male attire. One defect in the composition is observable. In the portrait which Jamesone first painted the hair is naturally parted and turned aside over the brow, so as completely to dis-cover it, and though full and curling is of moderate length. But in that now described, while the auburn locks descend in voluminous waves to the shoulder, the hair in front is cut straight across and very close to the eyebrows, according to a most unbecoming fashion of the day, which Jamesone and other masters too frequently submitted to. This and the black calotte cap on the crown of the head constitute a striking resemblance between the Camstraddan portrait and the one at Buchanan House to be presently noticed, besides great similarity in the features.

"Both of Jamesone's portraits possess the advantage of representing Montrose in the very dress he wore. In this respect all the other portraits of him that we have seen and the whole herd of prints are merely figurative. It was not the habit at that time to be cased in armour like the knights of old, although it was the right of every great military commander to be so portrayed. The English Tinoret and Ghevardo dalle Notte, whose portraits we have next to discuss, have given us sublime historical representations of the hero. From George Jamesone we have biographical delineations of the individual as boy and man."

The portrait was ultimately acquired by His Grace the Duke of Montrose, in 1871, on the death of Sir Robert G. Colquhoun, K.C.B.

The portrait is one of the set of beautifully perfect engraved portraits in Mr. Napier's "Life of Montrose," 1856, p. 289.

C. STIRLING HOME DRUMMOND MORAY, ESQ., OF BLAIR-DRUMMOND AND ABERCAIRNY.

136. Sir Patrick Drummond. (Knighted before 1640.)

A tradition of the house is that this portrait is genuine. The author has only seen the lithograph of it in the "Red Book of Menteith," and its pose and general aspect favour the idea. It is inscribed, "Nolens Parui 1634."

Sir Patrick was Lord Conservator of the Scots' Privileges at Campvere in 1650.

137. TWO OF THE ARTIST'S CHILDREN.

This picture formerly belonged to Charles Kirkpatrick Sharp, Esq., who left it to his sister, the late Mrs. Bedford, at whose sale it was bought by the present owner.

Intimation of the existence of this portrait having only been received as these last sheets were in the press, there has been no opportunity of inspecting it, and therefore no opinion is given in support of its ascription to Jamesone. It is inserted here in the hope that its genuineness may yet be verified.

MAJOR MORISON, OF MONTBLAIRY, ABERDEENSHIRE.

138. Sir JAMES CRICHTON, of Frendraught. (D. 1636.)

Inscribed, "Anno 1634 Ætatis 36." This is presumably the Laird of Frendraught in whose day Frendraught Castle was burned on the 27th September, 1630.

This picture has been slightly tampered with. The face has been at least varnished out, and the lace collar repainted in an inferior manner. The dress of black stuff, slashed with white silk, has not been touched. Sir James is a very plain, low-browed, rather sad-visaged gentleman, and if the *suspect* on account of the Frendraught tragedy, was at this very time undergoing much trouble on account of it.

139. Lady FRENDRAUGHT, wife of Sir James Crichton, of Frendraught.

Inscribed, "ANNO 1637 Ætatis 34." This picture has also been slightly tampered with—it remains, however, substantially as Jamesone left it. The hair is brought over the brow in a series of detached fringes or curls with a good effect, and a dark snood or veil partly covers the head, falling gracefully down the lady's back. A very large and particularly rich lace collar reaches from the neck, leaving only a long narrow stripe of the breast exposed. A stately handsome picture.

She was the beautiful daughter of the Earl of Sutherland, and nearly related to the Marquis of Huntly, to whom she went the morning after the burning of Frendraught. This pathetic incident is carefully related by Spalding, who says "that upon the morn, after this woeful fire, the lady Frendraught, backed in a white plaid, and riding on a small nag having a boy leading her horse, without any more in her company. In this pitiful manner she came weeping and mourning to the Bog [now Gordon Castle] desiring to speak with my Lord ; but this was refused, so she returned back to her own house, the same gate she came, comfortless."

140. Lady FRENDRAUGHT.

It is somewhat difficult to identify this lady, but she is more than probably the wife of the 1st Lord Frendraught. She is quite young, and very beautiful— dark brown eyes and wavy auburn hair, which is confined by a black velvet band above her rolled brow. Over a dark dress she wears an ample plain linen collar close up to the throat. The artist has excelled himself in producing a most attractive portrait, which happily remains in its original condition, absolutely untouched, and in no need of touching.

141. JOHN URQUHART, of Craigston. (1547-1631.)

This is probably a portrait of the "Tutor of Cromarty," so called from the circumstance that, as grand-uncle of the eccentric translator of Rabelais, Sir Thomas Urquhart, of Cromarty, he became tutor or trustee of that gentleman's affairs. He died in November, 1631, and in an epitaph in King-Edward Church, Arthur Johnston bewails him thus :—

> " Posteritas, cui liquit agros et praedia, disce
> Illius exemple vivere disce mori."

The portrait has, perhaps, been slightly touched, but remains an excellent example of Jamesone. He has long hair flowing to his shoulders, a piercing dark eye, and a happy expression. A Cromwellian collar over a dark coat forms his simple attire.

142. Mrs. URQUHART, of Craigston, wife of "The Tutor."

Inscribed, "Anno 1625 Ætatis 43." The picture represents a portly, dignified matron with well modelled features. A black snood or veil forms a background to a massive head of hair. A linen cape surrounds the shoulders and neck, round which hangs a string of pendant ornaments.

This lady, Elizabeth Seton, was of the family of Meldrum. She was entailed in the whole of that estate by her uncle, William Seton.

ALEXANDER ERSKINE MURRAY, ESQ., SHERIFF-SUBSTITUTE OF GLASGOW, SUNDOWN, MONTGOMERIE DRIVE, GLASGOW.

The authentication of this large and very fine collection of portraits by Jamesone is thus given by Sheriff Erskine Murray—himself a lineal descendant of Lord Treasurer Mar :—

" Lady Marie Stuart, Countess of Mar, second wife of John, 7th Earl of

Mar, Lord Treasurer of Scotland, had a large family. Of most of these she got pictures made. She left her pictures, cabinets, &c., &c., by will to a younger son of hers, Charles Erskine, by whom they came by descent to my mother, and thus to me."

The mother of this family, Marie Stuart, was the daughter of Esme, Duke of Lennox, and a "very imperative and autocratic little person." When young, she first captivated and then *liberated*, much against his will, John Erskine, 7th Earl of Mar. The story goes that the earl sickened of vexation. The King (James VI.) hearing of the plight of the companion of his boyish years, exclaimed, "Be my saul, Mar shanna dee for e'er a lass in the land." The King succeeded in effecting a change in the maiden's attitude, and she became to Mar an excellent wife and a fruitful mother.

143. Lady MARY ERSKINE, Countess of Marischal and Panmure.

Inscribed, "Anno 1626. June 29 Marie Ersken Count. Marschaill." This is probably the finest picture by Jamesone extant. The subject of it is comely, it has been painted with the utmost care, and it happily remains unimpaired in its original charm, exempt from the arts of the restorer. The lady's darkish hair is bound by a circlet of gold at the back of the head, and a pin seems to fasten the whole. The face is charmingly painted, and there is a fine shading together of delicate flesh tints. The features are regular and pleasing. The brow is expansive, the eyes bright, the nose well drawn, the mouth firm but not severe, and the chin well moulded. From the right ear depends an ornament which rests on an ample ruff colour, painted in such a delicate manner as to lessen its inherent awkwardness. A triangular portion of the breast is shown. A goffered and Vandycked collar is gracefully laid on the shoulders. The dress is a dark green, brocaded with gold lace, the sleeves being puffed and slashed, showing a white fabric beneath. The head is well poised, and the *tout ensemble* of this charming picture is that of easy dignity.

Lady Mary was married first to William, 6th Earl Marischal, and second to the Earl of Panmure. As wife of the former she was necessarily much at Aberdeen, where her husband was a citizen, and must have been personally well known to the artist. In 1639, Dr. Wm. Guild dedicated the first part of his book, "An Antidote against Popery," to

"Dame Marie Stewart Countess of Marre—The Mother
Dame Marie Erskin Countess of Marischal—The Daughter
and Dame Ieane Keith Ladie Petslego—The Niece."

144. Lady ANN ERSKINE, Countess of Rothes.

A characteristic and untouched sample of Jamesone. She possesses the same

21

cast of features as her sister (No. 143), but it is treated somewhat differently. There is exhibited a great breadth of bosom—the dress being cut square across it. The picture is unnamed and undated. It was probably done before she was married to the Earl of Rothes, and represents the same lady delineated in No. 164.

She was the second daughter of the Lord Treasurer, wife of John, the 5th Earl of Rothes, who was a great Covenanter, and especial friend of Jamesone's. She was mother of the only Duke of Rothes, who was in his day a staunch Royalist.

145. Lady MARGARET ERSKINE, Countess of Kinghorn and Strathmore.

Mistakenly inscribed, "Lady Martha Erskine." Painted with great elaboration of detail, and after all is but an average though untouched example. It is not in a state of first-rate preservation, and the treatment is thin and flattish. She is dressed in the height of fashion. The collar is of the richest lace, and extends in wing-like dimensions on either side, worn over a russet-coloured, striped silk dress, with widely-puffed sleeves. A double necklace and pendant jewel contrast with her fair skin, and a large brooch joins the collar in front. Lady Margaret was the third daughter.

146. Lady CATHERINE ERSKINE, Countess of Haddington.

An average, untouched example. A very erect, sprightly lady, with hair of the reddish family tint, brushed back from her forehead. A small feather is pinned to the right side of her head, and from her ear hangs several ornaments. A linen winged collar gives tone to her fair complexion. A necklace of pendant jewels surrounds her neck, and an enormous, squarish brooch is suspended by gold chains. The bodice of her dress is braided, and the sleeves puffed and slashed. She was the fourth daughter (No. 98).

147. Sir ALEXANDER ERSKINE, of Cambuskenneth.

Inscribed, "Anno 1638 Ætatis 26." A mailed figure, older like than the age indicated. A mass of curly, reddish hair surrounds the head, and he wears his moustache and beard *a la* Charles I. The face is almost full. A high collar is worn of moderate dimensions, and there is a scarf round his right shoulder. The attitude is somewhat stiff and formal, but the picture is, on the whole, a favourable example.

He was a colonel in the army, and with his brother-in-law, the Earl of Haddington (No. 97), was blown up at Dunglass Castle in 1640. He is described as one of the handsomest of men, with a noble and expressive countenance. The superstitious notion of his day was that his tragic death. along with some eighty other persons, was the signal vengeance of Heaven on him for his betrayal of Ann Bothwell, the youthful daughter of the Bishop of Orkney. The pathetic and well-known ballad, "Balloo, my boy," per petuates the memory of the liason. It is supposed to have been written by the victim herself, who gives an almost prophetic forecast to the event that "laid the dear deceiver low." The fourth son of the Treasurer and Lady Marie Stuart.

148. Sir JOHN ERSKINE, of Otterstoun. (D. 1654.)

Inscribed "Jamesone." An undoubted work of Jamesone's, but it has under-gone a partial restoration. It represents an erect, bright-eyed man of about twenty-five. He wears a stiffish, fluted collar, sloping down almost from his ears. His doublet is richly brocaded with designs of the pine-leaf pattern. Fifth son of the Lord Treasurer Mar. "The bairn John," as his mother calls him, acquired Otterstoun by marriage.

149. Sir ARTHUR ERSKINE, of Scotscraig.

An excellent example, and pronounced by some to be too good to be the work of Jamesone. Such is not the case, for the artist who painted the lovely Countess of Marischal, in the same apartment, was quite equal to this picture. It represents a long-visaged man, with a short moustache and reddish hair flowing to his shoulders. The unbecoming fashion of concealing the brow with hair detracts from his intellectuality, but not from the artistic value of the canvas. The usual collar, scolloped with lace over a dark stuff tunic, completes his simple costume. The sixth son of this family.

150. The Hon. WILLIAM ERSKINE.

A genuine and untouched example. He is represented with a profusion of long, reddish hair, parted in the middle. The brow is low, and the countenance of the rueful type and quite bare. His shoulders are much sloped for a man, and over a loose tunic he wears a neat collar with lace scollops.

This gentleman was the youngest son of the family. He was cup-bearer to King Charles II., and Master of the Charter House, London.

COLONEL JOHN MURRAY, POLMAISE CASTLE.

151. Sir ALEXANDER GIBSON, of Durie. (D. 1644.)

Much re-painted, but is unquestionably by Jamesone. He wears the lace-trimmed cap usually adopted by the legal profession, with a fluted collar over

a cloak with tippet.   He has a moustache and rounded beard—from ear to
ear.   (See No. 71.)

152. Sir HARRY NISBET, of Dean.

Inscribed, " Sir Hairy Nisbet of Dean."   A characteristic portrait.   Dark hair,
neatly trimmed to the ears, moustache and chin beard.   He wears a fluted
collar over a dark green doublet, slashed with white.

The subject was Lord Provost of Edinburgh, whose daughter was
married to a Murray, of Polmaise, which readily accounts for the presence
of the portrait.

153. UNKNOWN GENTLEMAN.

Inscribed, " 1627."   This picture, although it possesses every suggestion of
Jamesone's work, has been entirely re-painted.   He has dark hair, which
hangs about the brow.   Fluted collar and plain doublet.   His right hand is
introduced at his breast.

THE HON. LORD NAPIER AND ETTRICK, THIRLESTANE CASTLE, SELKIRKSHIRE.

154. ARCHIBALD, 1st Lord Napier.

A fine, manly portrait.   Black hair, moustache, and beard.   Features are well
modelled.   He wears a thick ruff over a dark doublet, slashed with white.
This picture has been well engraved for Mr. Mark Napier's " Life of
Montrose," and his remarks are as follows :—

"As the first Lord Napier was highly distinguished both as a courtier
and as a statesman in the reign of James VI. (whom he served for seventeen
years in the Bedchamber), and also in the reign of Charles I. (who selected
him as the first Scotsman whom he honoured with elevation to the Peerage),
it was not likely that the omission should have occurred of no portrait of him
having been taken by the Vandyck of Scotland.   Accordingly, two portraits
of this Lord Napier by Jamesone are yet preserved, the one which has been
admirably engraved for this biography by Mr. Banks being that possessed
by the family, and the other, that found among the fine collection of
portraits by Jamesone, which decorate the baronial halls of Taymouth
[No. 43, misnamed John, in the Family Collection at Taymouth].   This
last, which we have only seen as a fixture forming a panel above a lofty door,
has every appearance of originality, and though obviously representing the

same individual, does not appear to be a duplicate of that possessed by Lord Napier. Why it is found at Taymouth Castle is accounted for by the fact that Alexander Napier, 6th of Merchiston, who fell at Pinkie, 1547, was married to Anabella Campbell, daughter of Sir Duncan Campbell, of Glenorchy. Both her husband's father (Alexander, 5th of Merchiston) and her own father, Sir Duncan, died at Flodden. Through this marriage the 1st Lord Napier was great-great grandson of Sir Duncan Campbell, of Glenorchy, the owner of the ancient Balloch, now called Taymouth. One of his successors, called Sir Colin Campbell, of Glenorchy, was, says Walpole, 'the chief and earliest patron of Jamesone, who had attended that gentleman on his travels.' Both of the portraits mentioned above are only head-sized, as here engraved. But that possessed by the present Lord Napier has not been well preserved, and presents much of the appearance of having been cut down from a large size. The healing of wounds in an ancient portrait was not so well understood in those days as now."

Archibald, 1st Lord Napier, was the eldest son of the inventor of logarithms.

155. ARCHIBALD, 2nd Lord Napier.

Represents a sweet-featured youth in his minority. A profusion of dark hair hangs over his shoulders, round which hangs a rich, artistic lace collar. Let Mr. Mark Napier again speak of this picture :—

"This interesting portrait of a very interesting personage has, like that of his father, suffered severely between gallery and garret in the hands of heedless though not headless generations. Fortunately the features, complexion, and costume of both have been so far preserved as to enable the engraver to accomplish accurate representations of the original. But in both of these instances, Jameson's tender backgrounds, never made for "The Trubles" either of nation or nursery, have nearly vanished, so as to baffle all attempts at discovering date or signature. Yet the hand of Jamesone may be detected under the ribs of death, and these melancholy remains have considerable life in them still. Moreover, the portrait of the 1st Lord Napier is mentioned in the catalogue of Jamesone's works, and that of the 2nd Lord is obviously from the same pallet."

In company with his cousin, the 2nd Marquis of Montrose, he attempted a rising in Scotland during the Usurpation, under the leadership of Middleton, who was second in command to David Leslie at Philiphaugh. After the failure of that ill-managed attempt he returned to Holland, where he died shortly before the Restoration, when about 36 years of age.

HIS GRACE THE DUKE OF RICHMOND AND GORDON,
GORDON CASTLE.

156. GEORGE, 1st Marquis of Huntly.　(1570-1636.)

Inscribed, " 1630 Æt 64."　A fine picture, although it has probably undergone
a slight retouching.　Represents a man of a stately and dignified bearing.
Dark hair, brushed back from an open brow, regular features, lightish
moustache and peaked beard.　He wears the fluted collar over a coat of mail,
relieved by a red sash.　Another portrait on a rather larger scale at Gordon
Castle possesses features that indicate the hand probably of Vandyck.　When
the Castle of Strathbogie, as well as Bog o' Gight, now Gordon Castle, were
both residences of the family, there was probably a portrait in each.

The life and character of the Marquis are matters of public notoriety.
He lived in crucial times, and, filling a prominent position as Royal Lieutenant
in the North, he played a high game.　The Cock of the North, "called with
the lukken hand," is said never to have drawn a sword in his own quarrel.
"In his youth a prodigal spender, in his old age more wise and worldly
. . .　A great householder ; a terror to his enemies, whom he ever with his
prideful ken held under subjection and obedience ; just in all his bargains ; and
never heard for his true debt.　He was mightily envied by the Kirk for his
religion, and by others for his greatness, and thereby had much trouble.　A
princely, enterprising man.　He was constantly building, repairing, and
planting, yet he died under a strange roof on his way home from Edinburgh,
to which he had been summoned to give an account of his loyalty."　He was
married to Henrietta Stewart, daughter to Esme, Duke of Lennox, whose
name, with his own, still decorates the magnificent ruin of Huntly Castle.

157. GEORGE, 2nd Marquis of Huntly.　(D. 1649.)

Inscribed, "1630."　A genuine Jamesone, although it has the peculiarity of
inclining to the right to pair with his Marchioness (No. 158).　The face is
very characteristic, and exhibits a timid, vacillating man.　He has long, dark
hair, which falls over his shoulders, with beard and moustache of Charles I.,
whose general cast of features his own resembles.　He is clad in steel and
gilt armour, with a deep point lace colour.

The Marquis had not the grit of his father.　He was always making vain
demonstrations of loyalty, always in trouble with the Kirk and the Parliament.　He allowed himself to be outwitted by the more nimble-minded
Montrose, whom he never forgave for his astuteness.　After many alternations of fortune, he was brought to the scaffold on the 16th March, 1649.
"The man," says Baillie, "is of good discourse, but neither trusted by King
nor country."　He was married to Lady Ann Campbell, daughter of the Duke
of Argyll.

158. The MARCHIONESS OF HUNTLY. (1608-1638.)

Inscribed, " 1626 Æt 18." Like her husband's (No. 157), this is a genuine example, and just as it left Jamesone's easel. It is very pure in tone, but somewhat thinly painted. The face is pale, with cherry lips. Around it is a mass of auburn hair, in which a black pin ornament is seen on the right. A long pendant ear-ring hangs on the neck. Chains surround her neck, and suspend a breast ornament, whilst a magnificent brooch unites a highly-ornamental point lace collar. She wears a Court dress of her time, a black velvet bodice, open over a rich white robe brocaded in colours. Her sleeves are studded with jewels. In short, an evident effort has been made to respond to the poetical invocation of Arthur Johnston (page 53), and the happy result is one of Jamesone's best portraits.

The Marchioness was a lady held in high esteem. Straloch speaks of her as " a pattern of piety and virtue."

Edward Raban, on 6th June, 1638, published a work which he had compiled himself, entitled " The Glorie of Man, consisting in the Excellencie and Perfection of Woman." It is dedicated to " Ladie Anna Cambel Ladie Marqves of Hvntley." A complimentary couplet says—

> " Let Honourable Woman live for ever
> In all that Arte that Tyme that Fame can give her."

Poor lady ! the ink was scarcely dry when she died at Old Aberdeen on the 14th of the month. Her sudden and dangerous sickness recalled the Marquis from Edinburgh, where he was deeply engaged. She died before her husband reached home, and she was buried in the Cathedral Church of Oldmachar with all usual solemnity eight days thereafter.

Her funeral card is subjoined, and possesses some interest :—

" Right assured Freynd

" It has pleased God of his mercie to call our bedfellow from this transitorie lyf to the fruitione of eternall joyes, whose corpes we intend God willing to interre in St Macher Kirke of auld Aberdeen vpon Tuysday the xxij of Junii instant. These ar therfoir to intreat yowr presens that day be eleivin houres to assist for doing of the last honour to the depairted as we shal be readie to acknowledge and acquyte your courtesie quhen occasion shall offer. In assurance of your comeing we rest. Your assured freynd

" HUNTLYE."

" Abed 18 Junii 1638."

159. JOHN GORDON, Viscount Melgum.

A youngish man, a half-length in steel armour. He was the second son of the

1st Marquis of Huntly. This portrait derives much interest from the circumstance that the subject of it was one of the victims who was burnt to death
in the House of Frendraught on the 18th October, 1630. He was married to
Lady Sophia Hay, a daughter of the Earl of Errol. The pathetic ballad
which describes the tragic event also relates the effect its narration had on
Lady Melgum. She upbraids the messenger :—

> " O wae be to you, George Gordon,
>   An ill death may ye dee ;
> Sae safe and sound as ye stand there,
>   And my lord bereaved from me.
>
> " I bade him loup ; I bade him come ;
>   I bade him come to me ;
> I'd catch him in my armis two ;
>   A foot I should not flee.
>
> " He threw me rings from his white fingers,
>   Which were so long and small,
> To give to you, his lady fair,
>   Where you sat in your hall.
>
> " Sophia Hay, Sophia Hay,
>   O bonnie Sophie was her name ;
> Her waiting maid put on her clothes,
>   But I wat she tore them off again."

MAJOR JOHN ROSS, OF KINCORTH, QUEEN'S GARDENS,
ABERDEEN.

160. ALEXANDER THOMSON, of Portlethen.

A replica of No. 25.

161. The ARTIST.

The genuineness of this beautiful and well-known picture has been doubted without any better reason than a lurking scepticism, based on ignorance, that
Jamesone could paint so well. It may with justice be said that Jamesone
has done little more for himself than paint his own portrait, but happily it is
a masterpiece. After his " greater master," he represents himself in a broad-
brimmed hat, gracefully set. His silky, light-brown hair flows out over his

ears, whilst the moustache and peaked beard attest the cavalier fashion of the time of Charles I. The face is the artist's usual three-quarter view.

The features are those of a refined, rather handsome, educated man, and bespeak him as a person of good nature, and easy of access. He is attired in a woollen stuff cloak, with some sort of embroidery, or, perhaps, gold lace round the edge of the tippet. Over the cloak is worn a close fluted linen collar of moderate dimensions.

The right arm emerges from the thick folds of the cloak, and in the linen, wrist-banded hand he holds an oval miniature, a style of art in which he sometimes indulged, although, unfortunately, there exist no known specimens in it to attest his skill. In the left hand his palette and pencils are held. The lines of the picture are all more or less easy, and its prevailing tones are well harmonised, and impart a rich mellow feeling to the whole canvas, which is in most excellent preservation. It has come into the hands of the present possessor by direct lineal descent through Mary Jamesone. The picture is engraved in Chambers's " Lives of Eminent Scotsmen."

THE RIGHT HON. THE COUNTESS OF ROTHES,
LESLIE HOUSE.

162. JOHN LESLIE, 5th Earl of Rothes. (1600-1641.)

An excellent example, characteristic in every respect. He has long dark hair brushed back behind his shoulders. He has a sedate expression, and resembles a Puritan divine. A fine linen collar, with deep lace border, covers a dark doublet, the inside of the sleeves being slit, showing white beneath.

The Earl was a great Covenanter, and took a most active, courageous, and consistent part in the affairs of Church and State. He has always been understood to be the personal friend of the artist, whom he probably met for the first time at the Coronation ceremonies of 1633, on which occasion Rothes carried the sceptre in the procession from the Castle to the Chapel Royal. Among the various public duties of importance that he filled in his day was that of Commissioner for the Scots at the Treaty of Ripon. He died at Richmond after a very sudden illness. He is described as a man of joyous habits, and with but little of the Puritan about him.

163. ANOTHER.

A full-length portrait. A careful inspection does not quite dispel a doubt as to

22

its genuineness. This may arise from its unwonted character. He is standing at a table on which is a large open volume, on which his hand rests, and a small clock, a pillar, and curtain occupy the right of the picture. In the background, on a wall, hangs a small framed picture. Over the picture is painted a piece of white paper, with one corner turned up, showing a man's hand, presumably that of the King, the Constitutional struggle with whom was probably far advanced before this portrait of the Earl was painted. It has been engraved by the Bannatyne Club in their quarto volume, containing "A Relation of proceedings concerning the affairs of the Kirk of Scotland, from 1637 to July, 1638," written by the Earl.

164. The COUNTESS of ROTHES and her Two CHILDREN, in full length.

This is a companion canvas to that of No. 163. The pose of the lady is very easy and natural. Her right hand rests on a table before an open window, and her left is grasped by one of her little daughters. She wears in her hair a small bunch of white feathers, and a large lozenge-shaped brooch on her breast. Her dress is a striped or plaited stuff, reaching to the ground, and scolloped at the foot. The children, Ladies Margaret and Mary, seem to be about four or five years old. They wear skull caps and high collars, with their dresses to the ground. The one has a lap full of flowers, and the other a bunch in her hand. The group is very pleasant and domestic. On the back wall of the room is a series of nine miniature portraits, very carefully painted. Overhead, and at the left side, is a festooned curtain. As Lady Ann Erskine (No. 144), Jamesone painted this lady before, that portrait remaining in the possession of her mother, the Countess of Mar.

165. UNKNOWN GENTLEMAN.

An undoubted work of Jamesone's, which, however, may have undergone some handling by another. He has dark hair brought over his brow. The collar is large, and with a deeply-indented, Gothic lace border. A coloured scarf crosses the shoulder.

It is surmised to be a portrait of Montrose, but it is wholly unlike his now familiar features ; nor is Leslie House just the place where one might expect to meet the Marquis. It is much more likely to be a portrait of Sir Alexander Gibson, of Durie, although certainly not a replica of either of the other portraits Jamesone painted of this gentleman. A portrait of Sir Alexander has been said to be at Leslie, but no picture there bears his name.

166. General ALEXANDER LESLIE, 1st Earl of Leven. (D. 1661.)
    See No. 128.

Inscribed, " Anno 1635 Ætatis 53," in the left corner, and the Leslie arms in the
right.   It is not quite in Jamesone's usual style.   The General is painted in
half length, standing with his right hand resting on a table in front.   Did we
not know that he was of a very diminutive stature, as well as deformed in
person, the large, bullet-shaped head would be quite disproportionate to the
body.   Baillie, "setting down naught in malice," calls him "an old, little,
crooked soldier."   The face has been much repainted, which helps to dis-
sociate Jamesone from it.   He is dressed in military uniform, with sword,
scarf, and belts.   As the most successful of all the Generals of the Covenanting arms, his life and career are well known.   By the Covenanting party his
services to the good cause were justly appreciated.   To his opponents he was
at once an object of scorn and of fear.

> " From Leslie's quondam excellence
> Who wants too long a recompence
> For his good : yet however
> Better he have it late than never.
>   .   .   .   .   .   .
>   Almighty God deliver us."

THE HON. THE LORD SALTOUN, PHILORTII,
FRASERBURGH.

167. ALEXANDER FRASER, Laird of Philorth. (1570-1636.)

Inscribed " 1623."   A well drawn head, but unfortunately in colour bears evident
trace of Giles' peculiar treatment.   The hair of the head is dark, that of the
moustache and brush-like beard lighter.   The collar is small and plain.   This
gentleman is usually designated *Sir* Alexander, but this appears to be an
error.   He was the son of Sir Alexander, 8th of Philorth, founder of
Fraserburgh, and was married to Margaret Abernethy, daughter of George,
7th Lord Saltoun, and afterwards to Isabel, daughter of Sir Robert
Gordon of Lochinvar.

168. WILLIAM FORBES, of Tolquhon.

Inscribed as above, and "JAMEISON" (sic).   An undoubted example.   An
oldish, spare man, with a cap worn in a jaunty way, somewhat to one side,

and a ruff.   Grayish moustache and chin beard.   The picture possesses a
good deal of character.

Forbes, of Tolquhon, is well known in the north as of a family at once
ancient and honourable, namely, that of the Lords Forbes.   The subject of
this picture built the Castle of Tolquhon.   His daughter was married to Sir
Alexander Fraser, of Philorth, hence his presence here.

THE REPRESENTATIVES OF THE RIGHT HON. THE LATE EARL OF SEAFIELD, CULLEN HOUSE, BANFFSHIRE.

169. PORTRAIT OF THE ARTIST IN HIS STUDIO, Surrounded by
Representations of his Principal Works.

This work is interesting from several points of view.   It contains the only known
specimens of Jamesone as a painter of mythological pictures and sea pieces ;
and if these miniatures are fair samples of the originals, in the loss of them
the artist's reputation has sustained some damage.   Nothing is now known
of the circumstances in which this picture was painted, or how it has come
into the possession of the Seafield Family (formerly Earls of Findlater), but it
may be considered a brand plucked from the burning.   In the year following
Jamesone's death, and during the fiercely contested civil war in which the
country was unhappily engaged, the troops of Montrose met with no resistance
in their spoliation of Elgin, Cullen, and Banff.   In the immediate vicinity of
Cullen lay the house of the Earl of Findlater, and, with its valuable contents,
this very picture, probably, being one of them, it was spared destruction by
fire, only by the payment of a heavy ransom.

A reference to this picture, as engraved for the first time in the present
volume, will render unnecessary any detailed description of it.   The features
of the artist are somewhat heavier than are those of No. 161, when Jamesone
was probably a younger man.   This is certainly the latest portrait of the
artist.   The pictures on the wall of his painting room are not easy to identify.
Three of them are said to be those of Charles I., Queen Henrietta Maria, and
Jamesone's own wife.   The King's portrait is the only one quite recognis-
able.   No conjecture has been hazarded as to the remaining four portraits.
The large classical piece has been supposed to be that of Perseus and
Andromeda, and with some reason.   Perseus seems just to have discovered the
naked Andromeda bound to a rock.   Underneath this picture is a suggestion
of a sea piece on one side, and a landscape on the other.   Beneath all, the
sand-glass, armour, and escutcheon with skull, the usual properties of an artist's
studio of the period, are introduced.   The picture is in excellent keeping.

THE HON. THE LORD SEMPILL, FINTRAY HOUSE, ABERDEENSHIRE.

170. Sir WILLIAM FORBES, cf Craigievar.

This picture has suffered restoration, but still retains much of the feeling of Jamesone. It represents a man approaching forty, with short hair and peaked beard and ruff.

Sir William took a keen interest in the politics of his day, ranging himself on the Covenanting side. He was taken prisoner at the battle of Aberdeen, in 1645, where he commanded a troop of horse. He had afterwards several public engagements.

171. Dr. PATRICK FORBES, of Corse, Bishop of Aberdeen. (1564-1632.)

This not very favourable example of Jamesone is rendered less interesting on account of the restorer's efforts. In this case the hand of Mr. Giles is apparent. The pose and general treatment are those of Jamesone. The Bishop wears a black skull cap over a broad expanse of forehead. A thick set beard covers the under part of the face, and a heavy ruff to his ears produces a very short-necked appearance.

The Bishop was of the same stock as the noble owner. It is given to few men to lead such an influential life as that of Dr. Patrick Forbes, who was probably the most distinguished Bishop that ever occupied the See of Aberdeen. The powerful head of this prelate in Marischal College has been mistakenly assigned to Jamesone. It does not in the least possess his peculiar manner.

THE RIGHT HON. THE EARL OF STAIR, K.T., OXENFOORD CASTLE, DALKEITH.

172. UNKNOWN GENTLEMAN.

Inscribed, "Ætatis 21." This represents a bare-faced, pale youth, whose paleness is enhanced by being set in a background of black hair resting on his shoulders and partly covering the collar. He is habited in a brocaded black stuff dress with white stripes. This is altogether a sombre portrait, but neither unpleasant nor uninteresting.

173. UNKNOWN GENTLEMAN.

The likeness of a sallow-complexioned man, copious yellow hair falling over his

shoulders. The subject is somewhat hard of feature, and wears a plain white
collar and black stuff dress with white stripes.

174. UNKNOWN LADY.

An excellent example of the artist. It is inscribed, "Ætatis 23." The head is
well posed ; the breast partially covered with frilled lace work. A chain,
with jewelled pendant, encircles the neck.

THE RIGHT HON. THE EARL OF SOUTHESK, KINNAIRD CASTLE, FORFARSHIRE.

175. Sir DAVID CARNEGIE, 1st Earl of Southesk.

This is a work of great merit, showing the artist in his best form. It is in the
artist's "wonted attitude," but there is an unusual care and solidness in the
modelling of the features, and the result is a well-relieved, splendid head,
such as befitted the founder of the noble House of Southesk. He wears a
round velvet cap, and looks the age indicated on the picture. His beard is
grizzly, and is cloven in shape. The picture is inscribed, "Ætatis 62, 1637."

Sir David was an eminent lawyer and a senator of the College of
Justice, under the title of Lord Carnegie, of Kinnaird, until raised to the
peerage as Earl of Southesk by Charles I. on his memorable visit to
Scotland in 1633. His mind was pre-eminently judicial in its caste, and he
bore the character of an upright judge, as well as of a "sagacious, prudent,
and honourable statesman." During the Constitutional struggles of the
period his moderation and capability well fitted him to act the part of
mediator between the King and the people. He was not successful in his
rôle of peacemaker, and enjoyed no more immunity from "The Trubles" than
the extremest of partisans. His calm and steady allegiance to King Charles
led to his imprisonment at the hands of the Covenanters, and, his
"wishing well to the King and monarchy," brought him under a fine of £3000
by Cromwell. Arthur Johnston characterises him in one of his Latin
epigrams—

"Nec numero clauduntur opes nec limite rura
Carnegi, servat mens tamen alta modum."

A lithographic copy of the portrait is reproduced in the "History of the
Carnegies," by William Fraser, LL.D., 1867.

176. Sir ALEXANDER CARNEGIE, of Balnamoon.

Inscribed, "Ætatis 50 . 1637." Jamesone's hand is very marked on this picture, which is painted with much freedom. Sir Alexander has an abundance of curly auburn hair, the rounded short beard showing it of a lighter colour. The face bespeaks a man of sprightly intelligence.

Sir Alexander was a public-spirited, liberal man, and carried through many useful measures in his district. Among others, he built the Church of Careston, and endowed it with the sum of 4000 merks.

177. Sir ROBERT CARNEGIE, of Dunnichen.

Inscribed, " Ætatis 41 . 1629." A fine head. The bare temples, the moustache and peaked beard, and general aspect, are all suggestive of Shakespeare. The costume is of a black material striped with silk, the sleeves being slashed with white shown beneath.

Sir Robert is the youngest of the Carnegie quartette of brothers, and the portrait was painted in the same year as his young nephew-in-law, the youthful Montrose.

178. Sir JOHN CARNEGIE, 1st Earl of Northesk.

Inscribed, " Ætatis 58 . 1637." This portrait bears a pretty strong family resemblance to that of his elder brother, Sir David, and it would be stronger but for the peculiar way that his hair, escaping from the velvet cap he wears, hangs over his brow. The beard is cut square and is of a dark brown colour. There is considerable character in the head.

Sir John took an active interest in public affairs, and his rewards for adhesion to the Royal cause were his ultimate elevation to the Earldom of Northesk by Charles I. in 1649, and the heavy fine of £6000 imposed by Cromwell in 1654. Part of his correspondence has been preserved, and it reveals him to have been a warm-hearted, affectionate man.

These four splendid portraits are massed together over the fire-place in the dining-room in this magnificent mansion.

179. JAMES GRAHAM, 5th Earl, afterwards 1st Marquis, of Montrose. (B. 1612, D. 1650.)

This painting represents Montrose at the youthful age of seventeen, still a student at St. Andrews, although just on the eve of his marriage. The picture is inscribed, "Anno 1629 Ætatis 17, Jamesone fecit." It is on a panel—somewhat thinly painted—and after well nigh three hundred years begins to assume that condition temptingly suggestive of restoration. How to *preserve* the painting in its present condition is, however, the all-important consideration.

The preservation of this first and invaluable portrait of Montrose is due

to the Southesk Family, whose castle walls at Kinnaird it has not once
quitted since it was first hung up on the 2nd December, 1629.   To the late
Mr. Mark Napier belongs the honour of revealing this painting as a veritable
portrait of the great Marquis.   In this Mr. Napier has been quite as successful as in his tireless efforts to rescue from unmerited obliquy the character of
his hero.   The story of the discovery is so interestingly narrated by Mr.
Napier that no apology is needed for giving it in his own words :—

"On the 3rd of November, 1629, Montrose rode to Aberdeen from
Morphie, the seat of Sir Robert Graham, one of his curators, and there had
his portrait painted.   At this time he was just seventeen years of age, and on
the 10th of November, 1629, as the same accounts prove, he was married to
the daughter of Lord Carnegie of Kinnaird (afterwards Earl of Southesk), in
the kirk within the park of Kinnaird.   The young couple immediately took
up their abode in the Castle of Kinnaird on 2nd Dec., 1629, and from a note
in the account books the picture would seem to have been a marriage
present from Graham of Morphie to the young Countess.   The artist's name
is not mentioned in the accounts, but as George Jamesone, Scotland's only
known artist of the period, was at that very time following the profession of a
portrait painter in his native town of Aberdeen, the reason of the young
nobleman riding to Aberdeen to sit for his portrait is manifest.   The discovery, of course, suggested the inquiry whether a portrait of Montrose was
yet preserved among the family pictures at Kinnaird Castle.   The desideratum was a portrait of Montrose painted in 1629, when he was seventeen
years of age, and painted by Jamesone.   The facts disclosed by accounts had
been with those neglected papers long buried in oblivion.   Yet the tradition
seems to have been transmitted in the family that the gallery of Kinnaird
could boast of a portrait of Montrose.   Tradition, however, had settled on a
wrong one.   When we first visited the castle in search of it, there was
pointed out as such the head and bust of a middle-aged, steel-clad warrior,
black and truculent as the Covenant could desire, but without any resemblance to Montrose in feature, expression, or complexion at any period of his
life.   A glance sufficed to reject the grim usurper ; a little more was required
by a more experienced eye to attract it to a portrait of the young Montrose
decorating the same wall.   A boy of fair and somewhat delicate complexion
was smiling at the spectator with an aspect that bespoke not of 'The
Trubles,' but the port, erect and lordly, the exuberant auburn hair of a
fairer hue than the later portraits, the 'penetrating grey eye,' the finely-
moulded nose, with its sensitive nostril, and the characteristic expression of
the pressed lips, as yet devoid of a shadow of a moustache, at once suggested
the young Montrose.   Then the sumptuous dress—a rich olive velvet
doublet, profusely slashed with white satin and edge trimmed with gold, and

over the collar a lace ruff of the most delicate texture—seemed to announce the Boy Benedict in his wedding bravery. A closer inspection discovered these dates painted by the original artist on the upper corner, to the right of the head—'Anno 1629.   Ætatis 17 ;' and in the background, near the left shoulder, this autograph—'Jamesone fecit.' The problem was solved.

"The pupil of Rubens and fellow-student of Vandyck might well put his name to this interesting and graceful portrait, which had been called Sir John Carnegie of the Craig, upon no better authority than if it had been dubbed Sir John Colvil of the Dale. It is a head size generally adopted (from necessity) by Jamesone, and in the usual conventional position, half in profile, with the right shoulder presented to the spectator. Like most of the early portraits of that master, it is painted on panel. A slight flaw down the centre, which fortunately mars no feature, is the only injury of any conse-quence incurred through the lapse of two centuries.   It is 'signed all over,' even had the artist not added his name.   For there is no mistaking the light rapid pencil, warm priming, and thin transparent colouring of Scotland's only artist in the great era of painting.

"No type or shadow of the warrrior's career is to be found in that portrait. Not even the hilt of a dagger.   The artist had only to deal with the lively schoolboy, who headed the sports at St. Andrews, and led the Christmas revels at Balcarres, and in many others of the ancient halls of Scotland, whose college fame was chronicled by a poor 'Hungarian Poet,' whose ancestral glories and early promise were lauded in more ambitious strains by William Lithgow, and who, wherever he went, was welcome to the rich and kind to the poor ; and fed his hunter with loaf-bread and ale ; and delighted in minstrels and mummery ; and who was now, while yet a boy, on the eve of separating himself from the ways and means of boyhood to settle as a married man at Kinnaird with sweet Mistress Magdalene Carnegie. The engraving of this long obscured work by a master of whom Scotland may well be proud, now for the first time attached to a biography of its illustrious subject, was executed, in 1848, for the historical collection which the author compiled under the munificent auspices of the Maitland Club, and entitled, 'Memorials of Montrose.'   The liberality of that great literary society was further extended to bestowing the plate upon this new biography of the hero."

Not a bad proof that Jamesone had thoroughly succeeded in catching the family likeness in this picture is to be found in the following testimony of Lady M. Carnegie in reference to it.   She says, "A member of the present family is so very like the portrait that it may be taken for an excellent likeness of his descendant after the lapse of two and a half centuries."

ARCHIBALD CAMPBELL SWINTON, ESQ., OF KIMMERGHAME, DUNS.

180. WILLIAM, Lord Alexander. (D. 1638.)

Inscribed, "Anno 1628 Ætatis 24." This is one of the few portraits in armour painted by Jamesone. The mail is relieved by a figured and fringed sash which crosses the shoulder. A lace collar, carefully done, also enlivens the subject. The portrait is characteristic.

This nobleman was the eldest son of the 1st Earl of Stirling, who was celebrated in his day as a poet, politician, and promoter of extensive schemes of colonisation. The Earl was Secretary of State for Scotland, and contrived, by his various enterprises, to amass an enormous fortune, which Lord Alexander, the subject of this picture, did not live to enjoy, having pre-deceased his father two years.

HIS GRACE THE DUKE OF SUTHERLAND, DUNROBIN CASTLE, SUTHERLANDSHIRE.

181. Lady JEAN GORDON, Countess of Bothwell, and afterwards Countess of Sutherland. (1544-1629.)

Few more interesting pictures are contained in this Catalogue. Dr. John Stuart, in "A Lost Chapter in the History of Mary Queen of Scots," where Lady Jean's portrait is engraved, says of it:—"Nothing is known of the artist, but it seems plain that the portrait was painted when Lady Jean was well advanced in years." Here there is a total ignoring of Jamesone, whose hand was, at least, not perfectly obvious on the picture. Still there is not much reason to doubt its genuineness. In the first place, Jamesone could not have painted Lady Jean before she was an elderly woman, and although this is no proof that he did it then, there is the evidence of style. This is somewhat difficult to judge of, as the picture has lost tone and become very brown from successive varnishings, applied with the mistaken view of refreshing it. So far, however, as size, drawing, and pose reveal anything, it is that Jamesone was the artist. Lady Jean is attired in a bonnet, with the deep veil of a widow— a widow for the third time. She is seated, and the high chair forms a sort of background. The features are rather marked, and exhibit a character of firmness, but one not devoid of feeling. The mouth is quite in Jamesone's manner. The face is very pale, and the hair perfectly silvered. Lady Jean, who clung tenaciously to the old faith, wears a rosary, which is suspended in her right hand, on the *back* of which an attached cross lies. The portrait, as a whole, enables us to realise the personal appearance of one who, as Dr. J. Hill Burton says, "was in a manner drifted in among the stormiest incidents of her day, and then floated off into calm waters."

The grave face of this tried, prudent, and amiable noblewoman carries a history with it. Lady Jean Gordon was the third daughter of George, 4th Earl of Huntly, who fell at Corrichie. She was consequently much about the Court and on very intimate terms with the Queen. In 1667, she married the profligate Earl of Bothwell, but not before a Papal dispensation was obtained, the pair being within the prohibited degrees. In no long time, Bothwell, in order that he might marry Queen Mary, sued successfully for a divorce from Lady Jean, the one plea being that their propinquity was too close for the holy state of matrimony into which they had drifted *without* a dispensation. When it is remembered that Lady Jean's marriage was "with aduis and expres counsale of our souerane lady Marie Quene of Scotland," who gave the bride a handsome dress of cloth of silver, lined with taffeta, as a wedding gift, a strange insight is obtained into the views of the married relation entertained by these three interested persons. Lady Jean's position is the most inexplicable, for she was in possession of the dispensation that would have established her wifely claim and did not use it, but quietly retired from the scene to the Castle of Strathbogie, carrying the precious document with her. Bothwell's marriage with the Queen, his disgrace and exile, are matters of general history. On a false report of the death of her worthless husband, Lady Jean imagined herself free to marry again, and she accepted the youthful Alexander, 11th Earl of Sutherland, as her second husband. To her new home at Dunrobin Castle she carried her dispensation with her, and there the interesting discovery was made of its actual existence in the Sutherland Charter Chest by Dr. Stuart a few years ago. The Earl's death, in 1594, left Lady Jean a widow a second time, with the added responsibility of rearing her family and managing her vast estates. All this she did with signal prudence and ability. In 1599, she contracted a third marriage with Alexander Ogilvie, of Boyne, a cadet of the Findlater Family, who had been formerly married to Mary Beaton (Bethune), one of the Queen's four Marys. Lady Jean survived her third husband, to whom she had no family, and died at Dunrobin in May, 1629. Her son, Sir Robert Gordon, of Gordonstoun, the historian of the House of Sutherland, pays this affectionate tribute to his worthy mother :— "A vertuous and comlie lady, judicious, of excellent memorie, and of great understanding above the capacitie of her sex."

THE MOST NOBLE THE MARQUIS OF TWEEDDALE,
YESTER, HADDINGTONSHIRE.

182. JOHN HAY, 1st Earl of Tweeddale. (D. 1654.)

Inscribed, "Ætatis 33, 1628." Little doubt exists on the question of the genuineness of this portrait, yet the restoration to which it has been subjected greatly effaces Jamesone's touch. Lord Tweeddale's hair is dark brown and long. His moustache and beard are of the Charles I. type. He wears a large ruff. His doublet is black and slashed with white.

When the portrait was executed, the subject was 8th Baron of Tweeddale. When "The Trubles" began, he commanded a regiment in the Royal Army; and, in 1646, King Charles rewarded his loyalty by elevating him to the dignity of an Earl. He was married first to a daughter of the Earl of Dunfermline, and secondly to a daughter of the Earl of Eglinton.

183. COUNTESS OF TWEEDDALE.

Inscribed, "1628." This portrait, like its companion, has been much injured by being repainted in the face by an inferior hand. The Countess looks to the right, and is attired in a veil and ruff. Her bodice is very flat and stiff, with but little fabric feeling. The sleeves are striped and slashed.

This lady is evidently the first Earl's first wife, Jane Abercromby, daughter of the Earl of Dunfermline.

184. UNKNOWN GENTLEMAN.

The picture is inscribed, "1644," the year of Jamesone's death, and is probably one of the last, as it is one of the finest, that ever came from his hand. The subject is handsome, and painted with a becoming dignity. His hair is auburn and flowing, with moustache and imperial. He wears a lace collar and sash over a coat of mail. The loss of the name and historical identity has in all likelihood led to such a neglect of this portrait that it happily stands revealed as an untouched and most characteristic specimen.

CAPTAIN F. E. POLLARD-URQUHART, OF CRAIGSTON,
CRAIGSTON CASTLE.

185. Sir DAVID LESLEY. (D. 1682.)

Inscribed, "Anno 1642." This fine picture is engraved in Pinkerton, but in a manner that is wholly misleading : the result, probably, of a faulty sketch.

The painting itself is not quite in its original condition, and betrays traces of Giles' hand. Sir David has sandy-coloured, lightly, flowing hair, with heavy moustache and peaked beard. His eye is keen, and his general aspect that of a soldier of purpose. A rich lace collar surmounts a coat of mail.

General David Lesley (or Leslie), next to his kinsman, Alexander Leslie, with whom he is often confounded, was one of the most celebrated Generals in the Covenanting Army. Bred in the military school of Gustavus Adolphus, he returned to Scotland on the outbreak of the Civil War, and, under the Earl of Leven, became a Major-General, and throughout the period took a leading part in all the military enterprises. It was he who, though with a far superior force, defeated Montrose at Philiphaugh, and at a later date pressed sore on Cromwell himself, and, had he not been urged by a committee to fight at Dunbar, might have out-generalled the Protector. As it was, he suffered signal defeat. He was at the Battle of Worcester in 1651, but in retreating was captured and committed to the Tower, where he remained nine years a prisoner, and besides suffered a fine of £4000. He was held in high esteem by his party for his services and his sufferings, and received many proofs of their goodwill. After the Restoration, Charles II. raised him to the peerage as Lord Newark, a title long since extinct.

186. Dr. WILLIAM FORBES, Bishop of Edinburgh. (1585-1634.)

Inscribed, "D Gulielmus Forbesius Primus Episcopus Edinburgensis Anno 1634 Ætatis 52." Is suggestive of Jamesone, but the picture has been repainted by an inferior hand, who has left it very raw. The date or the age is wrong, for the date of his birth was 1585.

It is unfortunate that no worthier portrait exists by Jamesone of this eminent prelate, to whom reference has been made in the text. His career and character are too well known to require any extended notice here. He was of the family of Forbes of Corsindae, in Aberdeenshire. He graduated at Marischal College at the early age of sixteen, and whilst still in his teens was appointed to the Chair of Logic there. This he filled for four years, and then ran the curriculum of the principal seats of learning on the Continent. On excellent natural endowments Forbes engrafted the cultured results of ardent study and wide reading. These he consecrated to the office of the ministry, and on his return home, in 1610, he was appointed, in succession to Alford, Monymusk, and St. Nicholas, Aberdeen. He was a distinguished preacher, not alone for his learning and eloquence, but for his unaffected piety, and was respected and beloved by all ranks. In 1618, he was appointed Principal of Marischal College, and taught in the Faculty of Divinity. He was translated to Edinburgh for a short time, but returned to

Aberdeen until appointed by King Charles first Bishop of Edinburgh, in 1634. Never a robust man, hard study and a fervid manner of preaching wore him out at the age of forty nine, when he died, leaving behind him the savour of a good name.

THE SCOTS COLLEGE, ROME.

Four historical pictures are freely exhibited by the authorities there as from the pencil of George Jamesone. The Most Noble the Marquis of Huntly kindly communicates the following information on this interesting subject :—" I have much pleasure in giving you the information I possess as to Jamesone's pictures in the College at Rome. The College was founded by the Marchioness of Huntly, the widow either of George, 2nd Marquis, or [more probably] of the 3rd Marquis, and in the Chapel there are four or five pictures by George Jamesone. They are placed rather high up on panel, and appear to have been painted there, or expressly for the places they are in. They seemed to me excellent examples of the artist, but not so good as his works at Kinnaird Castle, which I consider his best." Then the Very Reverend Monsignore Campbell, Principal of the College, obligingly furnishes the following details of the paintings :—" The works attributed to Jamesone in the Church of St. Andrew, at the Scots College in Rome, are four oblong paintings on canvas, two metres in length by one metre in height, placed in compartments on the lateral walls of the church, two on each side. We have nothing but tradition and the style of art in proof of their authorship. The figures are life-size half lengths.

I. On the Gospel or left side, next the High Altar :—

SAINTLY KINGS.

A King in royal mantle, crowned, and holding in his right hand a naked sword with his left raised, seems to address a younger man similarly crowned and robed who carries the model of a church. In the background another King and noble attendants (King Malcolm Caenmore and David I. ?).

II. On the Epistle side, facing No. I. :—

SAINTLY BISHOPS.

A bishop mitred and carrying his crozier, a white dove hovering near his shoulder. Behind him another bishop with a branch of palm in his right hand and crozier in his left. In the background four other bishops with croziers and attendants.

III. On the Gospel side, farthest from the High Altar :—

SAINTLY QUEENS.

A queen (Saint Margaret?) holding an open book and contemplating the symbol of the Holy Trinity in the clouds. Near her another princess, crowned, regards her with veneration. In the background a number of noble ladies.

IV. On the Epistle side, opposite to No. III. :—

SAINTLY RELIGIOUS WOMEN.

St. Ursula bearing a banner in her left and a palm branch in her right. On one side a noble lady having a palm branch, on the other a religious, with a branch of lilies in her hand. In the background a number of female figures carrying palms."

Such is the historical evidence that awaits the confirmation of critical examination in proof of the genuineness of these pictures. The former is not strong and scarcely such as to *presage* support from the latter. Certainly the 2nd Marchioness of Huntly (No. 158), the daughter of the Covenanting Marquis of Argyll, neither founded the Scots College at Rome nor did she commission an artist to paint such pictures. Granting that the 3rd Marchioness was the foundress, the chronology will scarcely admit of our believing that Jamesone executed the pictures for her. Very much cannot be said as to the probability or otherwise of Jamesone executing such a class of paintings ; but, pending the report of an expert on the internal evidence of their style, they may be left unnumbered and our judgment suspended.

APPENDIX.

PAGE 29. The following are extracts from the Sasines Books of the Burgh of Aberdeen. They all refer to the properties in which the Jamesones had an interest, and are to some extent corrective of hitherto received statements of the family history.

No. 1, under date 27th May, 1586, describes the Schoolhill property by Andre Watsoun in favour of "Andre Jameson latomo libero artifici dicti burgi," the artist's father :—

Totam et Integram Terra sua anteriorem tam subtur q^m supra jacen infra dictu burgu in vico Scholari ex boreali parte eiusdem vici Inter terra Daudis Indeaucht ex orientali ex vica terra olim Adami Mair nunc vero heredid quondam Magistris Villelmi Carmichaell ex occidentali partibus ab altera Terra Interiorem dicti Andre Watsoun versus borea et toiem viam regiam versus austim.

No. 2 is in favour of Meriorie Anderson, during her life, of land by Andrew Jamesone, her husband. It is seemingly the same property as the above, and is a provision for Mrs. Jamesone in the event of her husband's death. It is dated 3rd December, 1607 :—

Totam et Integram terra suam anteriorem tam subtur q^m supra Jacen infra dictu burgu in vico Scholari ex boreali parte eiusdem via Inter terra anteriore quondam Dauidis Indeaucht nec vero roberti forbes te mendatarii de Monymusk ex orientali ex vica terra quondam Adami Mair ex occiendatali partibus ab altera terra Interiorem Andree Watsoun fabri liguarii vertis borea et toiem viam regiam vertis austris. Necnon terram sua de Novo edificatam cespitibus coopertam de prefecto Inhabitat per dictis Andream Jacen in australi latero dicti via scholaris Inter terra quondam James robertson nec vero . . . ex occidentali ex vica cum terra dicti burgi ex australi partibus ab altera et toies vias regi ab versus oriens et boream.

No. 3 occurs under the same date, and is also a sasine by Andrew Jamesone to his son Andrew Jamesone, and it relates that it is given in

21

"gratiam et favore delecti filii sui *senioris* legitim Andre Jamesoun."
The sasine relates to a house on a portion of the same ground described
above :—

> Totam et Integram Terram suam de Novo edificatum cespitibus coopertam de
> prefecto heredid Andrea . . .   Jacen infra dictu burgu in vico scholari ex australi
> parte eiusdem vici Inter terra quondam Joannes robertsoun vero heredum quondam
> Thome Straquhan ex occidendali ex vica cum terus ecclesia parochialis dùis Nicolas
> dicti burgi ex australi partibus ab altra et toies vias regias vertis boream et oriens.

No. 4, still under the same date, is also by Andrew Jamesone in
favour of George, who is distinctly described as the second son—" in
favore delecti filii sui *secundo* geniti Georgii Jamesoun " :—

> Totam et Integram terra suam anteriorem ad terras tegulis coopertam Jacen
> infra dictu burgu in vico scholari ex boreali parte eiusdem vici Inter terram olim
> quondam Davudis endeauct nec tero roberti forbes te mendatarii de Monymusk
> ex orientali ex vica terra quondam Adami Mair ex occiendentali partibus ab altera
> terra Interiore Andree Watsoun carpentaris vertis boream et toiem viam regiam
> vertis austra.

No. 5 is dated 25th January, 1625, and is in favour of Georgii
Jamesone and Isabelle Toshe his wife, of his late father's property,
described at length :—

> Supplicationem probi et Ingenui Juvenis Georgii Jamesone pictoris heredus
> legitime deseniti quondam Andree Jamesone fratrus sui germani de Terra Inferius
> bondat accessit personater cum dicto Georgio ad illam Terram de novo edificatam
> cespitibus coopertam in qua dictus quondam Andreas legitime Infer datus et saseus
> sue per Resignationem quondam Andree Jamesone Latomi Jucole dicti burgi sui patris
> Jacen infra dictum burgum de Aberdén in vico scholari ex australi parte eiusdem
> vici Inter teram quondam Joanis Robertsone postea quondam Thome Strathauchan
> et nunc Joanis Caddell ex occidentali ex vica Cimeterium ecclesie parochialis diui
> Nicolai dicti burgi ex australi partibus ab altera et comunes vias regias versus Boream
> et oriens. . . . .
> Totam et integram antedatam Terram suam de novo edificatam ac cespitibus
> coopertam cum pertinen bondat et jacen ut . . . .   Necnon aliam Terram suam
> anteriorem tegulis coopertam cum pertinen Jacen infra dictum burgum in dicto vico
> Scholari ex Boreali parte eiusdem vici Inter terra quondam Dauidis endauch nunc
> vero heredam quondam Thome forbes de Rubislaw ex Orientali ex vica Terram
> quondam Adami Mair ex Occidentali partibus ab altera Terra Interorem quondam
> Andree Watsone carpentarii nunc vero Joannes Liddell versus Boream et Dinunem
> viam regiam versu austrim.

No. 6, dated 7th June, 1627, is a sasine in favour of the artist, of land by Alexandri Gray :—

> Totam et integram illam Terram suam Anteriorem tam subtur quam supra cum pertinén per eiusdem Mg⁽ᵒ⁾ Duncane Forbes de Balnagask ocuptám et conquestám Jaceñ infra dictum burgum in vico Scholari ex australi latere eiusdem vici Inter terra comunitatus dicti burgi vocat ly kirkludge ex australi ex una Terram Roberti Alexander ex Orientali partibus ab altra et comúnes vias regias versus Boream et occidens.

No. 7 is dated 29th May, 1635, and docquetted " Sasina Georgii Jameson de feudefarma et portione Claustri Meluillis et Liddell :—

> Tota et integra illa Terra anteriore nunc ad Georgium Jameson pictorem burgen de Aberdén spectán, Jacen infra dictum burgum in vico montis Scholaris ex Boreali parte eiusdem vici Inter terram heredum quondam Thome forbes de Robislaw ex Orientali ex vica, Terram aliquando Andree Howat et nunc Joannes Nivn ex occidentali partibus ab altera Terram Interiorem quondam Andree Watson nunc vero dictorum Mg⁽ᵗⁱ⁾ Thome et Dauidis Meluillis versus Boream et comunem viam ᵗegiam versus austrum Ac etiam illam portionem Claustris predicte terre Interioris aliquando ad dictum quondam Andream Watson et nunc ad dictos Mg⁽ᵗⁱ⁾ Thomam et Dauidem Meluillis heruditure spectán Contogus adeatén terre anteriori supralimitat nunc dicto Georgis Jameson . . . . et Comprehendén Tres vluas in Longitudine a muro posterio dicte Terre anterioris versus australe gabulum vulgo the south gabill predicte Terre, Interoris Refernando jarnen dictis Mg⁽ᵗⁱ⁾ Thome et Dauidi Meluillis . . . . heredibus et assignatus ; Lberum Introitium et exitum ad predictam terram Interiorem per Jaimam Anteriorem eiusdem toties quoties.

No. 8 is a sasine, dated 5th November, 1641, by which Jamesone acquires a house in the "vico lemurum ly Gestraw " (*i.e.*, the street of Ghosts) from James Tosche, a merchant burgess, probably his brother-in-law.

No. 9 is a sasine, dated 6th January, 1645, referred to at page 104 of the text. It is a long instrument, and describes afresh all the properties above noted in the preceding sasines. The noticeable circumstance about it is the occurrence of the name of Elizabeth as co-heiress with two of her sisters, Isabella and Mary. The sasine is in true legal form " per terre et lapidis," by " Elizabetham Isobellam et Mariam Jamesones in veras ltunas et propinquiores coheredes prefati quondam Georgii Jamesone carum patris de terris tenementis aliisque supralimitat cum pertinen Eisdem Elizabethe Isobelle et Marie Jamesones." &c., &c.

Elizabeth's position in the eyes of the law may be inferred from the fact that on the 11th December, 1644, a few days probably after Jamesone's death, when Mary by herself, and Isabella and Marjory together, went forward and served themselves his heirs-at-law, Elizabeth did not. She had right to take sasine of the heritable property left her by her father, but established no next-of-kin claim like her sisters. This field of enquiry is, however, not exhausted, and it is hard to say what additional light may yet be thrown on the subject.

Page 30. Jamesone's Arms are described as Argent—a fessi wavy, azure, between three anchors. Motto, "Sine Metu" (Without Fear). The crest is a ship in full sail with a flag displayed. The shield, with bearings, is emblazoned in one of the eighty-four compartments into which the roof of the Aberdeen Town-Hall is divided.

Page 37. Extracts from the Baillie Court Books—Under 4th May, 1621 :—

Alex^r Gareauche is said to be restand auchtand to Williame Jamesone *secune* sone to umqll Andre Jamesone meason Indwellar in Abdñ the soume of fourtiene pundis Scottis money (vol. xlix., p. 827).

Under 22nd March, 1624 :—

The Quilk day in pñ of Mr Alex Cullen Baillie compeirit personallie George Jamesone paynter *eldest* Laüll sone to umqll Andro Jamesone measone Indwellar in Abdñ (vol. l., p. 871).

It is clearly to be understood that George was eldest and William second son at the above respective dates, because their elder brother had already pre-deceased them.

Page 57. In the second paragraph Jamesone's family has, by mistake, been limited to six. He had at least *seven* children, of whom *four* were sons, and of these *two* were unnamed (see the Pedigree).

Page 104. The following are the terms on which the Playfield was leased to Jamesone's representatives, as granted by the Town Council on 15th January, 1645 (Council Reg., vol. 53, pp. 36-37) :—

The said day anent the supplication gevin in be Mr John Alex^r Advocat in Edr, makand mention that q^r that peice of ground callit the Playfeild besyd the Womanhill (q^{lk} wes set to vmq^{ll} George Jameson, painter burges of Edr, in liferent and buildit be him in a garden) Is now vnprofitable, and that the said Mr John Alex^r sone-in-law to the said vmq^{ll} George Is desyreous to have the same peice ground set to him in few heretablie, to be hauldin of the Provest baillies Counsell and Comunitie of the burghe of Abēr and y^r successors for payment of a reasoneable few deutie yeirly y^{r}foir : Humblie y^{r}foir supplicating y^t honors of the counsell to set in few heretablie to him the foirsaid peice of ground for payment of a reasoneable few deutie yeirlie as in the said supplication at mair lenth is contenit : Q^{lk} being red, sein, and considerit be the said Counsell and they y^{r}with ryplie and at lenth advised The saide Provest, Baillies, and Counsell Ordanes ane heretable few charter to be past and exped To the said Mr John Alex^r, his aires maill, and successors of the foirsaid plot of ground callit the Playfeild, or garden sometyme possest be the said vmq^{ll} George Jameson, for payment of four punds scots money yeirlie of few deutie to the touns thesaurar and his successors at Witsunday and Martimes in Winter, be equall portions The first termes payment to be and begin at the feast and terme of . . . nixt to come, and sua furth, yeirlie in all tymes heirefter and ordanes the limits of the said Garden to be set doun and boundit in the foirsaid charter efter the sichting of the ground be the saide Provest and baillies, q^{lk} the Counsell appoints to be visited the morne, and that in respect the haill inhabitants of this burghe being convenit within the tolbuith of the same, vpon the sewint day of January instant They all in ane voice but any contradiction gave y^r expres consent and assent to the heretable fewing of the said peice of ground vpon sic conditiones and for payment of sic yeirlie few deutie as the magistrats and Councell sould think expedient.

Page 114. In 1617, the artist lent the sum of 500 merks to Alexander Jamesone, who was probably his uncle. As a security for this loan Jamesone obtained the disposition of a house and ground situated in the Green. The money was repaid on the 22nd March, 1624, and an entry is made in the Baillie Court Books, signed by Jamesone, granting the borrower a discharge. The signature on page 114 is copied from this discharge. On the 25th January, 1625, following a

custom of that period, Jamesone gives a propinquity proof, before an
assize, of his relationship to his late brother, Andrew, who is described
as "quondam Andreas Jamesoni filius senior quondam Andree Jameson
latomi Jucole burgi de Abёr, frater germanis Georgii pictoris latomo
putium " [vol li? p. 129].

Page 125. Dr. Dun's portrait in the Town House is a copy by
Mr. John Moir, who worked in Aberdeen in the beginning of the present
century. He was a son of the Rev. Dr. George Moir, of Peterhead.
He studied his profession partly on the Continent, and acquired very
considerable technical skill. His portraits are not numerous, but they
exhibit much care and finish.

No reference has been made in the preceding pages to Dr. Duncan
Liddell's interesting monumental brass in St. Nicholas (West) Church,
Aberdeen. The plate measures five and a half feet long by about three
broad. The upper half consists of an elaborate portrait of Liddell,
surrounded by many of the insignia of learning and science. The lower
half and border contain a lengthened Latin inscription. Mr. Andrew
Gibb gives a complete description of it, with illustrations, in the Proceedings of the Society of Antiquaries of Scotland, 13th March, 1876,
and ventures the opinion that the brass was probably designed by
Jamesone, who had just returned from Antwerp, and was at the time
(1623) in close friendship with Sir Paul Menzies, Provosts Nicholson,
Jaffray, and Dr. Patrick Dun, who were charged with its execution. It
was engraved at Antwerp, and Mr. Gibb contends that it may rank as
a work of Jamesone's. With regard to the portrait, it is not in the least
in the mode Jamesone would have chosen, nor are the circumstantial
accessories in the least degree like those of his known works. We think
that if Jamesone furnished the pen-and-ink sketch for the engraver, it
must have been copied from an existing portrait of Liddell painted by
a Continental artist, where he spent the best part of his life.

Two members of the Alexander branch of Jamesone's descendants inherited his artistic qualities. John Alexander, the son of Marjory Jamesone, became a picture engraver, and it is to his burin that we are indebted for the well-known engraving of the Jamesone family group (No. 119). Another descendant, Cosmo John Alexander, followed an artist's career during the last century. He studied at Florence, and, returning to his native country, followed in the same peripatetic way, the footsteps of his illustrious relative. His pictures, which are freely scattered about the mansions of the north of Scotland, possess no special merit of any kind. They may be described as matter of fact, and wholly lack the delicate handling of Jamesone. Let justice be done to Alexander, he did possess one great merit, but it is observable on the back of his canvases, where is usually to be found a historical record of the subject, the artist, and the date of the picture. He copied some of Jamesone's pictures, and, as in No. 24, commendably noted the fact. It may be suspected that in some cases he played the restorer's part, and is probably responsible for some of the perplexity now experienced in identifying Jamesone's works.

Sir George Chalmers, who married a descendant of Jamesone's, in the person of Marjory's great grand-daughter, was also a disciple of Apelles. He was born at Edinburgh, and was representative of the baronets of Cults, whose estate was confiscated for their adhesion to the Stuarts. Sir George first studied at Edinburgh under Allan Ramsay, and afterwards at Rome. He was patronised by General Blakeney at Minorca, where he painted the portrait of that officer, which was afterwards engraved and published. After his return home, Sir George established himself in his profession, first at Hull, and then in London. He died in 1791. Through his wife Sir George inherited the original picture of the Jamesone family group (No. 119), over which some mystery hangs.

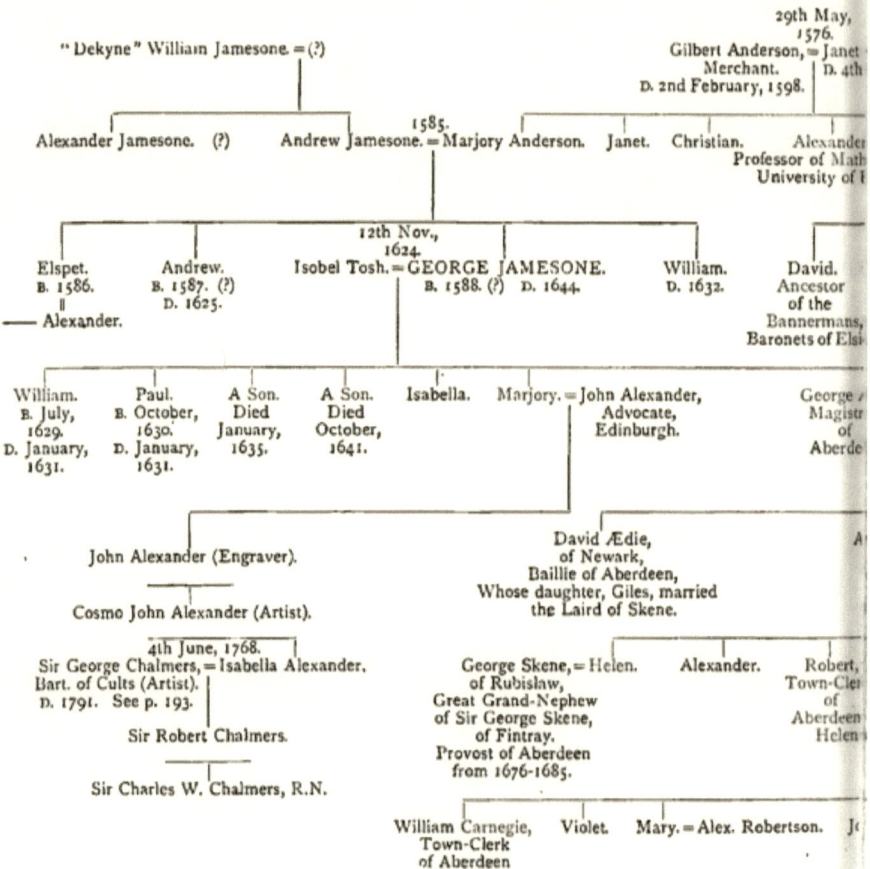

"Dekyne" William Jamesone. = (?)

29th May,
1576.
Gilbert Anderson, = Janet
Merchant.   D. 4th
D. 2nd February, 1598.

Alexander Jamesone.   (?)   Andrew Jamesone. = Marjory Anderson.   Janet.   Christian.   Alexander
1585.   Professor of Math
                                                 University of I

12th Nov.,
1624.
Elspet.   Andrew.   Isobel Tosh. = GEORGE JAMESONE.   William.   David.
B. 1586.   B. 1587. (?)   B. 1588. (?) D. 1644.   D. 1632.   Ancestor
   ‖   D. 1625.   of the
— Alexander.   Bannermans,
                                                                            Baronets of Elsi

William.   Paul.   A Son.   A Son.   Isabella.   Marjory. = John Alexander,   George /
B. July,   B. October, Died   Died   Advocate,   Magistr
1629.   1630.   January,   October,   Edinburgh.   of
D. January, D. January, 1635.   1641.   Aberde
1631.   1631.

John Alexander (Engraver).   David Ædie,   A
                                                   of Newark,
                                                   Baillie of Aberdeen,
Cosmo John Alexander (Artist).   Whose daughter, Giles, married
                                                   the Laird of Skene.

4th June, 1768.
Sir George Chalmers, = Isabella Alexander.   George Skene, = Helen.   Alexander.   Robert,
Bart. of Cults (Artist).   of Rubislaw,   Town-Cle
D. 1791. See p. 193.   Great Grand-Nephew   of
                                                   of Sir George Skene,   Aberdeen
Sir Robert Chalmers.   of Fintray.   Helen
                                                   Provost of Aberdeen
Sir Charles W. Chalmers, R.N.   from 1676-1685.

                                   William Carnegie,   Violet.   Mary. = Alex. Robertson.   J
                                   Town-Clerk
                                   of Aberdeen

PEDIGREE.

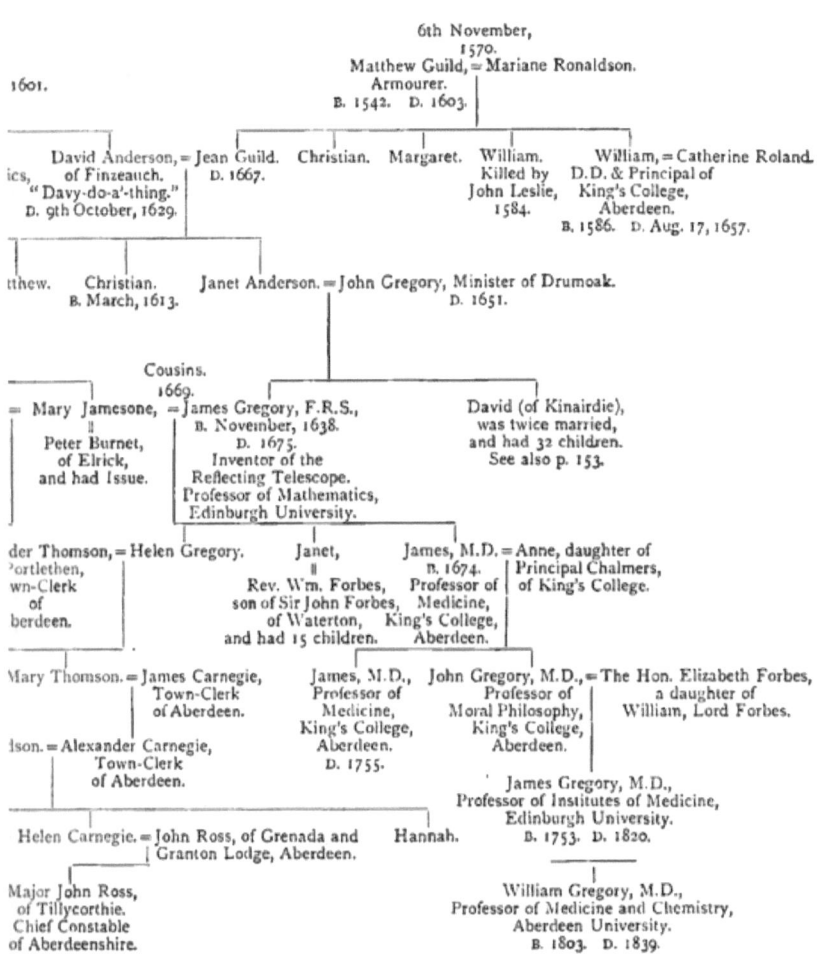

6th November,
1570.
Matthew Guild, = Mariane Ronaldson.
1601.   Armourer.
                    B. 1542.   D. 1603.

David Anderson, = Jean Guild.   Christian.   Margaret.   William.   William, = Catherine Roland.
ics,   of Finzeauch.   D. 1667.   Killed by   D.D. & Principal of
"Davy-do-a'-thing."   John Leslie,   King's College,
D. 9th October, 1629.   1584.   Aberdeen.
                                                                        B, 1586.   D. Aug. 17, 1657.

tthew.   Christian.   Janet Anderson. = John Gregory, Minister of Drumoak.
        B. March, 1613.   D. 1651.

              Cousins.
              1669.
= Mary Jamesone, = James Gregory, F.R.S.,   David (of Kinairdie),
   ‖   B. November, 1638.   was twice married,
  Peter Burnet,   D. 1675.   and had 32 children.
  of Elrick,   Inventor of the   See also p. 153.
  and had Issue.   Reflecting Telescope.
                     Professor of Mathematics,
                     Edinburgh University.

der Thomson, = Helen Gregory.   Janet,   James, M.D. = Anne, daughter of
'ortlethen,   ‖   B. 1674. | Principal Chalmers,
wn-Clerk   Rev. Wm. Forbes, Professor of | of King's College.
   of   son of Sir John Forbes, Medicine,
berdeen.   of Waterton,   King's College,
                                  and had 15 children. Aberdeen.

Mary Thomson. = James Carnegie,   James, M.D.,   John Gregory, M.D., = The Hon. Elizabeth Forbes,
              | Town-Clerk   Professor of   Professor of | a daughter of
              | of Aberdeen.   Medicine,   Moral Philosophy, | William, Lord Forbes.
              | King's College, King's College,
ison. = Alexander Carnegie,   Aberdeen.   Aberdeen.
        Town-Clerk   D. 1755.
        of Aberdeen.   James Gregory, M.D.,
                                                    Professor of Institutes of Medicine,
                                                         Edinburgh University.
                                                         B. 1753. D. 1820.
  Helen Carnegie. = John Ross, of Grenada and   Hannah.
                  | Granton Lodge, Aberdeen.
                  | William Gregory, M.D.,
Major John Ross,   Professor of Medicine and Chemistry,
of Tillycorthie.   Aberdeen University.
Chief Constable   B. 1803. D. 1839.
of Aberdeenshire.

INDEX.

PRINTED AT THE FREE PRESS OFFICE.
ABERDEEN.